INTO THE
GATES OF HELL
STUG COMMAND '41

BY BOB CARRUTHERS
AND SINCLAIR McLAY

EDITED BY MARK FARR

BASED ON AN ORIGINAL MANUSCRIPT
BY RITTER VON KRAUSS

PEN & SWORD
FICTION

D0273374

This edition published in 2013 by

Pen & Sword Fiction
An imprint of
Pen & Sword Books Ltd
47 Church Street
Barnsley
South Yorkshire
S70 2AS

First published in Great Britain in 2012 by Coda Books Ltd.

ISBN: 9781783462421

Printed and bound in England
By CPI Group (UK) Ltd, Croydon, CR0 4YY

Pen & Sword Books Ltd incorporates the imprints of Pen & Sword Aviation, Pen &
Sword Family History, Pen & Sword Maritime, Pen & Sword Military, Pen & Sword
Discovery, Pen & Sword Politics, Pen & Sword Atlas, Pen & Sword Archaeology,
Wharncliffe Local History, Wharncliffe True Crime, Wharncliffe Transport, Pen
& Sword Select, Pen & Sword Military Classics, Leo Cooper, The Praetorian Press,
Claymore Press, Remember When, Seaforth Publishing and Frontline Publishing

For a complete list of Pen & Sword titles please contact
PEN & SWORD BOOKS LIMITED
47 Church Street, Barnsley, South Yorkshire, S70 2AS, England
E-mail: enquiries@pen-and-sword.co.uk
Website: www.pen-and-sword.co.uk

Contents

For Mr McWhinnie whom we are both privileged to have as friend.

- CHAPTER 1 -

Die Welt wird Seinen Atem halten

"BREATH." SS-Hauptsturmführer Hans von Schroif had no idea why this single word should enter his mind at this time. Perhaps it was because in the still silence of the pine forest, amongst all these men and machines, all he could hear at that moment was the sound of his own breathing. Breath; life begins with the first violent inhalation and ends with the fight for our dying breath. Yet, for something so vital, so fundamental, we spend our lives so unaware of its presence; except in moments like these. How could it be possible? Three and a half million men, countless tanks, trucks, artillery pieces, horses and aircraft along a 3,000 kilometre front — stretching across almost the whole span of the continent of Europe, from Memel to Rumania — and, despite everything, for one fleeting moment all von Schroif could hear was the sound of his own breathing.

In this briefest of lulls before the coming storm, von Schroif sensed that many of the men in this colossal human chain were attuned to the same delicate sound, the sound of their own breathing. The *Führer* had been right — he was always right — in finding the exact words and phrases when speaking to the German people and the fighting men of the Reich. "When Barbarossa begins, the world will hold its breath".

Now, at 00:45 on Sunday the 22nd of June 1941, it seemed as if the world was indeed holding its breath. The flow of time itself seemed to have stopped. For the hundredth time SS-Hauptsturmführer Hans von Schroif glanced quickly at his watch — still two hours to go! He was waiting for the moment when all hell would be unleashed on, what he hoped would be, the unsuspecting Russian forces on the other side of the Bug River, and the war against the Reds would begin at last.

His thoughts turned to his command. Arranged in the trees along the roadside were the three batteries of mobile assault guns which, together with his own command half-track, should have made up the eighteen vehicle strong *Sturmgeschütz* battalion. That was the theory, at least. According to the official established tables, there *should* have been eighteen machines standing by under the fir trees. The fighting efficiency of the battalion was a matter of overwhelming private and professional pride to Hans von Schroif, but even the fabled German efficiency sometimes failed, and no army got everything right. So far, the factory had delivered only fifteen *Sturmgeschütze* with the depressing result that, before a blow had even been struck, each battery was reduced to just five machines. Nonetheless, von Schroif took strength from the knowledge that each of the three *abteilungen* consisted of five brand new machines of the Ausf C type and each was well run by his subordinate commanders who were clear about their duties.

As the key component of the newly formed

Kampfgruppe von Schroif, he planned to issue his command with their final orders at 02:00 hours. For now, there was nothing to do but wait. He had seen to everything personally. The smooth running of the battalion was all that mattered in his life. He was satisfied that the battery and platoon leaders were all hand-picked and extremely able.

The Sturmgeschütze were armoured fighting vehicles that had been created for a specific tactical purpose that was very different to that of the Panzer formations. Whereas the Panzers were intended to force a breakthrough and keep going, deep into enemy territory, the Sturmgeschütze were intended to stick close to the grenadiers and provide close infantry support against enemy field defences using direct fire from their formidable 75mm main guns. The StuG, as it was widely known, was intended to provide a movable, well-armoured, artillery piece for close infantry support in the gritty frontline assaults, and these life or death struggles were the life's work of Hans von Schroif.

Despite the gloom of this dark moonless night, the bright canopy of stars visible through the gaps in the forest provided a contrast against the black shapes of the trees, and the stark shapes of the waiting Sturmgeschütze were easily identifiable. To a layman, this squat, oblong-shaped machine with its short, stubby main gun looked like a tank that was lacking a turret. To the infuriation of the more pedantic members of their crews, the public often mistook them for tanks. However, the absence of a turret, combined with the grey uniforms of its crew, marked the Sturmgeschütz out as a mobile artillery piece. Here was the latest innovation in the *Wehrmacht* armoury, an assault gun crewed by only the bravest and the most daring, trained to rumble up to the enemy's strong points and fearlessly fight it out, toe-to-toe with the toughest defences, right there in the frontline.

To be fair to the layman, there was a familiar element to the StuG. It was not entirely a purpose-designed machine. It was built on the recognised chassis of the Panzer III tank. This proven chassis had only recently been adapted to provide this new type of armoured fighting vehicle for a very specific role. The Sturmgeschütz was simply an armour-plated and highly mobile gun platform designed to trundle up to the heaviest of field defences and blast them into oblivion at short range.

In common with his revered Führer, von Schroif was inclined to look back at German history for echoes of a heroic past, and in his mind he identified his troop with the siege trains of the Teutonic Knights who, in the medieval era, had expanded the eastern boundaries of the German world. He viewed the determined men who manned the Sturmgeschütze as the successors to the hardy foot soldiers who had battered at the defences of the strongholds that had been wrested from the Slavs by the Teutons. What was the StuG after all but a modern battering ram? It was certainly an effective machine. Following their successful deployment in France and Greece, the StuGs were now rightfully hailed as potent infantry support weapons, ready to be called into action wherever there was a particularly tough nut to crack.

The thoughts of Hans von Schroif now returned to the men who manned his command half-track as he began to walk along the sand-strewn road towards the dumpy shape of his own machine. The thick sand deposited on the road surface absorbed the sound of thousands of hobnailed boots that had been passing all day long. With them had come thousands of trucks and endless lines of horse-drawn wagons and guns. Now there was silence.

Von Schroif was lost in thought as he walked and was oblivious to the figure that slipped out of the trees and began to follow in his footsteps. Unmindful of everything around him, von Schroif was focused on the disparate elements of the task ahead. Should he give his own crew a few last words of encouragement, or leave them alone with their thoughts? He decided to leave them undisturbed. What possible need could he meet at this time? Now it was all about confidence and trust. He believed in these men and there was nothing he could offer them now that they couldn't offer themselves. Some of them had been with him since before the war, before Poland, France and Greece. They had proved themselves to him, not just by responding dutifully and manfully to the planned and the expected, but also by rising courageously to the unplanned and the unexpected. Doggedness, improvisation and teamwork had marked them as out of the ordinary and von Schroif was confident that the trend would continue.

Despite his long and successful combat experience, even von Schroif now betrayed a degree of nervousness. As he reached the first in the long line of silent vehicles his fingers drummed rhythmically on the cold, unforgiving hardened steel roof of the fighting compartment of the Sturmgeschütz. It was reassuringly solid and a source of immense comfort, and it reflected his pride in German engineering. The Sturmgeschütz was a radically different machine and only a chosen few were awarded the privilege of commanding one. Von Schroif took huge satisfaction in being given command of an entire battalion.

His years in the wilderness, unable to find a place in the tiny post-war *Reichswehr*, were now behind him. The SS-VT had provided him with a soldier's career and now here he was, proudly in command of the twentieth century's latest advance, the herald of a new age of warfare. He took great satisfaction from the fact that he had been chosen to lead a battalion of these priceless new weapons. Armed with a short-barrelled 75mm howitzer, the Sturmgeschütz was the cutting edge of German military engineering. It represented the very latest in military technology, and if anyone was qualified to judge the effectiveness of the new machine then Hans von Schroif was that man. However, that man was now so lost in thought that even in the stillness of the forest he did not notice the soft approach of the figure from behind his right shoulder.

"Everything in order, Hauptsturmführer?"

Startled by the unexpected sound, von Schroif spun

around to find the figure of SS-Kannonier Otto Wohl doing his stint of sentry duty.

"Yes Wohl, all is good, thank you… just remembering.…"

"I understand you lost some good comrades here, Hauptsturmführer?" Wohl asked.

"We did, Wohl. They're still here, biting into the grass. I remember all of them, but something else, too…" There was a pause, then, in apparent *non sequitur*, von Schroif suddenly asked an unexpected question. "How old are you, Wohl?"

"I'm twenty-one, Hauptsturmführer," stated Wohl earnestly.

The young man was something of a concern for von Schroif. SS-Kannonier Otto Wohl was a well-meaning joker from Munich who typified the *laissez faire* attitude of that time-honoured city. He served as the loader and radio operator for number 1 gun of the first *abteilung*. Wohl was something of an enigma. He had volunteered to serve in the *Waffen SS*, but for a political soldier he appeared to have no interest in politics beyond a basic admiration for the Führer, which was almost universally shared by the youth of his age. His disparaging remarks concerning the other party bigwigs and his non-stop flow of highly questionable jokes was a source of concern for von Schroif.

Wohl had been drafted in to number 1 gun in Wefer's battery just before the opening of the campaign in Greece. He had joined as a replacement for Karl Wendorff, a

11

Franconian and a genius with the radio who had, to von Schroif's intense frustration, been urgently seconded to *Abwehr* on some secret mission or other. No amount of pleading or cajoling had been able to prevent Wendorf from being spirited away from the battalion.

The replacement was the hapless Otto Wohl, who was a great asset as a loader, but criminally incompetent with a radio set. This was doubly frustrating because von Schroif and his team were charged with testing the next generation of radio, the transceiver, a single machine which could transmit as well as receive. Wendorf had been in command of the project and was achieving great results, but following the invasion of France in the previous year he had been abruptly transferred to mysterious specialist duties with Abwehr.

Unbeknown to SS-Hauptsturmführer Hans von Schroif and the millions of men either side of him, German operations had already begun, and Wendorff was one of those men who were to play a part.

* * * * *

In the dark skies over eastern Poland, the side door of the lumbering Ju-52 transport aircraft was thrown open.

"Jump!" came the curt command.

Karl Wendorff threw himself out of the plane.

In marked contrast to the technical superiority they had achieved in most arms and equipment, the style of parachute harness used by the German *fallschirmjäger* was vastly inferior to that used by the British; and that truth now came home to Karl Wendorff. *Wehrmacht* paratroopers were required to throw themselves forward out of the aeroplane, and in the resulting face-down position, when the chute opened, control was nearly impossible. The necessity of landing on knees and elbows reduced the amount of equipment the trooper could carry and increased the chance of injury. As a result, they jumped armed only with a holstered pistol and a small 'gravity knife'. Rifles and other weapons were dropped in separate containers and, until these were recovered, the soldiers were poorly armed.

Now, floating down in the darkness over Russian lines and completely out of his comfort zone, Karl Wendorff felt very alone and very afraid. As he fought to control the chute his heart was pounding fit to burst his chest. During his whirlwind training programme Wendorff had found the intricacies of the parachute jump difficult enough in daylight. Now, as the cool night air swirled around him and the ground seemed to race upwards, all the familiar terrors seemed tripled. To make matters worse, he was disguised as a Red Army bandsman and he was expected to find and retrieve a canister containing a shortwave transceiver.

Wendorff and his comrades formed one of many units of Brandenburger commandos now being parachuted behind enemy lines to disrupt Soviet operations. These tough men specialised in seizing vital rail and road bridges and were trained to kill with guns, knives, grenades and, if necessary, their bare hands. As the plane lumbered through Soviet airspace the others had jumped out to carry out their unspecified missions.

Karl Wendorff was the last to jump. He did not naturally fit the profile of the hard as nails Brandenburgers. He had been seconded because of his command of the Russian language and unrivalled skills as a radio operator. His mission did not involve any form of military mayhem. All he had to do was to set up the radio set and make contact with the contact known as Cobra. He was then to hand over the package of documents strapped to his waist. Exactly what he was supposed to do next was unclear. All he had been told was that unspecified events would be set in motion that would work in his favour, and that he was to adapt to the situation as it unfolded. Wendorff assumed that he was to play a role in some kind of counter-revolution designed to overthrow the Soviet government. He couldn't have been more wrong.

* * * * *

In Wendorff's absence, Wohl, already pushed to his limits, had not taken well to this new concept which he christened the 'schiesseiver'. Out of earshot of von Schroif, he had made his insubordinate feelings clear to anyone who would listen.

"Load it in the gun and fire it over to the bloody Reds! It'll fuck up their communication system — it certainly fucks up ours!" was Wohl's hopeful but forlorn suggestion to SS-Hauptscharführer Michael Knispel, his StuG's gunner.

Radio duties apart, von Schroif was aware that Wohl formed a deadly gunnery team with Knispel. He was lightning fast to load and reload the main gun and seemed to have an innate understanding of what type of ammunition was required, even though he had no visual terms of reference from his position inside the StuG. In action, he and Knispel became part of a triangular machine that was two parts flesh and blood and one part steel. Once in action, he combined with Knispel and the gun in such an all-consuming manner that they were without doubt the most deadly and efficient gunnery combination he had ever seen.

However, this had to be counterbalanced by Wohl's worrying habit of leaving the transceiver on transmit, which stopped the flow of incoming messages and bombarded the rest of the battery with a confusing stream of babble from inside the fighting compartment of number 1 gun. So far, nothing fatal had resulted, but in action it only needed to happen once, so von Schroif kept a constant wary eye on him.

A less intuitive commander would have transferred Wohl to one of the other guns in the battery — SS-Kannonier Halle from Hofmann's vehicle was an outstanding soldier and would make the crew world class — but Knispel was adamant that he should remain. In addition, von Schroif knew that he couldn't select the best candidates for his favoured machine and still command the respect of the battery. There was no other option — Wohl had to stay on as a work in progress for both Knispel and von Schroif.

While von Schroif's mind was elsewhere the pause in the conversation continued until he dimly became aware of Wohl shifting uneasily from foot to foot. The subtle, almost imperceptible movement was not accidental. Wohl hated sentry duty and would do anything to alleviate the hours of monotony. He was therefore eager to continue the conversation, but he said no more for the moment, hoping von Schroif would pick up the thread.

The thoughts of his commander, however, had moved on and he was now far away from the uncertain present. His roving mind had moved on from the Sturmgeschütze and was now cast back twenty-three years to the Great War, 1918, just before Wohl was born. That was the time when von Schroif had first rumbled into battle in the A7V, Germany's first battle tank, a lumbering colossus as big as a house and filled with the chaos of noise, fumes and the stench of seventeen sweating, choking crewmen.

Eventually Wohl's impatience overcame him and he decided to re-kindle the conversation with a question.

"Will there be anything else, Hauptsturmführer?"

"Not for now, Wohl…" came the disappointing reply. "I was just reflecting on what progress has been made in so few years." Von Schroif rapped on the armour of the Sturmgeschütz.

Wohl decided it was worth one last try.

"I regret I do not follow you, Hauptsturmführer."

"I mean this, Wohl… the StuG," said von Schroif, taking the bait. "You lack the necessary experience to comprehend it, Wohl, but trust me, this great leap in engineering is surely the mark of how great Germany has become under the Führer! When I was your age, I entered an armoured battle in our first Panzer. You know what happened, Wohl?"

"No, I don't, Hauptsturmführer," said the young man expectantly.

"We toppled over into a shell hole during our first combat!" Von Schroif was smiling. "It was so massive, so top-heavy, that it was unmanageable, and there were eighteen of us packed in there. Definitely not the Fatherland's finest moment! But now, in just one generation, we have this marvel, eh? Evolution at the pace of lightning, SS-Kannonier Wohl!"

Wohl looked back uncomprehendingly at von Schroif, who continued his exposition.

"Look how low it is, how agile, and how well-armoured. Tempered steel too, not the feeble plates we had to hide behind back then — they could just about stop a rifle bullet, but nothing else. You see, Wohl, the *Sturmgeschütz*, when compared to the A7V, is a like a greyhound compared to a mammoth, but this greyhound has an armoured skin and really sharp teeth. It is so much better armed and so highly efficient that it needs just four men to do the work that even a battalion of the old A7Vs could never have attempted, and all of this in just twenty-three years! That's why we'll hammer the Reds into the ground."

* * * * *

The incessant ringing of telephones and the constant bustle of messages being delivered in the busy main office of the *Abwehr* Headquarters in Berlin was in marked contrast to the silence of the pine forests packed with men waiting nervously in the frontlines.

"Still over an hour to go, Sir," shouted RSHA Kriminalassistent Walter Lehmann above the din.

"I appreciate that. We had the Dortmund signal at 13.00 hours," said Admiral Wilhelm Canaris, head of Hitler's secret service in Berlin. He was a man who took nothing for granted. He also checked his watch — 01:30. Looking for all the world like a kindly old gentleman who would not be out of place sitting placidly in his local church, he smiled at Lehmann and in an unspoken signal of solidarity gestured towards the quiet sanctuary of his private office. Once inside, he gestured towards a waiting tray and Lehmann poured a stiff measure of brandy into two waiting glasses.

Canaris too was conscious of his own breathing, but not in the same way as von Schroif or the millions of other German soldiers who sat poised in the East. His rapid breaths did not sound as if they followed one after the other, but more as if they were set against each other, the breathing of a man at war with himself, of a man living two separate lives. He and Lehmann were unlikely allies trying to stay inside the system and simultaneously trying to bring it down, carrying out acts which appalled his own Christian conscience in order to be in the position to enact small mercies to appease the very same conscience. He was a man who was slowly being strangled by the tightrope he had forced himself to walk. A man fighting for breath. It was Canaris who had sent Wendorff and the rest of the Brandenburgers behind enemy lines. Should operation Barbarossa be postponed, the coded message 'Altona' would be transmitted, but something told Canaris that this operation would not be cancelled.

"I respect your decision to join us, Admiral," said Lehmann, raising his glass. "I'm still surprised that you should come to such a juncture. Formerly, you were such an enthusiastic supporter of the Führer…"

"I know it seems strange, Lehmann," replied the older man with the air of someone delighted to unburden a weight of his mind, "but it was all so different back then. Who would not have been a supporter, given the shameless treatment we suffered at Versailles?"

"So why the change?"

"I suppose I first became disillusioned when I learned of the corporal's plans to invade the Sudetenland. It was then I felt the first suspicions that we could be dealing with a gambler and an egomaniac. Why risk the Reich for the Sudetenland?"

"Surely not *such* a big gamble?" replied Lehmann, enjoying the taste of the finest brandy France could offer.

"You didn't have the advantage of the intelligence,

Lehmann. The Führer had not only underestimated the power of the Czech forces, but risked intervention by the Western powers. *Finis Germania* — and for what? It was reckless in the extreme, and that was just the first glimmering. Now look where he is taking us!"

"I take it there's nothing, er… concrete we can do?" asked Lehmann with the air of a man holding out little hope.

"There may come a time, but not now. As you know, Lehmann, I had all the right people lined up. We had laid the most immaculate plan to launch a *putsch*, right down to organising a shock troop to arrest Hitler when the time came. But then that fool Chamberlain came along and waved Hitler in. Hitler's popularity soared and this ludicrous cult of hero worship made it impossible to carry out the plan."

"Damn that fool Chamberlain!" cursed Lehmann. "When the history of this needless, appalling war is written, sign it off in that idiot's blood!"

"I couldn't agree more," replied Canaris with a glance towards the closed door. "Don't forget I was in Poland, and don't forget that I fought in the last lot too. I've seen some sights, but even an old warhorse like me was shocked by what I saw there. Add to that what my agents have been telling me — it's not just burning synagogues anymore. Trains are moving from France, from Holland, from Greece."

"The Jews were always going to pay a hefty price," observed Lehmann.

"This is going to be a bigger price than anyone bargained for," hissed Canaris. "It's not just about the Jews. No one cares about them. The trains are bringing hundreds of thousands of 'guest workers' into the Reich, but they are not guests and they're not workers… they're slaves. Dutchmen, Frenchmen, Danes, and women too. The whole of Europe has been enslaved. It's a new Dark Age and one day — soon — Germany will be reviled and cursed for what is happening in the name of the Empire."

Lehmann changed tack back to his original point. "But surely the reports of the killings… we've both read them. OKW and OKH are aware. The Madagascar option seems to have been abandoned… the Jews in Poland."

"I told you, no one at OKW cares. What matters to them is winning the war. Of course I've complained to Keitel, but nothing had been done. Believe me, this is just an indication of how this war will be conducted. Do you know they have even given a command to that psychopath Dirlewanger! A man so depraved he has been kicked out of the Nazi party! Convicted paedophiles commanding German units… God forgive us!"

"Surely there must be some possibility…" replied Lehmann.

"As you know, Lehmann," came the quick response, "since the outbreak of war, like you, in our own way we've done all that we can. We gave the dates of both the attack on Norway and the invasion of France to our Dutch contact. As regards the British, we did what we could, sending some Poles to London with the cover that they were agents for the Reich. Then instructing them to tell all who would listen that not all Germans were as abominable as Hitler and his craven cronies and to try to make alliances with those good Germans who remained and had influence and bearing. But all this has produced nothing next to the insanity that Hitler is now embarking on. This madness, this apocalypse, this Barbarossa! What is that lunatic thinking of?"

Canaris again was forced to fight for breath. He knew that he had to be seen to be doing everything to aid the war effort whilst doing what he could to undermine it.

"This puts me in a very unsavoury position and it means that I have to deal with some very insalubrious characters. If the Secret Field Police turn against me, who knows what harm could come to my family? I have come to the decision, tack with the wind. You, Lehmann, must do what you can. One day you will have to answer to a power higher than the earthly demon you presently obey…"

"As you are aware, Admiral," said Lehmann, "I am doing my best. If the contents of Plan Ost become public knowledge, then the whole international community will soon close ranks…. I'm sure he won't survive."

"Hmm, I wouldn't count on it," replied Canaris. "It's a small start, but a good one. There's not much else of practical value we can do. How did you get it from Heydrich?"

"I suspect he doesn't yet know that we have it. Let's

just say his personal safe isn't as impregnable as he thinks. There will be hell to pay when he opens it and finds out that it's gone."

"I certainly hope so. It is certainly strong evidence of a criminal conspiracy, but is it big enough to blow Hitler and his cronies away?" queried Canaris.

"These lunatics have a detailed plan for genocide. They propose to exterminate all those who they term *untermenschen*. It's a criminal act. They can't be allowed to get away with what's proposed here, and once the world knows about it I'm sure they will close ranks against him… The Americans would join for sure."

"Perhaps… the Jewish lobby is certainly influential there," Canaris mused.

"Governments will stand for expulsion, they'll stand for a Madagascar option of exile, but surely no one will stand by and allow a cold-blooded programme of mass extermination."

"It makes for such painful reading," continued Canaris sorrowfully. "Secret extermination camps to be established within the borders of the Reich! I have family in the East. They live near this Auschwitz, featured in the plan. What kind of a reputation is that place going to have for future generations? And Bergen-belsen too… Good God, I never thought I'd live to experience such ignominy. Well, we can at least take some solace from the fact that by the time Heydrich finds out that Plan Ost has gone missing it will be in the hands of someone who will make sure that it gets to the right people in Moscow."

Lehmann fought back the urge to ask who that might be, but in any event there was no need — he was an expert in reading upside down. Canaris volunteered no further information but the brown file on the desk in front of him told the whole story. The name immediately jumped off the page. Dimitri Korsak, aka Wilhelm Stenner.

Canaris, unaware that Lehmann had all the information he required, guardedly ventured some details.

"I have known this agent since our time in the *Freikorps* together. He was a keen National Socialist but he grew to hate Hitler over the murder of Gregor Strasser, whom he considered to be the one true leader of the far left in Germany. He then fled Germany to take up the common cause by joining the Communist Party in Soviet Russia."

"My enemy's enemy..." thought Lehmann to himself. By staying silent he hoped to elicit more from Canaris. Perhaps it was the excitement of the moment, but Canaris was giving away far more than the taciturn Admiral normally did. Now he fell frustratingly silent.

"So you plan to get Plan Ost to Moscow? Surely that will be impossible once the Corporal's war is unleashed."

"Quite the contrary, my dear Lehmann. The latest intelligence confirms that our agent has been seconded to an NKVD unit based in the old citadel at Brest-Litovsk. A courier with the only known copy of Plan Ost is already on the way to him — by tomorrow it should be in Moscow. Let's hope that the international outcry it provokes will be enough to overthrow these criminals."

* * * * *

"Can't it be done tomorrow?" replied Captain Zubachyov. "I can arrange it if I must, but why the rush? Who actually needs a single T-26 light tank at 04:00 on a Saturday night, or should I say a Sunday morning? In peace time! Look, tomorrow is another day... we'll sort it for then... alright?"

Tomorrow was always another day for Captain Zubachyov. The 22nd of June was a Sunday and he hoped it would prove to be a lazy Sunday. He anticipated a deep and painful hangover as he drained the last drops of vodka from his tumbler and watched the dancers in idle boredom. He hoped that his stint of Sunday duty would prove uneventful. At least if he produced the tank and sent the troublesome commissar on his way he would be rid of this confounded political meddler with his relentless string of requests.

The band was sawing its way through the last few numbers as the midsummer ball in the fortress of Brest-Litovsk drew towards its very late conclusion. He glanced at his watch. The enthusiasm of the participants in the all night dance showed no sign of letting up. The slow waltz provided the opportunity for a close-up clinch and the remaining couples were in various advanced states of amorous intensity. Whispered conversations pointed towards moonlit trysts. The dance hall was still busy. The nurses from the garrison hospital that served the 4th Red Army and the girls from the town acted like magnets

25

for the unattached officers, and those officers pretending to be unattached. There was fun to be had for those not going on duty in six hours' time and Captain Zubachyov had no intention of letting this latest request interrupt his evening.

He had not allowed for the unyielding attitude of Dimitri Korsak.

"My orders come straight from Moscow, Comrade Zubachyov. Either the T-26 is provided, fully fuelled and functioning, or I have you placed under arrest. There is no other option."

The Commissar's words cut like a knife through the alcoholic fuzz enfolding the Captain's vodka-soaked system. He suddenly realised that the formerly pleasant man in front of him was deadly serious.

"As you wish, Comrade Korsak. Bring me the telephone, Corporal."

This change of heart saved the life of Captain Zubachyov. Had he not provided the machine, Korsak had the authority and the will to bring him to summary justice, and Korsak was not a man who dealt in idle threats.

Following a brief conversation, the Captain turned to Korsak.

"The machine will be ready at the gatehouse, with a full crew."

"I did not request a crew. I will personally drive the machine to the destination."

"As you wish, Comrade Korsak," said the captain,

returning the salute of Dimitri Korsak who turned on his heel and marched quickly out of the building.

Captain Zubachyov returned to watching the dance and his eye alighted on a slim young nurse with stunning blond hair. She was sitting alone by the side of the dance floor. In his new state of sobriety Zubachyov resolved to make his move while there was still time. Moving swiftly across the floor, Zubachyov was immediately into his stride.

"Forgive the intrusion, Miss. Would you honour me with the pleasure of a dance?"

"Sorry, no, I have to leave when my friend returns. I am on duty at nine in the morning," replied the young woman.

Despite the rebuff, something in her manner suggested that she was not altogether uninterested in him. Everything about her seemed perfect to Zubachyov, who could hardly believe he'd missed her all evening.

"That's a coincidence, so am I," replied Zubachyov with a smile.

"I regret I have to be in charge of a ward in five hours' time."

"I regret I have to be in charge of the whole fortress in five hours' time... so I can always come round and order you to dance with me," replied Zubachyov, now warming to his theme.

"Then perhaps it might be easier if I did dance after all," said the pretty young nurse with the fine blond hair and striking blue eyes.

"A gracious decision, by which I'm honoured, Miss…?" said Zubachyov, inviting the missing information.

"Er… Ostermann… Bettina Ostermann," replied the young woman with the air of someone who is about to embark on a depressingly familiar conversation.

"Are you German?" asked Zubachyov, posing the inevitable question. "You certainly look it."

"Perhaps I may have been, one day long ago," sighed Bettina, "but my family has lived in eastern Volhnyia for three hundred years. I'm as Russian as you, but we still do keep some of our old German customs and language. In Germany they call us the *Volksdeutsche*."

"It certainly is a mixed up world we live in," said Zubachyov warmly. "I grew up in Saratov on the middle Volga. When I was young there were so many families of German extraction that it was originally an autonomous republic. It was called the Soviet Socialist Republic of the Volga Germans." With that he offered his hand and was about to give his own name when it was shouted out from across the dance floor.

"Captain Zubachyov! Urgent message for Captain Zubachyov!"

A breathless corporal rushed up.

"This had better be good, Corporal," said Zubachyov.

"Your presence is urgently required at the Terespol gate. There are massed German infantry and tanks moving through the woods on the other side of the river. Artillery of the highest calibre is being deployed. Cavalry is moving up."

"And what do you want me to do? It's their side of the river. They can do what they like. They can carry out as many manoeuvres as they like on any scale they like. There's no war."

"Lieutenant Orlov is concerned that the Germans plan to attack us by surprise."

Captain Zubachyov was aware of the growing circle of listeners. The orders from Moscow were very clear — under no circumstances were provocative actions to be taken.

"That's enough, Corporal. Thank the lieutenant for his report and ask him to remain vigilant. Dismissed."

As the Corporal dutifully turned to depart, his place was taken by a young private.

"I dutifully report, sir, that Sergeant Siminov requests your presence in the western bunker. There are very large troop movements on the other side of the Bug River."

"I order you to stop now, Private!" barked Zubachyov. "I will not hear one more word about German troop movements. Let the Germans do as they wish —"

Before Captain Zubachyov could go any further he was interrupted by Commissar Fomin who, noticing a further bevvy of messengers assembling in the foyer, stopped the band and raised his arms.

"Comrades! Captain Zubachyov is correct. It is true that we have recently seen an increase in activity in the German sphere of activity. However, the peace treaty remains in force. The standing orders remain as before.

We are at peace with the friends of the Soviet Union. There must be no provocation or anything remotely like an act which could be misinterpreted and lead to an unnecessary war."

"Thank you for the clarification, Comrade Fomin," said Zubachyov. Turning to the band leader, he gestured with his left hand while leading Bettina Ostermann to the middle of the dance floor. "Maestro, if you please. I believe we were in the middle of a slow waltz."

The eager young couples soon forgot the intrusion and began to dance once more. However, as they circled the floor the rumours of impending war were heard under discussion.

"So the Germans will definitely not attack us?" asked Bettina who had clearly been troubled by what she had heard.

"They are our allies. They'll never attack us... Well, not on a Sunday," said Zubachyov, seeking to lighten the mood.

"I hope there's no war. My family suffered enough last time."

"Look, it's a Sunday. We both have time in the afternoon. Why don't we take a no-war picnic down by the river and watch the silly real Germans run around and tire themselves out?"

Bettina gave a soft laugh. "Oh, I'm not too sure."

"If I made it an order, you'd have to come."

From the corner of his eye Captain Zubachyov saw Bettina exchange glances with a very plump nursing sister who coyly waved back by wiggling her fingertips and gestured with her eyes towards the door.

"All right, Captain Garrison Commander. I dutifully report that I will attend the picnic... and so will my friend Anastasia."

* * * * *

As von Schroif walked back along the column of Sturmgeschütze to where his own vehicle awaited him Wohl fell in and kept pace, hoping that the conversation might spark up again and break the mind-numbing tedium of life as a patrolling sentry.

For his part however, von Schroif was again lost in contemplation. His mind, racing in all directions, somehow found its way back to January of the previous year when SS-Sturmbannführer Helmut Voss had first introduced him to the new machine of which he was now so proud. He could visualise the scene perfectly and recalled almost word for word the old man's final summing up. In his mind's eye he could visualise Voss standing on the engine deck as he concluded his speech.

"So that, gentlemen, is the Sturmgeschütz, the new breed of *Sturmartillerie*. The Führer has been kind enough to trust you with 80,000 Reichsmarks' worth of modern fighting vehicle, so please don't let him down, eh? Like every good commander, you will take care to play to its strengths and, of course, take careful note of the weaknesses of which you must be constantly aware.

Note that, unlike the main battle tanks that the public so often mistake them for, which as you know are crewed by five men, the absence of a turret means a much reduced fighting compartment has to be fitted inside the Sturmgeschütz, and this in turn of course dictates that the vehicle can only be crewed by four men which, let's face it gentlemen, is a bad thing. Something had to give, and in consequence the radio has to be operated by the loader. Not ideal, but it allows you to take to the field in an armoured vehicle no taller than an average man, which makes you very hard to hit, which I'm sure you'll agree, gentlemen, is a very good thing!"

In his mind's eye, von Schroif could picture the old man pausing to allow the laughter to die down and remembered how, despite himself, Voss couldn't help but give in to the natural urge to smile and how his wrinkly countenance soon broke into one of his characteristic grins. Voss was the owner of a face which could only be described as 'lived in'. Years of battle, hardship and a life spent outdoors had produced a craggy but somehow genial countenance which was part of the charm of the man who commanded such loyalty. As silence resumed, Voss at last felt ready to continue his briefing.

"The other major concern for all of you is the armour on the sides and rear which seems disconcertingly thin. So be alert! Make sure your driver is awake. I can't say this often enough — you must keep your front to the enemy at all times. You may have noticed that you have to do that — or you can't shoot them!"

A faint current of appreciation flowed through the audience and Voss, sensing that he had their attention, continued with his simple lesson.

"The lack of a turret also means that the driver has to spin the vehicle to acquire new targets, with the constant risk of throwing a track, so be vigilant at all times… Any questions before we go?"

"Forgive me, SS-Sturmbannführer, but, if the enemy approaches the vehicle, there doesn't seem to be much of an option for self-defence?"

The question was obvious, and the nervous young Wehrmacht officer who spoke was clearly uncomfortable, but Voss was understanding.

"First, you give the supporting grenadiers a good kick in the ass! We know from Spain and Poland that obviously there may be times when a machine gun will come in handy. I have made that representation on your behalf and I can assure you that the team at Krupp are investigating, and no doubt innovating as we speak, but for now you must make do with a 9mm machine pistol… Just open the pistol port or the hatch and take a pop at them. They'll soon clear off!"

There was more laughter but SS-Sturmbannführer Helmut Voss was aware that his audience was less than impressed with the situation and he continued with some words of comfort.

"Once it's been exposed to the realities of combat, much will be learned about the new machine. Trust me, gentlemen, much of it will be good. All of the exercises and tests confirm that the low silhouette makes it very hard to hit and the 50 mm frontal armour seems man enough for the job," said Voss with a knowing shrug of the shoulders, "give or take!"

Again there was sympathetic laughter at Voss' characteristic display of candour.

"Bear in mind, gentlemen, that your maximum speed cross-country is about 10 kilometres per hour. On roads, it is about 35 kilometres per hour. On normal roads its radius of action is about 130 kilometres. Cross-country, about 65 kilometres, no more — don't believe everything the manufacturer says." ♦

The smiles around the room told him that the men were listening.

"And, above all, think about the fuel you are using. To move a six gun battery 100 kilometres requires 4,000 litres of petrol. If you run out, you are stuck. So, be aware."

Nods and grins from the officers confirmed that they were familiar with the nightmare scenario of running out of fuel.

"You need to exercise the same caution when it comes to ammunition," continued Voss. "The manual claims that the maximum range of the 7.5 cm KwK short-barrelled tank gun, with which this weapon is equipped, is how much?"

"About 6,000 metres, SS-Sturmbannführer," replied the young lieutenant upon whom the piercing gaze of SS-Sturmbannführer Voss had come to rest.

"Perhaps that may be true on a good day with a following wind on the firing range, but really you are just wasting ammunition. 500 Reichsmarks wasted! Don't even think about it. Clear?"

"Yes, SS-Sturmbannführer, perfectly clear," came the swift response.

"Good. Well, there we have it," continued Voss, warming to his theme. "The basic principles and role of the new weapon are as follows; you shall hear this only once, so listen carefully." He paused briefly for effect and then continued. "The assault gun on an armoured self-propelled mount is an *offensive* weapon. I don't have to remind you that it can fire only in which general direction?"

"Forwards," replied the young lieutenant without hesitation.

"Correct!" replied Voss with a twinkle of a smile. "The direction in which the vehicle is pointing is also where your strongest armour is, so fix it in your mind! It could save your life. Now," continued Voss, who was in full flow, "owing to its cross-country performance and its armour, the Sturmgeschütze is able to follow anywhere its own infantry or armoured troops can go. The moral support that the infantry receives through its presence is vitally important. It does not fire on the move and you should never attempt to fire on the move, Herr Leutnant, is that clear?"

"Crystal clear, SS-Sturmbannführer."

"Well, that's all very good," replied the older man

with his customary warmth, "but in close fighting it is vulnerable because its sides are light and the roof is thin. Besides, as we have seen, it has no real facilities for defending itself at close quarters. It is therefore not in a position to carry out independent reconnaissance and fighting tasks. This weapon must always be supported by infantry. Never forget that. Splitting up assault-gun units into small parts such as platoons or single guns jeopardizes the firepower and facilitates enemy defence, so don't do it."

After a pause in which he carefully scanned the assembled officers Voss continued.

"That's enough of the negative stuff. I believe absolutely in the worth of this machine. We are working towards the principle of establishing assault gun battalions which will consist of a battalion headquarters and three batteries. In this room are the men who will lead those battalions" — his eyes were now fixed on von Schroif — "so make sure and give a good account of yourselves when the time comes. In the meantime, we will continue with the current basic organisation of the battery which will continue to have six guns split into three platoons, each of two guns.

"The command vehicles for battery and platoon commanders are armoured half-tracks. They make it possible, therefore, to move right up to the foremost infantry line to direct the fire. But as complete a picture as possible must be obtained of the enemy's armour-piercing weapons and the positions of his mines; hasty employment without sufficient reconnaissance means death. Premature deployment must also be avoided.

"After an engagement, assault guns must not be given security missions, especially at night. They must be withdrawn for refuelling, overhauling, and resupply. After four to five days in action, they must be thoroughly serviced. If this is not possible, it must be expected that some will not be fit for action and may fall out. When in rear areas, they must be allotted space near repair shops so that they are readily accessible to maintenance facilities.

"Surprise is essential for the successful employment of assault-gun battalions. It is therefore most important for them to move up and into firing positions under cover and generally to commence fire without warning. With the allotment of smoke ammunition, which we have set at 23 percent of the total ammunition issue, it is possible to lay smoke and to blind enemy weapons which, for example, are sited on the flank.

"The fifteen per cent supply of armour-piercing shells doesn't mean you are expected to fight armour battles. It's for use against concrete positions and the like. Assault guns should be used to engage casemates, not tanks! Take it from me; cooperation with assault engineers using flamethrowers is very effective in these cases. So, do we go charging into the attack in towns and villages, Leutnant?"

"Never, SS-Sturmbannführer," replied the Wehrmacht officer.

"Good man! Assault guns are only to be used in towns and woods in exceptional circumstances only, and only in conjunction with particularly strong and close infantry support. Remember, assault guns are not suitable for use in darkness, so at least you should get some sleep!"

Voss allowed a moment's pause to let the small ripple of laughter die down before continuing.

"It is the special role of the assault-gun battery to assist the infantry in fighting its way through deep enemy defence zones. Therefore, it must not be committed until the divisional artillery and the heavy infantry weapons can no longer render adequate support. When in action the battery commander, together with his platoon commanders, must at all times be familiar with the hostile situation, and must reconnoitre the ground over which he is to move and attack."

Voss was now on the home straight and he paused briefly to allow the information to sink in.

"I see faces here that I know from Spain and Poland. I'm sure you'll agree that it looks superior to the Panzer I we had out there, eh, von Schroif?"

Von Schroif nodded his assent and Voss continued.

"And we still shook up the Reds, even with that. The proof of the tapas is in the eating gentlemen. One day soon I think you'll get a chance to compare the two. I think you'll find our new friend, the StuG, up to the task."

* * * * *

The promised day had arrived very soon indeed. By May 1940 von Schroif and his crew were rolling into action for the first time. As he stood in the stillness of a Polish pine forest on the eve of Barbarossa, von Schroif could hardly credit the fact that it was just over a year since the day when they had first moved into combat in the Sturmgeschütz. It seemed simultaneously like yesterday and a life time ago.

During the long pause in which von Schroif had been lost in thought, SS-Kannonier Wohl had stood perfectly still, patiently awaiting the next word from von Schroif, but his commander's thoughts were far away from eastern Poland. In his mind's eye von Schroif was 1,000 kilometres away to the west, he was back in the green fields and pleasant towns of rural France. Once again he recalled the tension of that first day in action.

For three agonising hours von Schroif had watched in nervous frustration as the grenadiers advanced methodically toward the village of Narbonne, meeting increasing resistance, and were finally stopped at the eastern edge by strong hostile fire. It was then that the company commander, after considering the situation for what seemed like a lifetime, had at last sent the oral message to the rear: "*Sturmgeschütze Vor!*" — Assault battery to the front!

The 1st Platoon of the armoured assault artillery battery needed no further invitation and dashed forward to engage in its first fight. To his intense frustration von Schroif, as battery commander, had not been allocated a Sturmgeschütz, but had instead been assigned a command vehicle known as a *Beobachtungskraftwagen*. It was a tiny and lightly armoured observation half-track with the official designation of Sd.Kfz. 253. The prevailing logic was that the actions of the assault guns should be directed by this flimsy tin can, but orders were orders, and von Schroif, in his command vehicle, gingerly followed assault guns number 5 and 6 into action.

There followed a nerve-jangling ride past the abandoned houses, every man alert for the crack of an anti-tank weapon. Fortunately, the platoon encountered no resistance until it arrived at the centre of town, when suddenly they heard the *rat-a-tat* of a heavy machine gun. The machine-gunner was highly accurate and in the cramped interior of the StuG tiny chips of steel detached themselves and flew around the compartment, cutting and tormenting the crewmembers, whose nerves were already strained to breaking point. With the limited vision from inside the vehicle the location of the gun and even the direction of fire was hard to pinpoint and the StuG continued to receive heavy machine-gun fire as it trundled obstinately forward.

Eventually the ever-vigilant von Schroif spotted the source of the bullets that streamed forth like angry wasps from the upper storey of the Town Hall. The machine gun bullets splayed and ricocheted off the strong frontal armour but not a single shot penetrated the hull and, to the mighty relief of the crew, the first test was passed.

From his command half-track von Schroif remained

intensely watchful and the exact source of the fire was quickly spotted — first floor, two windows along from the main door. SS-Oberkannonier Karl Wendorff relayed von Schroif's orders over by radio.

"Machine gun nest, 11 o'clock, first floor elevation."

Inside the StuG a high-explosive shell was rammed into the semi-automatic breach and as quick as lightning the gun was fired by marksman SS-Hauptscharführer Michael Knispel. The death-dealing response was served upon the Frenchmen as two high-explosive rounds from assault gun number 5 crashed into the building, immediately silencing the machine guns. The StuG had drawn its first blood.

Under the expert guidance of von Schroif, assault gun number 6 then went into action. The command came over the radio. "Enemy artillery. 2 o'clock. Range 400 meters."

The French artillery von Schroif had spotted were sheltering behind the nearby buildings. He watched in satisfaction as one shell exploded in a courtyard among the horses of the gun teams. The uninjured animals galloped away, frightened by the explosion.

Assault gun number 5 then swung into position in the churchyard to silence hostile machine guns which were firing from two windows in a large building. From close by von Schroif, remaining exposed in the commander's hatch of his half-track, relayed the order to fire on this target and a further two high-explosive rounds from the assault gun served to silence them.

Dismayed by the accurate fire from this effective new weapon the French quickly evacuated the main street and the centre of the town, but machine-gun resistance was renewed at the western edge of the village and the infantry commander requested that the assault guns should be sent ahead again.

The assault guns, now six strong, soon reached a destroyed bridge across a tributary of the Semois River. The pioneers, although hard at work, had not yet completed their task here, but the guns managed to ford the river. The half-track however was unable to follow, and von Schroif took matters into his own hands. He abandoned his *Beobachtungskraftwagen* and pulled rank to oust the startled commander of assault gun number 5 from his machine, leaving Wendorff to maintain communications.

Slipping down into the poky interior von Schroif immediately entered the claustrophobic world of the fighting vehicle. Every millimetre of space was occupied with controls, levers, dials, projecting metal, ammunition and gear of every description, which left no room for anything more than the lithe frames of the crew. The poorly ventilated sweat-soaked interior was uninviting in the extreme. It was a miniature version of hell and the brimstone in the atmosphere was real; the air was literally thick with smoke and cordite from the shells which had already been fired in it — it was hot to breathe and produced a searing on the lungs which made it painful to inhale. Even an old hand like von Schroif needed a few seconds to adjust to his fetid surroundings.

However, for his pains he did receive a welcoming and cheery nod from the gunner, SS-Hauptscharführer Knispel, who was well known to him from their days together in Spain and Poland. He hadn't chosen this gun by accident. Von Schroif was confident of the fact that, if anyone was going to make this new fighting vehicle a success, it was SS-Hauptscharführer Michael Knispel. Never taking his eyes off the viewing device, von Schroif gave the command "*Sturmgeschütze Vor!*" and the StuG moved forward purposefully. Von Schroif was now back in his element.

After fording the stream, the assault guns came to a barricade of tree trunks which obstructed the road leading up a slope in one of the southern spurs of the Ardennes Forest. However, Bobby Junge, at the controls of assault gun number 5, simply stepped on his accelerator, dashed against the obstacle, and opened the way upon emerging into the clearing. Here they were fired upon from the direction of Suxy and quickly came to a halt. Infantrymen streamed past the vehicle as the leading company deployed promptly and, supported by an anti-tank platoon, began to advance. The advance was short-lived however as the *tack-tack-tack* of a French machine gun sent four men tumbling to the ground. The landsers were now checked on the banks of the stream just west of the town. It was time for the StuGs to do their work. They were ordered up; tasks were assigned, and positions designated. As the heavy infantry weapons and armoured assault guns were heard approaching from the rear, the lead battalion commander, in a quick decision, signalled his advancing reserve company to turn off and attack in the new direction.

The new army was once again performing like a well-oiled machine, just as it had done in Poland. Von Schroif and the armoured assault artillery battery continued to the front to assist the leading rifle companies. The riflemen slowly worked their way ahead, pressing hard against the French forces, driving them off the high ground to the right front. Finally, one of the assault guns moved up on to this commanding terrain and quickly fired eleven rounds at a range of 800 metres into a battery of enemy horse artillery going into action. The assault gun itself, however, was then taken under fire by a French anti-tank battery.

In the meantime, more German artillery opened fire and the battalion began to advance across the Vierre River. As usual, all the bridges had been destroyed and all the trucks had to be left behind, although the water was no obstacle for the infantry and the armoured assault artillery. After crossing the river, the advance was checked again by resistance coming principally from a fortified house which stood along the route of advance. Assault gun number 5 went into action against this house. The first round hit the lower left window. The second entered the attic window. The third went over the house but, as von Schroif noted with satisfaction, exploded among some of the now retreating Frenchmen.

By 17:30 all resistance in this vicinity had been overcome. The French reconnaissance battalion, which had attempted to stop the regiment, was completely destroyed. Von Schroif recalled with satisfaction that the performance of the armoured assault artillery battery, in its initial engagements at Narbonne, had completely won the confidence of the infantrymen. In the top pocket of his battle tunic von Schroif still carried the after-action report which Voss had prepared. It had become his talisman and he knew the words by heart.

Von Schroif's long reverie was interrupted by a short cough from Wohl and he was catapulted back into the present, a warm summer night in Poland with the stars shining through the canopy of trees, and he once again had to confront the uncomfortable fact that heroic events soon became faded by history. The events of the battle for France were irrelevant now, what mattered was the forthcoming battle for Russia.

"With machines like these, the fortress will again fall to us tomorrow. Mark my words, Wohl," said von Schroif, beginning the conversation anew.

"I believe it will, Hauptsturmführer," said Wohl, keen to re-engage the conversation and skip another boring circuit of the perimeter. "Was it a tough fight, last time?" asked Wohl, who had attended the briefing and, with a battle looming, for once had paid half attention to what was being said. Following his baptism of fire and the excitement of Greece, he was palpably aware that the next adventure might prove somewhat more challenging.

Despite his nervousness, Wohl took comfort from the fact that von Schroif radiated such genuine confidence. It was obvious that he felt confidence in the fact that he controlled the men and the machines for the job. He, and some of his crews, had literally been here before and he now gave vent to his frustrations.

"We were here in September '39, not even two years ago," said von Schroif, finally answering Wohl's question. "We had next to no time to draw ammunition and supplies when we found ourselves seconded from the SS-VT to Guderian's corps."

Wohl was now genuinely interested and, faced with the prospect of a similar experience, he now wanted to know all the details. Like soldiers everywhere, von Schroif was only too willing to fill a few empty minutes with reminiscence for the benefit of eager ears.

"We quickly crammed into the old Sd.Kfz. 232... You know the type, the one with the heavy 'bedstead' type antenna over the body of the car, so everyone can see it for miles around?"

"Well, at least it gives the enemy something else to aim at, Hauptsturmführer," said Wohl, always happy to lighten the mood. "We could have done with a few of them around us in Greece. Everyone in the Greek army seemed to be after me down there... and the Tommies too!"

"Don't take it personally, Wohl. I don't think you are

on Herr Churchill's hate list. I'm sure the Reds will have a welcoming bullet or two for you to remember them by."

"I'm not so worried, as long as I'm burrowed down in the StuG. It's the damn snipers I can't stand."

"I'm sure you'll be alright, Wohl. You have a lucky face."

"I intend to keep it that way. Was the armoured car a good fighting vehicle, Hauptsturmführer?"

"*Good* isn't the first word that springs to mind. Artillery splinters shoot through them like a knife through paper. Anyway, that's what we were issued with, so we clattered into Poland with Guderian and swept down on the old fortress over there," said von Schroif, pointing towards the east. "It was known to the Poles as *Brześć Litewski*. We surprised them by arriving from the north-east. We call it the Battle of Brest-Litovsk. It was fought out just over there, between the 14th and 17th of September '39."

As von Schroif recounted the events of the battle the pair were joined by driver Bobby Junge who clambered down from the driver's hatch at the front of vehicle.

"Everything in order, Junge?" asked von Schroif, by way of welcome.

"I've checked everything I can think of, Hauptsturmführer. The bus is in great running order."

The driver, SS-Kannonier Bobby Junge, from Heidelberg, served in number 1 gun of the first battery, commanded by SS-Obersturmführer Werfer. He was an absolute master of his craft; there really was no better driver. Junge liked the mechanical robustness of the Sturmgeschütz. He also liked its surprising turn of speed — and speed was something which Junge knew all about. In civilian life he was a professional race driver and his performances against Rudolf Caracciola and the tragic Bernd Rosemeyer at the Nürburgring before the war indicated a trajectory of great success. Now, in the last few moments before the world would change forever for better or worse, the talents of this remarkable son of Baden-Württemberg were put to work on the machine known as the StuG.

"Remember last time we were here, Junge?" asked von Schroif, inviting the driver into the discussion.

"I'll never forget it, sir. This is where we lost Biermann, Oehler and Eggers."

"Good comrades all," replied von Schroif solemnly. "It certainly was a grind. Three days and nights of heavy fighting for the indestructible island stronghold surrounded by three heavily fortified islands, comrades falling around us... We win the battle, then we give the prize to the Ivans. They keep it for a couple of years, build up the fortifications, make the place even more impregnable. Then they order us to take it back!"

"I'm not a politician, Hauptsturmführer, but it seems to me like von Ribbentrop blundered... Maybe too much wine in his cellar?"

As usual, Wohl had overstepped the mark with his oblique reference to the Reichsminister's days as a wine salesman and von Schroif was quick to snuff out any suggestion of dissent. "That's enough, Wohl. It is not our place to question the workings of the party." Despite the sharpness of his tone, von Schroif was content to let the remark pass as he continued to ruminate with Junge on the painful events which had occurred nearby. "You know it is what I learned after the battle that still irks me. Initially at least, the Poles did not even plan to defend the damned fortress. It's also ironic that we should have even been in the vicinity of Brest-Litovsk."

"May I enquire as to the reason?" asked the chastened Wohl.

"You may, Wohl. We now know that, as the storm clouds of war were gathering around us, in a brilliant piece of diplomacy an understanding was reached by von Ribbentrop and Molotov. The result was that Poland was covertly carved up between us and the Reds. It was agreed that our attack from the west would be matched by a Soviet advance from the east, which would neatly slice up Poland between us. The region of Brest-Litovsk was assigned to what was to be the Soviet 'sphere of interest'. However, our rapid advance was not matched by the expected attack by the Soviets, who did not begin their own invasion of Poland until later."

"Once we had done all the hard work!" interjected Junge.

"As you say, SS-Kannonier Junge," continued von Schroif, "and in the continuing absence of the Reds, Guderian decided there was a need to secure the fortress. Today, Brest-Litovsk is the frontline formed by the partition of Poland, but at the beginning of the surprise attack in '39 the fortress was actually located deep behind the Polish frontlines. Our intelligence had reported it to be a supply depot and organisation centre rather than a defensible fortress. However, no one had allowed for the genius of General Heinz Guderian. Under his guidance we won the swift victories at Wizna and Mława and broke through Polish lines and sped southward with the aim of flanking Warsaw from the East and cutting Poland in two. This swift attack is now known to a trembling world as Lightning War; it's a devastating military operational doctrine, which was developed by Guderian between the World Wars. For us participants it was a thrilling experience. The situation changed dramatically when we reached Brest-Litovsk."

"Did you see the General in action?" asked Wohl.

"For sure we did," replied von Schroif. "The armoured cars had been pushed to the limits. As the last few drops rattled around in the tanks I finally had to order a stop near the Muchawiec river bridge. No sooner had we halted when a staff car roared up and a General bellowed across, 'What is the reason for this delay? You must push on!' I could only reply with something along the lines of 'We must have fuel, our tanks are dry...' He shouted back at me 'Do I have to take care of everything?' and three fuel cans were immediately produced. While Junge here filled the tank I was summoned into the presence of Guderian. He wasted no time and got straight to the point. His grasp of detail was impressive. I still recall his every word.

"'We need to seize the fortress in order to prevent elements of the Narew Operational Group from retreating southwards and re-joining the rest of the Polish forces,' he said. 'We understand the fortress is currently housing the battalions of the Polish 82nd and 35th infantry regiments and elements of various smaller units. If you move fast, all you will be faced with will be the rear-echelon units of an infantry regiment — all the tabors, field kitchen staff, reserve soldiers, military police, commander's reserves, guards, aides, and raw recruits who did not arrive at the mobilization centre before the unit to which they were attached left for the front.'

"But you must be aware that a large number of newly mobilised reservists had also started to arrive at the fortress, awaiting forward deployment to their units. General Guderian was obviously not aware of it at the time, but from these units, the Polish General Plisowski had somehow managed to organized a force of roughly three infantry battalions, aided by an engineering battalion, several batteries of artillery and two companies equipped with the old French FT tanks. As we were about to discover, there was also somewhat unorthodox assistance available in the form of two armoured trains."

"So what is it like to fight a train?" asked Wohl in amazement.

"Frightening!" Junge interjected. "We had no sooner noticed this strange train in the distance than we immediately started to receive some really big calibre shells. Powerful stuff. That was where Oehler and his crew bought it. Direct hit from a high-calibre shell. The car just blew apart."

"Yes, the train was certainly a strange adversary," continued von Schroif, "because it also carried a platoon of five scout tanks. You know, the old French FT type. They left the train and attacked our armoured cars. That's where we lost Biermann, but they hadn't reckoned with our SS-Hauptscharführer Knispel. After losing three tanks to the cannon in those expert hands the other two wisely withdrew. Fortunately for us, the Poles have no sense of cohesion. We then had to endure a further attack by an assault platoon from the train, but without the tanks that also failed, but only after the loss of more brave comrades. It was then that we learned that the armour on the Sd.Kfz. 232 can just about stop a bullet, but nothing else. So never overlook the humble anti-tank rifle, Wohl! Anyway, after a combined attack of the assault platoon and the heavy artillery from the train, it looked as if we would be forced to leave the area of the Muchawiec Bridge, but by then General Guderian had pushed the 5th Tank Regiment forward. The train withdrew towards Brest town and the train station was left in our hands. That was the last we saw of the armoured trains, and thank God for that too!"

"So, did the fortress surrender?" asked Wohl, now wrapped up in the tale.

"Sadly, no. We reached the area of Brest and attempted to capture the fortress on the bounce. We lacked infantry and heavy weapons so the probe attack was easily repelled by Polish infantry and a company of those funny little FT tanks. With Knispel on form, all the Polish tanks which dared show themselves were destroyed, but we were still forced to retreat towards the part of town we controlled.

"Later that day the artillery arrived at last and they started the bombardment of both the fortress and the town. Heavy street-fighting broke out again. Our forces were soon mixed up with the Poles, so no one really knew what was happening. The little ammunition we had soon ran out, so we fought through the night from house to house until dawn with grenades, rifle butts and daggers. By dawn approximately half of the town was in German hands, the other half was still being defended by Polish infantry. They could have held on but on the following day Polish defenders had taken such a beating that they withdrew from the town.

"Our heavy casualties prevented us from continuing the attacks on the fortress. Instead, it was constantly shelled with artillery and even bombed by the Luftwaffe. It was all hell and fury, but it was little use to us as the forts are built over a series of caverns and tunnels. In its ruined state, this place affords countless positions for snipers. On the surface, bombing just creates rubble and the Poles were able to take advantage of innumerable hiding places.

"Our casualties were already considerable and they rose even higher when the main assault finally started in the early morning on the 16th of September. We soon discovered that the Poles had plenty of small arms ammunition and light arms, thanks to the munitions depot in the fortress, but had almost no anti-tank weapons. However, our advance was halted by the last of the FT tanks which were piled up, sealing the northern gate of the fortress. By nightfall, despite further heavy losses, we finally captured the northern part of the citadel. We had killed around 2,000 Poles, almost half of the defenders."

"So that's when they gave in?" asked Wohl.

"A sane man would have done, but we were faced with fanatical lunatics. At dawn the next day General Plisowski ordered part of the Polish forces to retreat from the easternmost fortifications and regroup to the other side of the river and southwards. We were too weak and too exhausted to continue fighting into the night. It was a big mistake. Most of the evacuation was completed by early morning. The only Polish unit to remain in the fortress was drawn from the 82nd Infantry Regiment under that crazy Captain Radziszewski, who decided to fight to the end. We fought on with these fanatics in the ruins and tunnels and cellars throughout the day of the 17th of September."

"The parade day," interjected Junge.

"Correct, Junge," said von Schroif. "This proved to be a significant day because that was the day when the Red Army finally crossed the Polish border and started its quick advance westwards. We had no sooner put the last bullet into the last of the Poles when the Soviet tank brigade reached us. I can't recall his name... What was his name, Junge?"

"He was Brigadier Krivoshein. They reached the area on the 17th and took over the fortress from us."

"At least we didn't have to bury the bodies," announced a deep booming voice from the darkness. "We left the Reds the job of burying the *untermenschen*."

The unmistakeable voice was that of SS-Hauptscharführer Knispel, who now levered himself free from the gunner's hatch and jumped down into their midst, snapping to attention and saluting as he did so.

"Ah, Knispel, just remembering a few of your past glories," said von Schroif, who was obviously pleased to welcome this celebrated member of his battalion.

SS-Hauptscharführer Michael Knispel, known to everyone as 'The Prussian', was a Berliner, born in 1910. He demonstrated all the stoic characteristics of that undemonstrative breed but, like many from that great city, he was as hard as iron underneath. By the age of seventeen he was already a veteran SA man and street fighter par excellence. His reputation as a fierce street brawler, the scourge of the Berlin communists, had projected him to local fame. Knispel had been picked up and processed by the party machine and turned into a formidable boxer. In the eyes of his comrades he had achieved lasting greatness in the boxing ring by beating the fearsome Max Diekmann in just six rounds, who himself had beaten the great Max Schmelling.

Knispel and von Schroif had been together for four

years, since their days in the Legion Condor. They saw eye to eye on most things, except Knispel's undying passion for poaching deer. They had exchanged words on the subject in Spain, Poland, France, Yugoslavia and Greece. To von Schroif's chagrin there was sure to be a Sauer hunting rifle stowed somewhere on board the StuG and, as a former land owner, von Schroif harboured an inborn grudge against poachers. Although he turned a semi-blind eye, Hans von Schroif was a proud man and his pride would not allow him to accept defeat. He was determined to find it one day. In the meantime, an uneasy truce prevailed. As long as Knispel was not too overt in his activities, von Schroif did not push too hard to discover the whereabouts of this unauthorised non-regulation weapon. He possessed a sense of soldierly duty which was too strong to give in and completely relent, and even the delicious aroma of fresh roast venison could not persuade von Schroif from pursuing his duty.

However, Knispel was an amazing marksman. His skills had made the difference between life and death in France and Greece and von Schroif knew when to lose the odd battle in order to win the war. Knispel's grey battle dress tunic was festooned with wound badges, assault badges, his Iron Cross second Class, and war merit medals. He also proudly displayed his Marksman's Lanyard, and it was well earned too. He was far too good a man to lose over such a minor issue as an infraction of one tiny section of military law. Therefore the policy adopted by von Schroif was to ask no questions and accept his portion of the 'roast horse meat' frequently proffered by Knispel when the vehicles went into laager for the evening in a forest glade.

"I can't recall much in the way of glory back there, Hauptsturmführer," said Knispel, gesturing in the vague direction of the fortress. "All I can remember is a bloody mess with no ammunition. As I remember, we had to fight with sharpened spades in those confounded tunnels with those maggots who didn't know how to surrender. We came out covered in their blood and shit and Guderian tells us we have one hour to get ready for a big parade! While we were still grappling with the bastards underground Junge was washing the armoured car and polishing our dress tunics! Crazy days, but that's war for you."

"Surely not?" queried Wohl, suspecting his leg was being pulled.

"I give you my word of honour, Wohl," said von Schroif. "Strange things happen in combat. Heaven and hell can coexist within yards of each other. While Wohl and Wendorff were getting ready for the parade, we killed their Captain Radziszewski, who was the last of them, with our daggers and went straight into the joint German-Soviet parade that was held in the town while his blood was still warm in our scabbards."

"It was certainly the weirdest day of my career," said Knispel. "We paraded once through the town and then kept going straight across the Bug River, over the bridge there, and started fighting the Poles again an hour later."

"Things were easier after Brest-Litovsk, until Plisowski pulled things together down in Moravia," said von Schroif, "but I don't think the Ivans will prove as tough as the Poles. The Radziszewski bunch were real lunatics."

"And full of shit too. It sprayed all over you when you carved them open with a sharpened spade," said Knispel, remembering the gruesome details of the horror of his underground fight.

"Well, let's try and use high-explosive this time, eh?" said von Schroif.

"I'd like nothing better, Hauptsturmführer," replied Knispel earnestly. "I don't go about looking to grapple with untermenschen in tunnels. But the tunnels are still there, the underground barracks are still there, the fortifications have all been repaired, and who's to say the Reds won't prove as tenacious as the Poles?"

"Well, the Finns kicked their asses," offered Wohl hopefully.

"That was in the snow and the trees. The Reds will have learned their lessons."

"You'll never know for sure with Ivan," said von Schroif. "I spent five years among them at KAMA. Some days they were bright and resourceful, on other days stupid and slothful. There were times when they appeared unable to grasp the most basic engineering concept, only to amaze you with an astonishing advance of their own."

"Never a truer word was spoken," said a strange

voice, and SS-Sturmbannführer Voss stepped out of the shadows. The group immediately sprang to attention. Before Wohl could ask what KAMA meant, Voss picked up the thread of the conversation.

"As you were," said the older man with familiar ease. "In my experience, it is possible to predict how virtually every soldier of the western world will behave in a given situation — but not the Russian. The characteristics of this semi-Asiatic *untermensch*, like those of his vast country, are strange and contradictory. Disregard for human beings and contempt for death are other characteristics of the Russian soldier. I fought on the Russian front in the last war and I have personally witnessed him climb, with complete indifference and cold bloodedness, over the bodies of hundreds of fallen comrades in order to take up the attack on exactly the same spot."

"We hadn't expected you, SS-Sturmbannführer," said von Schroif.

"Well, you might have done. You didn't think I'd let you take my precious *Sturmgeschütze* into something this big without giving you a little advice on what to expect? You are about to face a foe who is radically different from the French or the Tommies. Ivan is a different animal altogether. I've seen him work, with wary apathy, all day burying his dead comrades after a battle and it seems to me he looks toward his own death with the same resignation. Even severe wounds impress him comparatively little. For instance, I recall seeing a wounded Russian sitting upright at the side of a street near Tannenberg, in spite of the fact that both lower legs were shot away, ask for a cigarette with a friendly smile.

"With stoic equanimity he endures cold and heat, hunger and thirst, dampness and mud, sickness and vermin. Because of his simple and primitive nature, all sorts of hardships bring him but few emotional reactions. His emotions run the gamut from animal ferocity to the utmost kindliness; odious and cruel in a group, he can be friendly and ready to help as an individual."

"That certainly mirrors my own experience, SS-Sturmbannführer," said von Schroif.

"Yes, but you haven't been in action against them yet! During the last war I fought them for three years and I couldn't let you enter into this campaign without giving you some kind of insight into what you are faced with. I witnessed many times units which one day repulsed a strong German attack with exemplary bravery, and on the next folded up completely. There were others which lost their nerve one day when the first shell exploded, and on the next fought like lions, forcing us, man by man, to literally cut them to pieces. The Russian is generally impervious to crises, but he can also be very sensitive to them. Normally, he has no fear of a threat to his flanks, but at times he can be most touchy about them. He disregards many of the old established rules of tactics, but clings obstinately to his own methods."

"Can you enlighten us as to what, in your opinion,

makes the Ivans so different to us Germans, SS-Sturmbannführer?" asked von Schroif.

"Well, I'll try," replied the old warrior. "In my experience, the key to this odd behaviour can be found in the native character of the Russian soldier who, as a fighter, possesses neither the judgment nor the ability to think independently. He is subject to moods which to a German are incomprehensible; he acts by instinct. The strength of the German soldier is conscious action, controlled by his own mind. Neither this action on his own, nor the consciousness which accompanies the action, is part of the mental make-up of the Russian. But the fact must not be ignored that a change is taking place also in this respect."

Singly and in small groups the crews from the waiting StuGs appeared and gradually formed a circle around Voss, all eager to drink in the experiences which might prove invaluable.

"The difference between the Russian units of the Tsar, who we faced in the last war, and those of the Bolshevists, who we now face, are likely to be considerable. Whereas in the earlier war the Russian Army was a more or less amorphous mass, immovable and without individuality, the indoctrination of the Red Army through communism will no doubt show itself clearly. In contrast to the situation which prevailed during the last war, the number of illiterates is now thought to be very small. The Russian masses today are thought to have acquired at least a measure of individuality, or at least were well on the way to acquiring it. The Russian is beginning to become a perceptive human being, and hence a soldier who is able to stand on his own feet.

"However, you may take heart from the fact that the number of good non-commissioned officers is still not large and the Russian masses have not yet overcome their sluggishness. But in my opinion the awakening of the Russian people cannot be far off. Whether this will work to the advantage or disadvantage of their soldierly qualities cannot yet be determined. For along with awareness flourish criticism and obstinacy. The arbitrary employment of masses resigned to their fate may become more difficult, and the basis of the typically Russian method of waging war may be lost. The force bringing about this change is communism, or more precisely, a psychic awakening of the people directed by a rigidly centralized state. The Russian is fundamentally non-political; at least that is true for the rural population, which supplies the majority of soldiers. He is not an active communist, not a political zealot, but always for his Motherland."

Taking advantage of the slight pause in the proceedings, von Schroif was able to make a quick request. "Do you mind, Sturmbannführer, if I summon the rest of the battalion?"

"No, the more the merrier as far as I'm concerned," replied Voss.

The messengers were quickly despatched. Orders were whispered into open hatches; Sturmbannführer

Voss would address the battalion. The eager men came tumbling out of the vehicles and arranged themselves in a densely packed ring around the careworn figure of their beloved Sturmbannführer. Once all was in readiness he continued with his impromptu lecture.

"As you know, men, you are about to embark on a titanic adventure where you will meet a very different foe. In judging the basic qualities of the Russian it should be stated that, by nature, he is brave. To this innate capacity for valour, our intelligence informs us that another determining factor has been introduced into the Red Army. It takes the form of the political commissar who demands unqualified obedience.

"Systematic training, drill, disregard for his own life, and the natural inclination of the Russian soldier to uncompromising compliance are the bedrock of the Red Army. The very real summary disciplinary powers available to the commissar are the steel ties which bind the Red Army to a culture of iron obedience. In this connection it must be understood that, unlike our fair and open National Socialist regime, Russia is an autocratically ruled state — an absolute dictatorship demanding and compelling the complete subordination of the individual. That blind obedience of the masses, the mainspring of the Red Army, is the triumph of communism and the foundation of its fighting capacity.

"Don't be fooled by some of the setbacks they suffered against the Finns last year. Ivan is a fast learner and those lessons will be adapted to in no time. In addition to the simplicity which is revealed in his limited household needs and his primitive mode of living, the Russian soldier has close kinship with nature. It is no exaggeration to say that the Russian soldier is unaffected by season and terrain. This immunity gives him a decisive advantage over us Germans, especially in Russian territory where season, temperature, and terrain will play such a decisive role. Unlike our elaborate supply system, providing you with all the comforts of home…"

"Yeah, except coffee, cigarettes, and good food!" thought Wohl, who wisely kept his council and continued to pay rapt attention, allowing Voss to continue uninterrupted.

"The problem of providing for the individual soldier in the Russian Army is of secondary importance, because the Russian soldier requires only very few provisions for his own use. The field kitchen, a sacred institution to our troops, is to the Russian soldier merely a pleasant surprise when it is available, but it can be dispensed with for days and weeks without undue hardship."

"Please forgive the interruption, Sturmbannführer," ventured von Schroif, "but do you have any intelligence on whether the Reds have improved their use of technology?"

"That's a very good point," said Voss. "The industrialization of the country, carried out in a comparatively short period of time, has made a large number of industrial workers with full command of technical skills available to the Red Army. The Russian has mastered all new weapons and fighting equipment, all the requirements of machine warfare, with amazing rapidity. Soldiers trained in technical subjects are carefully distributed through the ranks where they are to teach the necessary rudiments to their duller urban comrades, and to those who came from rural areas. The technical skill of the Russian is especially notable in the field of signal communications.

"Mark my words, the longer the war lasts, the better the Russians will become at handling this type of equipment. Their communications have improved steadily since the end of the last war, and with noteworthy skill the Russians will soon make themselves familiar with German signal communications. Whereas in the last war the telephone was still magic to the average Russian, in the coming battles we must assume that he no longer regards the complicated radio as an amusing toy." Voss turned to von Schroif and continued his lecture. "As you will no doubt recall from our time at KAMA, monitoring and tuning in, jamming and deception, all were arts which the Reds understood very well."

Wohl could stand the mystery no longer. He just had to know. "Permission to speak, Sturmbannführer?"

"Granted," replied Voss.

"I keep hearing mention of KAMA. Can you please explain, Sturmbannführer?"

"Certainly I can, SS-Kannonier. During the Weimar years, when we were not permitted to develop tanks, a number of *Reichswehr* officers and various specialists attended a secret development facility at Kazan in

Soviet Russia. I was one of those who spent a number of years among our former adversaries and it gave me a great insight into the working of the Russian mind." With a warm smile Voss turned his attention once more to von Schroif. "You will all be familiar with the events of the beer hall putsch of 1923. Well, following that unfortunate series of events it was decided that your Hauptsturmführer might benefit from a few years outside the Reich… and KAMA was the best fit."

"It was there that we developed the Panzer I and laid the foundations for the Panzer II," continued von Schroif, drawing a veil over the reasons why he urgently had to absent himself from Bavaria.

"During our time out there we learned a great deal about Ivan," said Voss, picking up where he had left off before Wohl's interruption. "In contrast to the good side of the Russian soldier, there were bad military aspects of equal significance. To us Germans, it was one of the imponderables about each Russian unit whether the good or bad would predominate. There still remained an appreciable residue of dullness, inflexibility, and apathy which had not yet been overcome, and which probably will not be overcome in the near future."

"We thank you for your generosity with your time, Hauptsturmführer," said von Schroif. "We are anxious not to detain you further. Is there anything else you'd care to impart?"

"I will leave you with a word about the craftiness of the Russian. He seldom employed large-scale ruses. The usual tricks, such as feigning the existence of troops by increased fire and other means, were just as common with the Russians as with all armies. They seldom carried out feint attacks. We found, however, that we had to be on guard against dishonesty and attempts at deception by individual Russian soldiers and small units. One trick, a particular favourite, was to feign surrender, or come over to us with raised hands, white flags, and all the rest. Anyone approaching in good faith would often be met by sudden surprise fire at close range. The Russian soldier, who can lie motionless for hours on end, often feigned death. An unguarded approach often cost a German soldier his life.

"Finally, I'd just say his emotions drive the Russian into the herd, which gives him strength and courage. The individual fighter created by modern warfare is rare among the Russians. Most of the time a Russian who has to stand on his own feet does not know what to do. During the last war, however, this serious weakness was compensated for by the large mass of men available. The unpredictability of the mood of the Russian soldier and his pronounced herd instinct at times brought on sudden panic in individual units. As inexplicable as the fanatic resistance of some units, was the mystery of their abrupt mass flights, or sudden wholesale surrender. So these, gentlemen, are some of the many faces of Ivan… Who knows which Ivan we'll meet tomorrow?"

- CHAPTER 2 -

Der sich versammelnde Sturm

A PLAN OF an altogether different kind formed the focus of attention as the StuG commanders and infantry liaison team from the 45th Infantry Division gathered round von Schroif in the farmhouse which served as his temporary battalion office. The lamps cast just enough light for the assembled officers to make out the details of the plan of the fortress spread out on the table in front of him.

For once, even OKH was in tune with the reality in the field and the general staff had correctly identified the fact that von Schroif was particularly well qualified for the task ahead. Less than two years previously von Schroif and his *abteilung* of armoured cars had been seconded to general Guderian's XIX Armoured Corps. They had played a key part in seizing the fortress of Brest-Litovsk from the Poles — only to see it handed over to the Soviets. For that logical reason the SS Sturmgeschütz battalion, now commanded by von Schroif, had been detached from its parent formation and formed into an ad hoc battle group which consisted of elements of the 45th Wehrmacht Infantry Division, a company of combat engineers and some supporting units and artillery all charged with seizing the fortress of Brest–Litovsk.

According to the most recent orders, Kampfgruppe

von Schroif was due to be joined by an SS 'Special' *Sonderkommando* who would provide rear area security and a battery of 'special mortars', but as yet there was still no sign of either unit. In the confusion of the unheralded preparations now engulfing the command system von Schroif could obtain no clear information as to the location, or even the identity, of the missing units.

In addition to the frustration produced by the absent reinforcements, the recurring sense of déjà vu irritated von Schroif. For the hundredth time that morning von Schroif's thoughts strayed to the two additional units had been promised to complete the Kampfgruppe. The purpose of the first was obvious, a Waffen SS formation to provide rear area security against partisans and the like; the other was intriguingly described as 'special mortars'.

Like soldiers everywhere, von Schroif and his team were anxious to discover exactly what made these new toys so 'special' — anything which gave an edge in combat was welcome and their interest was piqued by an insatiable demand for the newest and the best. In all the hubbub surrounding the preparations for Barbarossa it had been impossible to obtain clarity; all von Schroif knew from the cagey intelligence officer was that the additional units were definitely on the way.

Not wishing to have to repeat himself, von Schroif waited before commencing his briefing. He made the correct decision, for just as he was about to commence the briefing the sound of ragged and ill-disciplined marching could be heard. The dim sounds of a hurried conversation with the sentry on duty outside the hut followed. Eventually the door opened and, squinting in the light, stood a gaunt Waffen SS-Obersturmführer. His skeletal features were scarred. His lank hair was slicked down and parted Führer-style. His battle dress was dripping with decorations. His Legion Condor medal marked him out as a combat veteran from Spain. He appeared to be in his mid-forties which was rather old for a rank which equated with a lieutenant.

For once Hans von Schroif was unable to maintain his steely self-control. The shock of recognition was clear to all. "Dirlewanger!" he gasped in stunned disbelief.

"Reporting for duty, Hauptsturmführer!" replied the skeletal SS-Obersturmführer in a strong Franconian accent.

Oskar Paul Dirlewanger hailed from Würzburg, a beautiful city in the region of Franconia, located in the northern tip of Bavaria. The legendary beauty of the city was in stark contrast to the ugly apparition which now stood before the assembled officers. His large, almost bulbous skull narrowed to a weak, pointed chin. His face carried Mansur scars and other gashes and cuts.

Even to those who were not familiar with the Waffen SS, SS-Obersturmführer Oskar Dirlewanger was an infamous name. Despite his official rehabilitation, his unsavoury reputation preceded him. There was no doubting his personal bravery, which was almost legendary. He had served as an infantry officer in World War I and had won both the Iron Cross 2nd Class and the

Iron Cross 1st Class. His military service in the trenches had been viewed as exemplary and he was known for his considerable courage in battle; his damaged features testified to the fact that he had been wounded over ten times. He always led his troops from the front and the decorations covering his chest were proof of that.

After the end of the World War, Dirlewanger had floated around the different Freikorps volunteer militias and fought in the Ruhr, at Saxony. His path had often crossed with von Schroif and they had actually fought together in Upper Silesia. Dirlewanger was an intelligent man. Von Schroif was aware that he had studied at the university in Frankfurt and had obtained a degree in political science in 1922. Their politics were similar too; both men had joined the NSDAP in 1923. It was a source of frustration for von Schroif that Dirlewanger could boast slightly longer service in both. Dirlewanger's party number was #1,098,716 and his later SS number was #357,267; beating von Schroif by roughly a thousand volunteers in each instance.

"Excuse me for one second, gentlemen," said von Schroif, who almost staggered into the kitchen where he found the familiar figure of Leutnant Vogel, the aptly named Luftwaffe liaison officer.

"Is everything in order, Hauptsturmführer?"

"No, it is not," said von Schroif, his eyes alighting on a bottle of schnapps. "Yours?"

"A gift from home," said Vogel.

"As a rule, I do not drink schnapps, Leutnant," said

von Schroif, "but on this one occasion, would you be so kind as to spare me one glass?"

"Certainly," said Vogel, picking up a glass and filling a generous measure. "Is there anything I can do?"

"No, it's Dirlewanger."

"Is there still a problem? Hasn't he been exonerated? He is a veteran after all," enquired Vogel.

"Sure, that's the official line, and it's true that he has seen more combat against the Reds than any other veteran, including Sepp Deitrich himself. He seems to have a nose for action and has been everywhere. To my certain knowledge, Dirlewanger fought against the communist general strike in 1919, and I can testify that he has fought with the Freikorps in Backnang, Kornwestheim, Esslingen, Untertürkheim, Aalen, Schorndorf, Heidenheim, in the Ruhr at Dortmund, Essen in 1920 and in eastern Germany in 1920 and 1921. I am certain that Dirlewanger had served faithfully and loyally in Freikorps Epp, Freikorps Haas, Freikorps Sprösser and Freikorps Holz."

"Then he sounds like the kind of man we need," suggested Vogel, tactfully keeping his options open and waiting to see which way the wind would blow.

"No one needs this man," said von Schroif.

"I understood Dirlewanger had combat experience with armour and had commanded an armoured car troop with some distinction?" continued Vogel.

"I can't deny it. On his own initiative, he set up the Württemberg 'Highway Watch'. It included many ex-members of Dirlewanger's machine-gun company, the one he had commanded at the end of the war. Regrettably, they were augmented by my own A7V veterans and it was these proper men who first brought me the reports of 'improper practices' concerning our friend Dirlewanger."

"Is he disloyal? To the party?" asked Vogel.

"I cannot even lay that charge at his door. There is no question that Dirlewanger has proved to be an active and dutiful servant in the fight against the Reds in Germany. His methods were… shall we say, *robust*."

"So the rumours are true, Hauptsturmführer?" asked Vogel.

"I don't deal in rumours," retorted von Schroif. "After the Kapp revolt had been beaten, you will no doubt recall how the murdering bandits of the 'Ruhr Red Army' controlled large parts of the Ruhr area."

"My knowledge is a little hazy. It was… er, a little before my time," replied the young officer.

"Of course… I must be getting long in the tooth," replied von Schroif before continuing with his explanation. "Anyway, what happened was that a regular army force, the Reichswehr-Brigade 13, under General Haas, and the Sprösser Volunteers were sent to combat the Reds. Unlike today, they were tempestuous times. Workers from Daimler-Benz in Untertürkheim intervened and tried to prevent the movement of these units by rail."

"Is that when Dirlewanger's men intervened?" asked Vogel.

"Yes, his armoured troop somewhat brutally

intervened. This permitted the transport of the Reichswehr units, but rumours of bloodthirsty vengeance and 'other acts' followed in the wake of the unit. We have to accept that revenge is sometimes part of the experience of a soldier in the heat of battle, but with him there were always 'other acts'. The same thing happened when they were deployed in Dortmund, then Iserlohn and then again in Essen."

"*Other acts*?" queried Vogel.

"Bestial, debased acts," replied von Schroif. "Dirlewanger and his men contributed fully to what has become known as the Reichswehr's regime of 'White Terror'. There was a massacre in Pelkum and 'Dirlewanger' armoured troop IV was involved."

Vogel, who had no interest in politics, said nothing and expectantly waited as the tale unfolded.

"My unit was nearby and I remember the occasion vividly. On Easter Sunday 1921 Dirlewanger and his troops moved towards Sangershausen, which had been occupied by workers. Rather embarrassingly, an attack led by Dirlewanger failed and the workers succeeded in cutting off and capturing some of his men. The next day, after Dirlewanger had been reinforced during the night, the town was taken and, in response to rumours that Freikorps men had been executed, the Dirlewanger troop wreaked a typically barbaric and horribly violent revenge on the remaining workers, many of whom were horribly mutilated."

"I recall something of a connection between the town

and SS-Obersturmführer Dirlewanger," offered Vogel. "I thought it was something positive?"

"You are right, to an extent. During this operation, Dirlewanger was grazed on the head by a gunshot. After the party gained power, Dirlewanger was celebrated as a 'liberator' from the Red revolutionaries, and a square in the town was named after him and he received the title of 'honorary citizen.'"

"So was he in the Reichswehr?" asked Vogel, his interest now fully roused.

"No. Like me, there was no place for him. He was out in the wilderness and that's where the problems began."

"With the law?" enquired Vogel, sensing the downward curve of the tale.

"With the law... and with humanity."

"I'm afraid I don't follow, Hauptsturmführer..." replied Vogel.

"Following the disbandment of the Freikorps it seems Dirlewanger held various jobs, which included working at a bank, a knitwear factory and, somewhat ominously, as a teacher. The rumours of 'improper' behaviour continued. In 1934, he was finally convicted of the rape of a 13-year-old Bund Deutscher Mädel girl. He was also accused of the illegal use of a government vehicle, and damaging that vehicle while under the influence of alcohol. For these crimes he was sentenced to two years' imprisonment. Dirlewanger then lost his job, his doctor title and all of the military honours he had won in the war. He was also expelled from the party. It came as no surprise to me and to the other Freikorps veterans to learn that, soon after his release, he was arrested again on similar charges."

"So why was he not sentenced to death?" asked Vogel.

"This time he was branded as a repeat sexual offender and a deviant. He was sent to the Welzheim concentration camp. That should have been that, as far as we were concerned, but amazingly our friend Dirlewanger was released and reinstated as a colonel in the General SS Reserve."

"Friends in the right places, then?"

"Very perceptive, Herr Leutnant. This was following the personal intervention of his influential friend, one Gottlob Berger, the Head of the SS-Hauptamt, and his long-time personal friend, one Heinrich Himmler."

Vogel's face remained a mask of calm but inwardly he was desperate to shout out: *"For God's sake man, this animal is so base he was thrown out of the fucking Nazi party!"*

However, Vogel was far too astute. He made no comment and his demeanour continued to suggest animated interest. One could not be too careful, even with a sympathetic ear. One word out of place could be fatal. He continued to listen, his impassive face somehow still managing to convey an air of interest, as von Schroif continued with his tale.

"The only stipulation was that he should travel to Spain to fight in the Condor Legion against the Reds in the Spanish Civil War. So our paths crossed once more.

Despite my contempt for the man, my own sense of duty meant that I had no alternative and we served side by side in the Condor Legion from 1936 to 1939. There were two unproven incidents of improper behaviour. I have my own opinions, based on what I saw, but Dirlewanger wriggled free. In combat, he was wounded three times."

"I recall that he was exonerated by the courts back home?" advanced Vogel.

"There's no denying it. For Dirlewanger, his stint in Spain served its real purpose. Following further intervention on his behalf by his patron, Berger, Dirlewanger successfully petitioned to have his case reconsidered in light of his service in Spain. The appeal was clearly a formality. To my eternal disgust, Dirlewanger was reinstated into the party, albeit with a higher party number. To the eternal shame of a renowned institution, his doctorate was also restored by the University of Frankfurt. While we were at war in Poland and France I became aware that Dirlewanger had volunteered for the Waffen-SS and that he had received the rank of Obersturmführer."

There was a short pause as von Schroif accepted another measure. The act of unburdening himself had obviously had the hoped for cathartic effect and the shock and bewilderment began to wear off. Unbeknown to Hans von Schroif, Otto Dirlewanger had initially been out of the way serving as an SS-VT commandant of the SS labour camp in Dzików. However, he was now embarking on active service once more as the commander of the

'Dirlewanger' penal battalion, and it was something which would place him on a collision course with the former landowner, Hans von Schroif.

The Dirlewanger battalion was moulded around the nucleus of a small group of former poachers recruited from jail. It was believed that the excellent tracking and shooting skills of the poachers could be put to constructive use in the fight against communist partisans. On this fateful night the unpleasant surprise still lay in the future and during the time it took to adjust to the shock of his unpleasant new arrival von Schroif was able to gather his composure. He left the comfort of the kitchen and re-entered the main room and went on the attack.

"You are late, Obersturmführer," said von Schroif. The tone was unwelcoming and hostile.

"I beg your forgiveness, Hauptsturmführer, but vehicular traffic is taking precedence and we were halted until the special weapons had passed."

"No matter, Obersturmführer," said von Schroif dismissively, "you have held us up enough."

Before he could say anymore, von Schroif was again interrupted, this time by the sound of motor engines and the clanking of half-track vehicle tracks, followed by the hasty arrival of a breathless Wehrmacht artillery captain. The smartly dressed young officer snapped to attention.

"Captain Grunewald reporting. My battery is now at your command, Hauptsturmführer."

"Is this the new secret weapon we've heard so much about — the mortar?" asked von Schroif.

"It has not been a well-kept secret, Hauptsturmführer, but it's not a mortar," replied the young officer.

"Well, what is it exactly, Captain? The time for secrecy is over. Please enlighten us."

"As you wish, Hauptsturmführer. It's a six-barrel rocket projector, sometimes called the Do-Gerät, also known as the Nebelwerfer."

The puzzled looks from the liaison officers of the 45th Infantry Division invited further explanation.

"I think it best if you were to explain. The floor is yours, Captain," said von Schroif.

"Thank you, Hauptsturmführer. Actually, this is not a particularly new weapon. Its name, moreover, is extremely misleading. In the first place, the Nebelwerfer 41 is not a mortar at all, and in the second place, it can accommodate both gas-charged and high-explosive projectiles, as well as smoke projectiles."

"Is it accurate?" asked von Schroif.

"This weapon does not demand pin-point accuracy."

"So what do you offer?"

"Power, Hauptsturmführer, awesome power. With us in the kampfgruppe, it's like having the might of Wotan behind you. Although fire from the Nebelwerfer is relatively inaccurate, the weapon's chief asset is the concussion effect of a cluster of high-explosive projectiles, which is considerable... devastating, actually."

"Glad to hear it,' replied von Schroif, warming to the captain, "but will you be able to keep up? We intend to snatch the fortress and keep going."

"Our battery is fully motorized and therefore extremely mobile. We will be right behind you. Our projectors are capable of playing a decisive part in any engagement. Our 3-ton prime mover is sufficient for traction purposes, and can also carry the gun crew and some of the ammunition...."

"You sound as if you really believe in your weapons."

"As I say, the Nebelwerfer 41 can fire three different types of projectiles: high-explosive shells, incendiary projectiles, and smoke projectiles. The high-explosive shells include those with supersensitive fuses and those with delayed-action fuses. The latter can penetrate reinforced cover. Because of their fragmentation and concussion effect, high-explosive shells are used primarily against personnel. It has been found that the concussion has not only been great enough to kill personnel, but occasionally has caused field fortifications and bunkers to collapse. The incendiary projectiles are psychologically effective, and under favourable conditions can start field and forest fires. The smoke projectiles are used to form smoke screens or smoke zones."

"Smoke is all very well, but for this mission I'd like to hear more of the high-explosive capability."

"Certainly, Hauptsturmführer. One of the main advantages of the Nebelwerfer 41 is that it can mass its projectiles on a very small target area. With advanced observers, the infantry can assure manoeuvrability for itself and a concentration of its firepower upon the most important points. Projectors are placed well toward the front, ahead of the artillery, so that they will be able to eliminate hostile command posts, destroy hostile positions, and even repulse sudden attacks effectively. It is essential that the firing positions of the projectors are always carefully built up so that the weapons can give strong support to the infantry."

"So do the rounds pack a punch in their own right, Captain?" asked von Schroif.

"They certainly do, particularly as my weapon's six barrels are fired successively, just one second apart. The high-explosive round contains over two kilograms of high-explosive; this is comparable — in weight, at least — to the high-explosive round used in the 105mm howitzer, but each of our pieces has the power of a battery falling in a small area."

"Well, glad to have you aboard, Captain," said von Schroif with a warmth that was missing from his exchanges with Dirlewanger. "Let's hope your new weapon repays the obvious faith you have in it. In just over one hour we shall see. Now, gentlemen, pay close attention." With that he turned his attention to the group.

"Gentlemen, I know that, like me, some of you have fought here before. We had some difficult days here, eh? Hard fighting and brave comrades, now biting into the grass. It's now just two years since we took the fortress of Brest-Litovsk from the Poles... then we handed it straight over to the Reds! And now we have to take it back again. I know there has been some grumbling out there. I don't need to remind you that, as soldiers, we don't ask questions — we simply obey orders. I'm afraid you must now put all memories of '39 behind you. What we are about to experience will make '39 seem like a stroll down the *Unter den Linden*. From the intelligence reports, the garrison has been expanded and reinforced. Last time we had to resort to these…" Von Schroif drew his finely wrought SS dagger from its sheath. "You may rest assured that Ivan will not just hand the place over."

Turning his attention to the map, he used his dagger to point out the salient features.

"The ancient fortress of Brześć lies at the confluence of the Muchawiec and Bug Rivers. It occupies the site of a medieval castle, and has been strengthened and reconstructed in Napoleonic times and then again in 1847. As you can see, gentlemen, the fortress is composed of a series of islands which are partly man-made and partly natural. It can be described as resembling a human eye. The citadel island is like the pupil while the concave sides of the three islands form the iris surrounding the pupil. The network of various rivers and canals are like the capillaries. The original Polish outermost defences of the west island are now on our side of the demarcation line, so that makes a natural jumping off point.

"The fortress occupies a strategic position in the Soviet lines. The Reds have strengthened it and will seek to hold it. Our task is to assist the 45th Infantry Division to seize the Brest fortress. It's not going to be a walkover this time around; intelligence has identified elements of seven rifle battalions, one reconnaissance battalion and two artillery battalions. There also appear to be some specialised subunits of rifle regiments and corps subunits of the 6th Orlov Redstandard and 42nd Infantry division of the 28th Infantry Corps of the 4th Army, subunits of the 17th Redstandard, the Brest Frontier Guard detachment, and strong elements of the 33rd Engineering Regiment. We believe they have a number of tanks of the T-26 type. In all, the garrison could be as strong as 7,000 men."

Von Schroif paused to allow the information to sink in.

"There are also a large number of civilians with many families located inside the fortress, and a large hospital."

"Permission to speak, Hauptsturmführer?" The voice was Dirlewanger's.

Von Schroif felt his heart sink into his boots, but decided in the interests of cohesion to allow the question. "Permission granted."

"How are we to deal with *untermensch* civilians?" asked Dirlewanger.

"What do you mean?" replied von Schroif brusquely.

"Are they to be summarily executed?"

"Of course not, they are to be rounded up and detained and sent to the rear."

"And the commissars?" asked Dirlewanger.

"The same applies," came the curt reply from von Schroif.

"I dutifully report, Hauptsturmführer, that you may have overlooked the recent guidelines issued by General Eugen Müller on the 6th of May concerning the treatment of political commissars. It demands that any Soviet political commissar identified among captured troops be shot immediately as an enforcer in military forces of the communist ideology and the Soviet Communist Party line. According to the guidelines issued only last month, all those prisoners, civilian or military, who can be identified as 'thoroughly bolshevized' or as 'active representatives of the Bolshevist ideology' should also be instantly executed. We were given to understand that the guidelines are to be interpreted widely when civilians are involved."

"You are correct. However, we do not expect to capture a large number of thoroughly bolshevized individuals."

"How are we to judge the extent to which they have been 'thoroughly bolshevized?'"

"You'll have to use your own judgement, but I expect you to exercise caution."

"But you do expect us to carry out the order issued by General Müller on the 6th of May?"

"I do not believe a written copy has been circulated," said von Schroif truthfully.

"You are correct, Hauptsturmführer. The order was expressly required to be promulgated orally. You were briefed, I take it?"

The nodding heads of the other officers indicated that the order had been circulated and von Schroif was forced to admit that this was indeed the case.

"We've all heard it and I must stress that we have been told to maintain discipline," said von Schroif.

"Discipline is a prerequisite. However, as I understand it, the shooting of all political commissars is necessary in order to avoid letting any captured commissar reach a POW camp in Germany where they might infect their own men and possibly find ways to communicate their ideas to the population of the Reich."

Von Schroif was aware that Dirlewanger was leading the conversation for his own purposes. He no doubt had his own dark scheme in mind but he was taking valuable time away from the military aspects of the briefing. However, Dirlewanger was a highly skilled operator with very strong political connections. There was always the possibility that he was acting on behalf of the Gestapo and sending back information and seeking out signs of political disaffection. This new viper in their midst had to be handled with extreme caution.

"You must urge caution and consider if I, as your commanding officer, would order an execution."

"You always were a good soldier, Hauptsturmführer. I shall make sure to ask myself the question when the need arises." There was something about the emphasis which Dirlewanger placed on the word 'good', the tiniest hint of an extra stress which produced an unspoken, almost imperceptible, but undeniable suggestion that Dirlewanger was cynical concerning von Schroif's approach.

"You mean *if* the need arises," said von Schroif.

"I stand corrected, Hauptsturmführer."

"Good. Well, that's all clear then," said von Schroif

dismissively, swiftly turning his attention to the role of his own command for the benefit of the infantry officers.

"Gentlemen, as you are well aware, assault guns are strong when concentrated, but have no effect when used in small numbers. They are capable of forward fire only, since they have no turrets. Therefore, they are sensitive to attack from the flanks. This is why the guns must never be employed by themselves, but always in conjunction with infantry. These weapons may be considerably restricted by marshy land, thick woods, and natural or artificial obstacles. Moreover, they constitute large targets. They can see and hear little. Even during a battle, the assault guns occasionally must withdraw to cover and obtain fresh supplies of ammunition and fuel."

Von Schroif scanned the faces to ensure that the infantry commanders were paying close attention. His very survival and that of his men was closely dependent on their understanding and cooperation.

"This brings us to the question of how the infantry should assist the assault guns. Infantrymen must draw the guns' attention to hostile tanks and other targets by means of the signal pistol, prearranged light and flag signals and, in desperation, even by shouting. Buttoned up inside our vehicles, we have a very limited field of vision. The infantry must therefore assume responsibility for neutralising any hostile anti-tank guns. The flanks of assault guns are particularly vulnerable and must at all times be covered and protected by the infantry against hostile tank-hunting detachments, which are always ready to operate against our assault guns. Such protection is especially necessary in built-up areas and in terrain where visibility is poor. The infantry must also warn the assault guns of the proximity of anti-tank obstacles and particularly mines, and must be prepared to guide the guns through such obstacles."

Von Schroif paused briefly to assure himself that this vital information was being absorbed. Satisfied that his words were being heeded, he continued with the briefing.

"The infantry must take advantage of the guns' firepower to advance in strength via pre-arranged lanes not under fire. The assault guns must be given sufficient time for reconnaissance. The guns and the infantry will formulate plans through personal consultation, and will ensure means of communications during battle. Infantry should not stay too close to the guns, and should not bunch. Instead, deployment is advised to lessen the danger of drawing hostile fire and to avoid injury by ricochets. Since the driver of an assault gun has limited vision, infantrymen must keep in mind the danger of being run down, and must move accordingly!"

There was a ripple of amusement at this statement.

"Remember, gentlemen, assault guns are 'sitting targets' when they have to wait for the infantry; infantrymen can find cover almost anywhere, but the assault guns cannot. Since the guns fire at the halt, the infantry must gain ground while the guns are firing. Although the assault guns are of great assistance when ground is being gained, it is the infantry that must *hold* the ground. Since the assault guns must also keep their ammunition available for unexpected or especially dangerous targets, the infantry must engage all the targets that it can possibly take on with its heavy and light weapons. Although the assault guns must withdraw after every engagement to prepare for the next engagement where their assistance will be required, the infantry will not withdraw. Is that clear?"

"Good. Time is short, gentlemen, and you'll be please to know that we can count on our comrades in the Luftwaffe. Leutnant Vogel is our appropriately named liaison officer. The floor is yours, Leutnant."

"Thank you, Hauptsturmführer," said Vogel, stepping forward to take up a position by the map. "Gentlemen, as you are aware, my role is to act as the link between what happens in the skies and with you down below. The system of visual communication between ground troops and aircraft is well developed. It must be remembered, however, that we take the precaution of changing the signals as often as possible. To speed up recognition, ground troops should possess detailed knowledge of our own aircraft types. In this sector you can expect to see the Heinkel 111, the Messerschmitt 109 and our old friend, the Stuka Junkers 87."

"Can you run through the signals protocol once more?" von Schroif asked, knowing how crucial this information could be.

"Certainly, Hauptsturmführer. In the daytime, ground

troops must give recognition signals when air units call for them by giving their own recognition signals, or if friendly aircraft threaten to attack. Orange-coloured smoke is the signal most easily recognised from the air. It means, 'own troops are here.' It is the chief recognition signal and should be used by all ground troops wherever possible."

"I take it everyone is also familiar with the protocols concerning identification panels?" interjected von Schroif.

Without pause, Vogel continued.

"Identification panels are vital. They should be laid out so that they may be read from aircraft flying toward the front. They must be arranged in good time, and on a background against which they can be picked out clearly from the air, so that the aircraft will not be obliged to circle over the battle area. The panels should be spread on open ground, wherever possible, since aircraft usually observe while approaching, and not when directly over a position. Trees, bushes, and other objects may prevent aircraft from seeing the signals obliquely. Every effort must be made to make the signals as large as possible. Panels may be lifted only when the aircraft are out of sight. Yellow cloths mean 'here is our own frontline.' They are to be used only for this message, so that the frontline will always be clearly indicated. The aircraft can draw its own conclusions as to the battle situation. In general, yellow is easily recognisable from a moderate height; a number of yellow cloths spread out side by side will make identification easier. When our own troops advance, the yellow cloths must not be left behind! In addition, the orange smoke signal is to be used as extensively as possible."

"Permission to speak?" The voice was Dirlewanger's.

Von Schroif was about to refuse when he thought better of the matter. "Granted," he said, his world-weary tone of voice betraying the grudging manner in which he granted the request.

"In the SS we fly the hooked cross flag. Why not use them?"

"Swastika flags can scarcely be identified at all from great heights," replied Vogel, "and only with difficulty from moderate heights. Although, if there is no alternative, they obviously mean 'own troops are here.' As a rule, they are used in rear positions, but may be used in the frontline if yellow cloths are not available or if no particular value is attached to a distinct recognition of the frontline as such. Since swastika flags alone are generally not sufficient for identification purposes, it is advisable to use the additional signal of orange smoke."

"And if no smoke is available?" asked Dirlewanger, clearly enjoying his moment.

"If the usual recognition signals are not available, troops may improvise signals, such as the waving of steel helmets, handkerchiefs, and so on. However, these signals afford no guarantee that the ground troops will be recognised."

"It might be helpful for us to go over the recognition

signals which our own aircraft will provide one last time," interjected von Schroif, now anxious to regain control of the proceedings.

"In the daytime, pilots of all of our aircraft must give recognition signals when fired on by friendly troops. Daytime signals may also be given by aircraft that suddenly emerge from clouds over friendly territory, or that wish to request signals from ground troops. Ground troops will generally be able to identify friendly aircraft by noting the type of plane, the national marking, or special painting. When security permits, messages will be dropped in message boxes that emit a yellow smoke while dropping and after reaching the ground. If these boxes are not available, messages will be dropped in message bags, to which a red and white streamer is attached. Aircraft may improvise such signals as the dipping up and down of the nose and tail of a plane, wing dipping, or repeated spurts of the motor which we call 'jackrabbiting.'"

"That takes care of the daytime scenario," stated von Schroif, bringing that section to a close. "Are we all clear on the night signals?"

"Aircraft must give night signals when there is the danger of being attacked by friendly troops. In the forthcoming operation we will use white, green, and red Very lights. White Very lights will be used to request ground troops to give recognition signals: green, when a plane is about to drop a message and wishes ground troops to indicate where they prefer to have it dropped, and red, to convey the message 'Beware of enemy anti-tank weapons', while blue or violet smoke signals will be used to indicate the presence of enemy tanks."

"Thank you, Leutnant," said von Schroif, drawing the briefing to a close. "Very comprehensive. Let's hope we don't need the blue signals, eh? That will be all, gentlemen, and may good luck stay with you all."

* * * * *

As the dance finally came to an end and the last drunken remnants edged their way towards their beds, Zubachyov found himself rather smitten. As a result, he had tried hard to get Bettina away from her hefty chaperone and on her own. He had tried very hard and eventually he had succeeded. By taking the longest possible route back to the nurses' home, he had tired the flagging Anastasia to the point where she had been forced to admit defeat and had reluctantly turned in.

"I presume you don't want me to wait up?" was Anastasia's testy parting remark.

Although Bettina too seemed weary, there was chink of light. She had warmly accepted his offer of one last turn round the grounds of Cholmsker, the southernmost island, where the 4th Army field hospital was situated. It gave them a last chance to enjoy the balmy summer air. She was clearly interested in him and his hopes grew as they walked and talked. Eventually he drew to a halt and began to listen intently to a very feint buzzing sound.

"Bees? Is that bees, out so late?" asked Bettina.

Forgetting himself for a moment, Zubachyov brusquely held his hand up and commanded her silence.

"Not bees — aircraft," said Zubachyov.

"Why so late?" asked Bettina.

"I fear it's not a question of late, but *early*," replied the commander.

"Are they our planes?" asked Bettina, a note of concern creeping into her voice.

"They're coming from the west, look," said Zubachyov, his own manner now displaying signs of nervousness. "They can only be the fascists."

Dimly, in the sky to the west, the lights of hundreds of aircraft could be seen, all heading in the same direction — eastwards, into Soviet territory. As they drew close there was the deafening drone of hundreds of Heinkel and Dornier engines, supplemented by the occasional higher pitched whine as their escorting Messerschmitt fighters zipped by. At the gates leading to Brest Fortress at that very moment, on June 22, 1941, the frontier guards observed many multi-coloured lights in the sky, moving quickly from the west. Soon they covered the entire horizon. Then the hum of motors could be heard. Hundreds of planes were crossing the border with their running lights on. Black crosses could be seen on their wings and fuselages.

"What does it mean?" asked Bettina.

"I think it means I was wrong. I must leave you," growled Zubachyov. Before he could react however, the sound of running footsteps heralded the approach of a breathless messenger.

"I regret to interrupt, comrade, but we need you at the gate."

* * * * *

All along the 3,000 kilometre stretch of front last minute briefings were taking place as information and instructions cascaded down from the highest level at OKW to individual squads in the front line. The Luftwaffe too stood ready to play its part. As the planes of their comrades droned overhead, heading for targets further to the east, the few remaining men of *Luftflotte* 2 who had not yet taken to the air were being addressed by their officers. The men of Stuka squadron Rossheim had only a short flight to their target and were now summoned to hear the last minute words of Major Kuhn.

Each man was by now well aware of the historical importance of the coming events as they stood round their commander in a tent lit by flickering oil lights. During the last few months there had been constant rumours flying around of a new campaign. The fact that numerous ground crews as well as entire flying formations had been moved east provided grist to the rumour mill.

During his five years of active service Oberleutnant Ludwig Rossheim had heard many rumours. He had heard them in Spain, Poland, Norway, France, the

Balkans and Greece. Sometimes they were accurate, sometimes akin to unbridled fantasy. Rossheim rightfully considered himself to be a knowledgeable veteran and therefore inclined to make a correct call. Exercising his own judgment, he had discarded all of the gossip about a surprise attack on the Soviets, but now, to his great surprise, he had to admit to himself how wrong he had been. Most of those with whom Rossheim had discussed the various rumours and counter-rumours believed that the Russians were going to allow the Germans to push forward across Russia to the Near East in order to threaten the British stranglehold on the oilfields and other raw materials. Given that the two countries were allies, this seemed to make perfect sense. A surprise stab in the back was not the German way, but now the exact opposite was being confirmed to all.

The pilots took turns to consult their own maps and once more noted the details of their objective.

"Take careful note, gentlemen, of the fortress of Brest-Litovsk, a sprawling collection of buildings, like a small town with parkland, strong points, training colleges and a hospital. A number of Russian formations have their headquarters here. On the ground, the main attack will be undertaken by the 45th Infantry Division and the SS led Kampfgruppe von Schroif."

At the mention of the name, OberLeutnant Ludwig Rossheim couldn't resist a wry smile.

"Does the name mean something to you, OberLeutnant?"

"Well, if it's the same von Schroif I'm thinking of, then he and I are great friends. We met in Spain, where von Schroif commanded one of the Legion Condor's light tanks. It caused a great deal of merriment to watch his gunner squeeze into the tiny Panzer I. The von Schroif I know is a hard fighting and highly efficient battlefield leader and I take heart from the fact that matters will progress well on the ground."

"That sounds very reassuring. The other good news is that we don't expect much in the way of anti-aircraft fire, but intelligence suggests there may be some elements of an anti-aircraft unit," said Major Ostermann. "We hope to have the element of surprise, but you can't be too sure. Whatever happens, gentlemen, you will be flying out in a few minutes, in advance of the greatest offensive of all time. Your job is to obliterate the fortress."

The pilots of the Stuka squadron, led by a grim-faced OberLeutnant Rossheim, now made their way to a line of dive bombers, formidable Ju-87s, each parked neatly in parade formation. No sooner were the crews aboard than the engines roared into life, the chocks were pulled away and the ungainly aircraft lumbered into the air. Their gull wings made them look like particularly sinister birds of prey as each raced along the grass and took off in the dark. In order to gain height before crossing the frontier the squadron headed westwards before turning in a large circle and setting a course eastwards to make towards the Soviet frontier, ready to be in position over their objective in the early dawn.

* * * * *

As von Schroif moved through the trees on the banks of the Bug towards his own vehicle he was forced to a halt by his mounting curiosity. His attention had been drawn to the prime movers for hauling the special mortars under Captain Grunewald's command. The column had halted and the weapons were in the process of being deployed in the designated clearing on the opposite side of the road from the waiting StuGs.

They appeared to be artillery pieces but these were the strangest pieces von Schroif had ever seen. The guns were multi-barrelled with short tubes that were arranged like the chambers of an old six-shooter revolver. Each of the six guns was swiftly unlimbered and placed in position by its crew, which appeared to consist of four men. The large calibre ammunition was stacked within easy reach to the left and right of the strange guns. The crews were loading the guns and von Schroif watched with interest as the shells were introduced two at a time, beginning with the lower barrels and continuing upward. Meanwhile, foxholes were being finished.

The spreading rumours of new and formidable developments in German ordnance had reached the ears of everyone in the Wehrmacht. The word was that spectacular results were being achieved with the six-barrelled tubular projector. This was von Schroif's first close-up glimpse of the new wonder weapon and

Captain Grunewald welcomed him to a rapid tour of inspection.

"As you can see, the projector is mounted on a rubber-tired artillery chassis with a split trail," said Grunewald with loving pride.

"Is the barrel rifled?" asked von Schroif with professional interest.

"No, Hauptsturmführer, there is no rifling; the projectiles are guided by three rails that run down the inside of the barrels. This reduces the calibre to approximately 150 mm. You will note that the barrels are open-breeched."

"I had noticed that," replied von Schroif.

"So this is no ordinary shell," continued Grunewald, "it's a rocket, Wotan's rocket from hell!"

"Well, we would certainly welcome his help," said von Schroif.

"It's the very latest in military technology," said Grunewald, "but I have to admit, the propellant is surprisingly old-fashioned. It's actually slow-burning black powder, such as Frederick the Great would have recognised. Each round uses six kilograms of high-explosive, set behind the nose cap. This propellant generates gas through twenty-six jets set at an angle. As a result, the projectiles rotate and travel at an ever-increasing speed, starting with the rocket blast. The burster, which is in the rear two-sevenths of the projectile, has its own time fuse."

"Does it have a long range?" enquired von Schroif.

"The maximum range is said to be about seven kilometres, but if we need to hit a target we like to be no more than two kilometres behind the front."

"It would be a brave man to pull the lanyard with that lot set to go off!" observed von Schroif with a flicker of a smile.

"There's no lanyard," replied the earnest young captain. "We like to be as far away as possible. The barrels are fired electrically, from a safe distance." Grunewald pointed to the men digging trenches, which were already deep enough to conceal a man in a standing position. Each trench had been dug in text book fashion, about 10 to 15 metres to the side and rear of the projector.

"All six barrels are fired at once?" enquired von Schroif.

"No, they are never fired simultaneously. The blast from six rockets at once would undoubtedly capsize the weapon. The order of fire is fixed at 1–4–6–2–3–5," replied the intense Captain Grunewald with the air of a man who was deeply proud of his expertise and anxious to share his passion. "The sighting and elevating mechanisms are located on the left-hand side of the barrels, immediately over this wheel, and are protected by this light-metal hinged box cover, which is raised like this when the weapon is to be used."

Noting that he had the full interest of his audience, the captain continued with his exhaustive exposition.

"As you can see, each barrel has a metal hook at the breech to hold the projectile in place, and a sparking device to ignite the rocket charge. This sparker can be turned to one side to permit loading and then turned back so that the 'spark jump' is directed to an electrical igniter placed in one of 24 rocket blast openings located on the projectile, about one-third of the way up from the base. About one-third of the length of the projectile extends below the breech of the weapon."

The enthusiastic captain now turned his attention to the projectile itself, which von Schroif noted resembled a small torpedo—without propeller or tail fins. The base of each was flat, with slightly rounded edges.

"You will note, Hauptsturmführer, that the rocket jets are located about one-third of the way up the projectile from the base, and encircle the casing. The jets are at an angle with the axis of the projectile so as to impart rotation in flight, in 'turbine' fashion. The ingenious thing about the construction of the missiles is that the propelling charge is housed in the forward part of the rocket. A detonating fuse is located in the base of the projectile to detonate the high-explosive charge. In this way, on impact, the high-explosive is set off above ground when the nose of the projectile penetrates the soil, making for a much more destructive blast area."

"Is it an efficient operation?" asked von Schroif.

"I like to think so. The gunners will remain in these foxholes while the weapon is being fired by electrical ignition. Within 10 seconds my battery can fire 36 projectiles. These make a kind of droning pipe-organ sound as they leave the barrels and, while in flight, leave a trail of smoke. After a salvo has been fired, the crew quickly returns to its projectors and reloads them."

"Thank you, Captain. That was most informative. I await the results of the first firing in anger with interest. It sounds terrific, but I regret that I am likely to be otherwise engaged," said von Schroif, gesturing towards his waiting StuGs. "When you begin the barrage on the fortress, please make sure not to hit my vehicles!" With that, he hopped aboard the waiting half-track.

Slipping down for a brief moment into the cramped interior, von Schroif was painfully aware of the smaller space even than in the fighting compartment of the StuG which housed the four man crew. The jumble of maps, radio equipment and bodies was quite a squash and he gratefully rose again to his command position in the open hatch.

Rumours abound in every army. Back in late '39, the rumour had gone round that von Schroif and his men were to be equipped with tanks. He had shown what he and Knispel could do even with the ridiculous Panzer I way back in Spain and the progression from armoured cars to tanks had seemed logical. The fact that the issue of the new Panzer III had eluded them had come as a blow at the time, but they had been seconded to the Wehrmacht and found themselves in the first of the StuGs and had rumbled into battle with the prototype. None of them could have predicted its effectiveness in France the previous year or in Greece just a few weeks ago.

Now, of course, the original feelings of disappointment

had been replaced with a newfound sense of pride, but still von Schroif wished they could be with Guderian just now, riding with the panzers! That was where the glory and the accolades were sure to be found, that was the tip of the spear! Aimed at Moscow, Guderian and his panzers were the modern equivalent of the Teutonic knights, leading the charge against the Slavic hordes, creating the *Grossraum*, the new living space for the German people, the foundations for the Third Empire which would last a thousand years! There was no point in wishing for the unattainable though. He and his men had their humdrum orders to support the 45th Infantry Division for the second attack of his career on the fortress at Brest-Litovsk.

Von Schroif looked at his watch again, not so much as to find the time but to take his mind off the frustration of not being at the very cutting edge of the greatest operation in German military history. 03:00 — still fifteen minutes to go....

* * * * *

Oblivious to the storm which was about to break, Dimitri Korsak drove his requisitioned T-26 tank through the dark fields. The headlamps burned merrily as he left the main Moscow highway road and made directly across country towards the designated rendezvous point. He hummed a melody and reflected on the mission in hand. His instructions were clear; rendezvous with a German parachutist dressed in a Russian bandsman's uniform and collect a sealed package from the radio operator. There was a slight twist to the instructions which appealed to Korsak. The words from his superior in Moscow were still ringing in his ears.

"Ensure that you have the package then turn your machine gun on the courier. Make sure there are no witnesses, from our side as well as theirs."

As the tank trundled its way through the darkness Korsak had time to reflect. *So it's come to this, a glorified postman!* But he qualified that thought, as postmen didn't usually kill their customers.

The first grey light of dawn was beginning to show in the sky to the east as Korsak drove straight on through a field on ripening corn. He could have gone round the edge, but for the sheer hell of it he carried on straight through, oblivious to the tell-tale tracks which marked his passage. He felt safe that no jumped up local official would dare lodge a complaint. All was peaceful when suddenly his world was turned upside down. At 04:15 Moscow time, the hurricane began.

- CHAPTER 3 -

Das Loslassens des Infernos

HANS VON Schroif looked at his watch for the last time — 03:15, 22nd June, a date and time he would never forget. He then inhaled, felt his mind go strangely empty and calm, then exhaled and it all began.

"Fire!" The command was simultaneously issued from thousands of throats, unleashing a barrage with the power to wake a sleeping world and crack a continent in two.

It was the light first, the red streaks rushing off to join their predecessors, the first red streaks of dawn, in the sky above them, and then the sound... Even as a veteran of the great war von Schroif was stunned. He thought to himself, *"No man has ever heard a cacophony like this before, no man should, and hopefully no man in the future ever would..."* and at that moment he snapped out of the role of mere spectator and snapped into the role he had been training all his life for....

Above the roar of the StuG engines he could hear Captain Grunewald call "Fire!" and the hell dance began.

As the command half-track rumbled forward the rockets shot skywards with a howling, wailing sound and the earth trembled. German artillery of all calibres joined in the barrage and the noise rose to a deafening crescendo which was immediately joined by the rumble of explosions in the nearby fortress.

Von Schroif tried to imagine the effect this wave of fiery hell would be having on the ramparts of the fortress, its buildings and gun emplacements. The shock waves could easily be felt at this distance. The unbelievable concussion was palpable. It was inconceivable that anyone or anything could survive under such a rain of destruction. Surely the fortress must have been pounded to dust. Perhaps, after all, they might be able to drive right past and chase after Guderian. Surely no living thing could withstand that barrage.

There is a phrase commonly used, often by those who have never served in any theatre of war, namely 'when the dust settles'. For those who have experienced, or rather survived, any kind of heavy bombardment — whether from the ground or the air — this phrase is completely devoid of meaning. The dust never settles. This is especially true if, like the garrison of the Brest fortress, you are holed up in a fortification made of brick and concrete which is exposed to sudden and unexpected bombardment. It hangs in the air and clogs the eyes and the lungs, the atmosphere almost as solid as the bricks from whence it came.

After the initial explosion the defenders did not stand and 'dust themselves off'. They lay where they had been thrown, some with their eardrums completely shattered, others with their lungs sucked out, many whose brains were so damaged it was as if they had been knocked straight back to infancy. Perhaps it was the lucky ones who were dead, either atomised or pulped. Most did survive however, though few could tell you how.

One of the stunned survivors was Bettina Wendorff. She had been disappointed to lose the newfound companionship of Captain Zubachyov, but her loss saved her life. The nurses' quarters were adjacent to the hospital complex, spread over a jumble of nearly forty buildings on Cholmsker Island, which lay within the boundaries of the fortress, but was known to the Germans as South Island. It was on South Island that the first volley of the fire from Grunewald's Nebelwerfer battery fell. As she walked disconsolately towards the hospital a terrible howling sound suddenly arose from the west. The noise reached a painful pitch as thirty-six high-powered rockets packed with high-explosive screamed down and exploded on the hospital complex. Two minutes earlier and Bettina would have been under the barrage. As it was, the horror of a Nebelwerfer attack threw her backward, pummelled her ear drums and sucked the air from her lungs as the cluster of explosions impacted and the succession of concussions pounded her prone frame with shock wave after shock wave.

Just up ahead from von Schroif and his battery of assault guns, even closer to the falling barrage, lay the 3rd Company of the 135th Infantry Regiment. In common with von Schroif's men, they had lain quiet and motionless in the reeds which fronted the Bug, the only sound before the bombardment the mating calls of frogs, their only thought the hopelessly undermanned bridge that lay before them.

At exactly 3:15 the grenadiers charged from their positions, past the empty customs hut, and surged across the bridge, the single Soviet sentry mown down before he could react. Tearing onwards across the open space, a burst of fire from the lead elements of the unit wiped out the remaining Soviets in the guard dugout then dashed on to form the perimeter of the first bridgehead. The next phase in the lightning-fast operation was for the engineers to clear the bridge of any explosives. A single charge! That was all they found! Once dealt with in a matter of seconds, a green lens over the torch — and that was it! Bridge clear!

"*Sturmgeschütze vor!*" called von Schroif. With the upper part of his arm extended horizontally to his right side and his fist in the air he jerked the limb downwards. Engines roared and revved and the whole column rolled across the bridge and into the territory of the Soviet Union.

All along the frontier the same element of surprise had been achieved. Frogmen, boats and assault engineers throwing makeshift pontoons all helped to cross the river obstacle.

None made their entry on to the battlefield in such a dramatic fashion as the tanks of the 18th Panzer Division commanded by Major Jurgen Rondorf. His machines were the *Tauchpanzers*, the underwater tanks developed for the abortive invasion of England. At

Milowitz, near Prague, in the spring of 1941, Rondorf had been charged with a programme under which the tanks had been modified to make them suitable for river crossing. With typical thoroughness he had risen to the challenge and both the tanks and crews were now adapted for a new campaign. Their mission, as had long been understood, was literally to submerge beneath the waters of the Bug and make a submarine crossing over the line near Patulin. Rumour travels fast in armies and it was an open secret that the Panzer III's of Jurgen's force were being modified for a surprise river crossing. To make it possible they were provided with an ingenious submersion kit. Air-intakes were fitted with locking covers, and the exhaust was fitted with non-return valves. The cupola, gun mantlet and hull machine gun were all sealed with waterproof fabric covers. An inflatable rubber tube surrounded the turret ring and made it waterproof.

Major Rondorf and his men had been through this manoeuvre dozens of times but, however efficient the preparation, the real thing was always a step into the unknown. 'Dortmund' was the signal which crackled over the airwaves.

"Panzer rollen!" called Rondorf in response and his command tank surged forward and was immediately submerged in the waters of the Bug.

There was so much to do in the eerie interior of a submerged tank crawling across the floor of a river that the understandable thoughts of a watery iron coffin were immediately banished by the routine which had been drilled into them. In any event, the crew was equipped with escape apparatus and this was one drill which everyone knew by heart. As it crept across the river bed the tank drew its air from a fixed snorkel pipe attached through the commander's cupola which remained on the surface. In the red lit interior of the tank a gyro-compass provided surprisingly accurate underwater navigation. The river was less than 200 metres wide.

"Steady, keep it steady," ordered Rondorf as the blind vehicle crawled across the river bed. "Are we getting traction?"

"Traction is good, Herr Major," replied the driver.

The submerged machines were relatively easy to steer as buoyancy lightened them, but the problem was to keep the momentum going forward on the soft floor of the river. Even with good traction, with no visual aids the short journey seemed to take an eternity. Major Jurgen Rondorf took comfort from the fact that the *Tauchpanzer* could operate in depths of up to fifteen metres and according to the best intelligence reports the river Bug was no deeper than five metres... But who knew for certain that there were no underwater trenches or potholes which could swallow up the tank? After what seemed like a lifetime, twenty-two tanks emerged from the river. A series of small explosions followed as the ignition wires blew off the covering sheets as soon as the tanks surfaced, leaving the vehicles ready for action.

"Now let's see what the Reds are made of," said Rondorf.

As the tanks forged ahead all along the frontier the German forces were experiencing success and beginning a war of movement. Pontoons, barges and emergency bridges joined the captured crossings and the river was almost immediately forded. Within minutes, armoured spearheads of Army Group Centre moved on in the direction of Minsk and Smolensk. South of Brest too, at Koden, following the successful assault on the bridge, the surprise attack of XXIV Panzer Corps, under General Freiherr Geyr von Schweppenburg, had gone according to schedule. The tanks crossed the bridge, which had been captured intact. The advanced units of Lieutenant-General Model's 3rd Panzer Division crossed on rapidly built emergency bridges, the commanders standing in the turrets, scanning the landscape for the rearguards of the retreating Soviet frontier troops, overrunning the first anti-tank-gun positions, waving the first prisoners to the rear and moving nearer and nearer to their objective for the day — Kobrin, on the Mukhavets.

The pattern of events was far less dynamic for von Schroif and his command. As they crossed the rail bridge and approached the fortress the receding darkness of the night was now lit by hundreds of fires raging in buildings and shattered vehicles. The scattered bodies in grey uniforms which littered the cobbled street bore mute witness to the ferocity of the defence. Rifle fire was coming thick and fast from behind the steep walls of the fortress. Machine-gun fire began to rattle on the sides of the vehicles, causing the crews to close and lock their hatches.

The initial ferocity of the surprise attack by the Germans was debilitating and disorientating for the Russian defenders. As they groped towards some kind of cohesive response a group of German submachine-gunners led by Leutnant Weissheim picked their way through the chaos of explosions, flames and falling masonry. Initially, they encountered only a few dazed survivors, many of whom were not even fully dressed.

"Don't stop for prisoners!" screamed the lieutenant again and again during their advance as time and again the hapless victims were cut down by a ruthless stream of submachine gun bullets which ripped their targets apart. In the initial confusion Weissheim and his command were able to penetrate the Terespol gate, leaving it to be secured by those coming behind them, and were able to use the ensuing chaos to stealthily make their way to the centre of the citadel. There, as ordered, the submachine-gunners occupied the regimental club building, which dominated the entire citadel. This building was situated on a piece of rising ground and stood above all the other buildings with a commanding all-round view of the environs of the fortress.

"Quickly!" Weissheim barked, "bring the transmitter over here and let's get it operational now!"

Under Weissheim's watchful eye the radio operators set up a radio transmitter inside the main room of the club. As soon as the device was in operation the artillery spotter from the 45th Infantry Division took control and without further ado began to guide the gunfire of the nearby German artillery units which soon became murderously accurate.

In the opening moments of Operation Barbarossa the defending units of the fortress of Brest-Litovsk suffered from the fact that they were not on a war footing and many didn't even occupy the positions within the ambit of the fortress. Some of the units were assigned to defence construction works and others were in training. On the night of the attack there were between 7,000 and 8,000 men from various units, including personnel of the garrison hospital and medical unit. In addition, the families of many of the servicemen were inside the fortress.

From the very first minute of the war the fortress was bombed and shelled by every available calibre of German artillery. Severe close quarters fighting also erupted throughout the fortress. The 45th Division formed in Hitler's Austrian homeland was chosen to deliver the full thrust of the attack. The division had been active in the occupation of Poland and France and served with distinction where it had suffered 462 casualties. Now it undertook the storming of the fortress, for which it was reinforced with five hundred guns, capable of firing four thousand shells per minute, all of which were trained on the fortress.

The barrage which broke upon the heads of the

Russian defenders came with a force that no one had ever experienced before. This gigantic concentration of firepower literally shook the earth. Four thousand shells per minute were fired into the four-square-kilometre fortress. Who was in the fortress when this fearful blow was struck? In the months before the war began, the garrison in the fortress numbered about 14,000 officers and men. At the end of June, however, many units were engaged in defensive construction works or were in training camps.

On the night before the attack, there were 7,000 to 8,000 men from various units, including the personnel of the garrison hospital and medical unit. Thousands of wives and children of the servicemen were also inside the fortress.

Despite the chaos which immediately ensued, in the first few hours of the war, just before the fortress was encircled, approximately half of the garrison managed to slip out of the fortress and avoid the closing German pincers. This left a force amounting to around 3,500 officers and men to defend the fortress. They were to write their names in legend.

Five to ten minutes before the beginning of the artillery fire, German assault units captured the bridges across the Bug River, which units of the 12th Army Corps then crossed, heading for Brest. A massive column of enemy panzers moved northwards and southwards of Brest, bypassing the city as they headed eastwards.

During the opening barrage the Germans had aimed

their artillery fire at the entrance gates, bridgehead fortifications, bridges, artillery and auto-parks, warehouses and the ammunition stores. The curtain of fire was moved 10 metres deeper every 4 minutes. It was followed by the assault groups of the 45th Infantry Division. The majority of the warehouses were ruined and destroyed. Within minutes the water supply was disrupted and there was no possibility of a connection with headquarters. The majority of the soldiers and officers were killed or wounded and the defence was fragmented into islands of resistance.

An already bleak situation began to look even more dangerous for the defenders as further groups of German submachine-gunners began to move towards the Cholm gates on the south island and the Brest gates on the northern Kobrin island. It was clear that these units would soon link up, with the aim of fully taking over the centre of the fortress.

Decisive measures were desperately needed, and the man for the hour arrived in the shape of the commissar of the 84th Rifle Regiment, Senior Political Instructor Yefim Fomin.

A thought flashed through Yefim Fomin's mind as he prepared to meet the threat to the fortress. *"I should not even be here."* It was certainly true. He was supposed to catch a train to Daugavpils to meet up with his family on that fateful Saturday, but due to the crowds at the railway station had been unable to get a ticket. *"Is this fate? Was I supposed to remain here, perhaps to die?"* Fomin quickly dismissed the thought. There were too many permutations and 'what might have been' scenarios to consider. It was this ability — this decisiveness — that had assured his rise through the ranks to become a political commissar. Born in Northern Belarus and orphaned at an early age, the Komosol had become his adopted family.

Fomin's regiment occupied the barracks on both sides of the Cholm gates. Unfortunately, most of its troops and their commanding officer and chief of staff were on duty outside the fortress when the Germans struck and the fortress was hit by enemy bombs and shells. However, seeing the extent of the chaos all around, Fomin was quick to react and soon took command of the motley band of men who were scraped together by the armoury. Fomin was trained to speak in public and this was precisely the moment when those hard won skills would be put to the test.

"Comrades, to arms! The fascists are here! Act now or it will be too late!" cried Fomin, who had climbed on to a sturdy table. "Break out the rifles and bayonets. Issue 100 rounds to every man!"

His instruction was swiftly followed by an alert quartermaster who was assisted by many eager hands. Once the bemused soldiery had a rifle and some ammunition in their grasp the situation was transformed and some semblance of order ensued. Under the clear guidance of Fomin the first confusion was quickly overcome. The surviving soldiers were quickly armed and grouped together in the safety of the basement where Fomin again spoke to them.

"Comrades, a terrible deed has been done this day. The fascists are invading our Motherland. Help will soon be on its way, but for now we must take matters into our own hands. We must make sure that no further reinforcements reach the fascists who have occupied the citadel. Are you with me? Shall we give them the bayonet?"

There was a roar of approval from the assembled soldiery and bayonets were locked into place.

"Then follow me!" screamed Fomin, placing himself at the head of his small army who rushed up the stairs and into the jaws of hell.

"Hurrrrahhhh!" The deep throated cry came from a hundred voices as Fomin's men launched their murderous bayonet attack. Their sudden appearance and the sheer savagery of their advance took the advancing Grenadiers of the 45th Infantry Division completely by surprise. Fomin personally led the rush and struck at a large German grenadier in the middle of the advancing enemy group. The group was soon split in two. Men from other Russian units, seeing the success of their colleagues, rushed to support the counter-attack. Some of the German infantrymen ran on the Officers' Club building while the others fell back towards the Terespol gate. A third smaller group retreated in the direction of the island's eastern shore, hoping to cross the Mukhavets. However, there was no escape from the attacking Soviet troops who defeated the enemy group, putting all survivors to the bayonet.

"Move on, comrades! On to the Terespol gate! Be quick!" urged Fomin, and his men responded like demons as they surged on to the gate, seizing it back from the stunned German sentries and thereby cutting off the German units already in the fortress. This was the first counter-attack struck at the German assault groups and under Fomin's energetic leadership. It would not be the last.

At the gate a confused group of Russian prisoners was found and released by Fomin and his soldiers from the 84th Rifle Regiment.

"Well done, comrades. We have shown them what the 84th is made of. You have launched a counter-attack which has destroyed the enemy assault detachment. Now, quickly set up the machine gun positions again and pass the ammunition. We must not allow a single fascist to pass these gates!"

Fomin's men were true to their task. Although the German infantry made numerous attempts to penetrate into the depths of the fortress, again and again attempting to cross the bridge, the withering fire of the defenders was too strong.

Sprinting over to the Cholm gate with a small detachment, Fomin was able to draw strength from his success and soon organised a clear defence plan for this gate too. He was just in the nick of time. As wave after wave of German assault troops tried to cross the bridge they were met by rifle and machine-gun fire from the 84th Regiment and fell on the bridge or on the riverbanks. German troops eventually fell back and opened fire again and again, peppering the walls beside the Cholm gate with bullet and shell holes.

The garrison's improvised yet stubborn resistance had brought the attacking German units to a halt. The victory won at dawn in re-taking the Terespol gate and cutting off Weissheim's submachine-gunners who had forced their way into the fortress gave a fresh impetus to the citadel's defenders.

Regimental Commissar Fomin now assumed responsibility for the defence and set up his command post next to the engineering headquarters building in the very middle of the citadel's courtyard. From here he tried to establish radio contact with divisional headquarters.

"What do you wish me to transmit, Comrade Commissar?" asked the radio operator.

"Transmit as follows. This is the fortress. We have contained the initial assault and we are fighting the fascists for every metre of ground. We request ammunition and reinforcements. Please respond."

Fomin stood by as the message was transmitted.

"Message transmitted. There's no reply, comrade," stated the radio operator.

"Transmit again," ordered Fomin and the operator repeated the process, again and again, without success.

"There is no mains electricity and we are running

low on battery power, Comrade Fomin,' said the radio operator disconsolately.

Fomin had wasted enough time and now urgently needed to be elsewhere.

"Comrade, I order you not to leave your post. Switch to text transmission broadcast, a single open text message, saying: 'This is the fortress. We are fighting. We have contained the initial assault and we are fighting the fascists for every metre of ground. We request ammunition and reinforcements. Please respond.' Continue to broadcast this message until you run out of power. Do I make myself clear?"

"Very clear, comrade, I shall continue to transmit the message."

"Good. Then I shall attend to our defences."

With that, Fomin rose and sprinted across the courtyard towards the entrance to the tunnel which led to the underground barracks. It was one of those split-second decisions which in battle can mean the difference between life and death. No sooner had Fomin reached the safety of the tunnel entrance when, with a noise like an express train passing within a few feet, a high-calibre shell smashed into the very spot he had just vacated. The resultant explosion blew the radio operator into a million pieces and with him went the last means of communicating with the outside world. As he got to his feet Fomin realised that the fortress was now cut off and surrounded on all sides with no means of knowing what was happening in the wider world.

Fomin would have been dejected to realise that in any event it made little difference whether the fortress continued to broadcast or not. The panzer divisions were striking ever deeper into Soviet territory, the fortress had already been bypassed, divisional HQ had been captured, and there was no one left within 50 kilometres to respond to the fortress' calls. Fomin's actions, however, had galvanised the defenders, who had retaken the Terespol tower. As a result, the grenadiers of the 45th Infantry Division, who should have been pressing into the citadel, were now held up and pinned down by the Terespol gate.

* * * * *

A few hundred metres back from the bridge lay von Schroif and his StuG battalion, awaiting the call to action. Suddenly the radio of the cramped interior of von Schroif's command half-track crackled into life as the infantry commander made his report which was only just about audible above the rattle of gunfire and the noise of ricochets hitting masonry.

"We are encountering fierce resistance and heavy machine-gun fire. The assault group reinforcements are pinned down in the buildings leading to the Terespol gate bridge. Request assistance from the assault guns!"

"Are there any anti-tank weapons in the vicinity?" came the reply from inside the *Beobachtungskraftwagen*.

"Negative," replied the Wehrmacht officer. "We have

conducted thorough reconnaissance, as much as the enemy fire has permitted, and have seen no sign of any anti-tank weapons."

"Very well. Assault guns are on their way to you. Hold your position. *Sturmgeschütze vor!*" cried von Schroif and the column set off in the direction of the fortress.

Huge columns of smoke and a relentless rolling cacophony of explosions marked their destination which was illuminated by countless fires that raged unchecked. As they reached the last of the buildings which stood next to the bridge leading to the Terespol gate and the formidable fortification known as the Terespol tower it soon became clear that the liaison officer from the 45th Infantry Division was not exaggerating the seriousness of the situation. The landsers were hopelessly pinned down and were powerless to advance. They desperately needed the intervention of von Schroif and the StuGs. With so much lead flying around, the advance to contact in his half-track made von Schroif extremely nervous, but he had to remain visible and exposed in the commander's hatch of his *Beobachtungskraftwagen* in order to get a feel for the situation and to communicate with the grenadiers, who were hunkered behind a wall.

Eventually a young infantry lieutenant plucked up courage and sprinted over to the vehicle. As he raced over he began to set out the situation. "There's a machine gun nest on either side of the gate. It's…"

The young man did not get the chance to complete his

sentence. A stream of bullets thudded into him, bowling him over and spraying blood over von Schroif, who quickly slid down into the relative safety of the packed interior.

"Machine gun nest in the wall, two o' clock," barked von Schroif and the details of the target were immediately relayed to the number 1 gun.

Inside assault gun number 1 Wohl had heard the message and responded in the affirmative. He had already selected a high-explosive round and slammed it into the breach. Junge expertly swung the StuG round to the required facing and Knispel spotted the tell-tale flicker of flame as the machine gun spat its message of death. The round hit home and there was a satisfying explosion, but as the smoke cleared Knispel could discern the tongue of flame as the machine gun continued to fire. A second round had no more effect on the tough concrete structure.

"*Scheisse!* Load with armour-piercing," barked SS-Untersturmführer Steiner, who commanded the gun.

"It's no use, sir," said Knispel, his eyes locked on to the aiming device, "there's too much of a heat haze from the fires. I can't get a clear aim on the target."

"Let me take a look," said Steiner, abandoning his viewing apparatus and opening the command hatch. These were the last words ever spoken by the young man from the Ruhr valley. No sooner had he surfaced from the relative safety of the inside of the vehicle than two machine guns were trained upon him. The result was horrific. Blood and innards were sprayed over the vehicle and spattered over the remaining crew members in the hot interior.

"Christ! Reload with high-explosive!" barked Knispel to Wohl as he assumed control of the vehicle. No sooner had the words left his mouth when an almighty explosion rocked the StuG.

From his limited viewpoint Junge could see that number 2 gun had burst into flames. He could hear screaming coming from inside the stricken StuG and watched anxiously for signs of life but none came. The escape hatches remained closed and the screaming ceased as those inside died the death that Junge most feared — to be trapped and immolated in a burning vehicle.

"Number 2 gun has been hit," said Junge, who had the view of the stricken machine.

"Anyone see what happened?" queried Knispel.

The radio inside von Schroif's command half-track blared into life with a babble of voices, all confirming that the source of the destruction was an anti-tank gun to the right of number 1 gun.

"Order them out of there," was von Schroif's instant response.

The message was swiftly relayed and the bulk of the battalion withdrew. The pace of the retreat was not fast enough for number 3 gun from the second abteilung. The rubble from a wall which had collapsed behind the Sturmgeschütz during the combat now made it impossible for the gun to reverse. In desperation the driver made a ninety degree turn, hoping to free the vehicle from its predicament. It was the worst possible decision. The powerful forces exerted by the sharp turn were too strong and the thin metal pins holding the track together split under the pressure, causing the StuG to throw its track and skid to a halt. As it did so, it presented a perfect side-on shot to the waiting anti-tank gun, which made it difficult for the gunners to miss. The crew were aware of their danger. The other guns had by now all withdrawn, except for the number 1 gun, which now attracted von Schroif's attention.

"What's he doing?" asked von Schroif rhetorically. Through his binoculars he could see Steiner's lifeless body hanging limply in the commander's hatch. Bullets were still intermittently striking the corpse, which was being mangled into an unrecognisable bloody pulp.

"Relay the order again," barked von Schroif.

The radio operator did as ordered but still there was still no movement from the number 1 gun.

"Are they alive?" asked von Schroif.

"Yes, Hauptsturmführer, I can hear them," said the radio operator. "I fear the radio is locked on transmit."

Inside number 1 gun there was no sound from the radio, which was indeed still switched to transmit mode.

"It's on fire. Looks like an anti-tank round," confirmed Junge as number 2 gun continued to blaze.

The corroboration of Junge's estimate of the source of the destruction came instantly. There was a tremendous blow on the front armour of the vehicle that sent shards of hot metal flying around the confined and stiflingly hot interior, now coated in the blood of its commander.

"Jesus! Anti-tank gun, two o' clock," bellowed Knispel. "Switch facing!"

Junge needed no second invitation and the assault gun was swiftly turned so that its heavy frontal armour faced its deadly adversary.

* * * * *

Fortunately for the defenders of the Terespol fortification, the 98th Independent Anti-Tank Artillery Battalion had its base in the fortress. Somehow the existence of this powerful formation had been overlooked by German intelligence. When fighting began, it was the surviving men of the battalion who immediately began to drag their guns towards the main fighting area. As they approached the Terespol gate, they had entered into battle at the same time as the enemy assault guns led by von Schroif. They now had the number 3 gun in their sights. The pistol port had been opened and a stream of submachine-gun fire was issuing forth from the vehicle as the crew prepared to make their next move. With the extremely limited field of vision the submachine-gun fire was woefully inadequate and there was now no supporting high-explosive fire from the remainder of the battalion who had promptly followed the order to withdraw. It would only take one round to deal with their almost helpless adversary.

SS-Hauptscharführer Schmidt was the man inside gun number 3 who was valiantly attempting to lay down covering fire with the submachine gun. He felt he was firing in the right direction and he hoped he had done enough to make the Soviet gunners keep their heads down.

"Right, go now!" he yelled.

Three hatches immediately flew open as the other crew members prepared to leap into action and repair the track under fire. No sooner had the commander's hatch opened than there was the crack of a high-powered rifle. The commander of the gun fell lifelessly into the interior of the gun.

"Sniper!" called Hauptscharführer Schmidt, but his warning came too late. The sniper quickly picked off the other two crewmen as they scrambled from their hatches.

The anti-tank gun now fired and registered a perfect hit, which ignited the fuel tank on number 3 gun. As Hauptscharführer Schmidt attempted to bail out, he too was gunned down.

All of this had been observed by Junge, in number 1 gun, who was still dutifully awaiting confirmation from Knispel. "Do you want me to back up? The others are withdrawing," he said calmly, revving the engine in preparation to move.

"No," replied Knispel calmly. "We're loaded with HE and we haven't had any orders to withdraw... right, Wohl?" As he spoke he pressed the firing button. At that range, Knispel was never going to miss. The anti-tank gun disappeared amidst the resultant explosion.

"Good shooting!" called the mightily relieved Junge. "Shall I take us out of here?"

"Not yet… not until ordered," replied Knispel. "Load HE, Wohl."

Wohl selected the appropriate round and rammed it home into the breach. As he did so he casually flipped the switch on the radio set to receive and a stream of commands instantly filled the vehicle.

"Let's make things a little more interesting for our Red friends," said Knispel, taking careful aim at the massive water tower that dominated the Terespol fortification.

His perfectly aimed round found its mark and the tower exploded, releasing thousands of gallons which instantly extinguished the fire in the building below. The huge volume of water swept all before it as it cascaded down the street.

"That should give them something to worry about," said Knispel. "Any orders, Wohl?"

"Withdraw with all speed," stammered Wohl.

"Good. Well, that's what we'll do then…. Take us home, Junge."

* * * * *

In the dark skies above eastern Poland Oberleutnant Rossheim had bided his time as he awaited the first glimmer of the rising sun in the east. It was still quite dark when the immense spectacle had presented itself to his disbelieving eyes. Suddenly, from one end of the immense horizon to the other, the combined weight of thousands of German artillery pieces had sprung into life and engaged in pulverising the Soviet positions. The line flickered and scintillated across the continent as if huge electrical discharges were taking place all along the length of the border and the display had grown more intense as he approached the fortress. Directly beneath him, the impacts could be seen lying close together. Wherever he looked, flames were shooting up. The explosions of the discharges and impacts joined together into an elemental roar, a deep resonating sound which, even at this distance and in the closeted confines of the cockpit, swallowed up the noise of the engine and rendered it even more ethereal.

Oberleutnant Rossheim had his squadron marshalled well together. Although it was still quite dark, it had become a little brighter by the time they were a short way off their objective. Rossheim looked at the clock again. The raid has been timed for 03:35. There were still a few minutes to go. He banked in a wide curve, so as not to be above the objective earlier than the set time. Rossheim looked back once more to where the colossal artillery barrage was proceeding below. It had risen to a hurricane of fury which could easily be recognized by the vastly increased concentration of fire. As a result of the overwhelming impression of the scene unfolding beneath him, the squadron leader almost forgot to approach his objective in time.

In the first glimmers of the light of the new day the fortress of Brest-Litovsk was revealed. It was rather a large place for a stronghold, even large for a village. It sprawled over an area which included four islands at the confluence of the two rivers. Explosions were smashing in to the buildings and fortifications. As the squadron swooped down to 1,500 metres numerous vehicles could be seen on the streets and the panic-stricken figures of individual soldiers could be clearly discerned as they scurried around, seeking cover. Fires raged everywhere.

It seemed the perfect target for a raid and full of choice targets, although the combined bombs of his squadron could not hope to completely cover the target. It was therefore left to the individual pilots to select their targets. The planes swooped down one after the other and the bombs exploded among the maelstrom below. There was virtually no anti-aircraft fire and the first aircraft came through unscathed and headed back towards the field to refuel and rearm. Rossheim noted with satisfaction that this first run had gone off as smoothly as a training run and most of the others followed with the same results.

Finally, OberLeutnant Rossheim completed his run. He looked back in satisfaction as the bomb scored a direct hit on a wooden-framed building. The objective was instantly enveloped in clouds of smoke in which fresh explosions could be discerned as targets exploded and fresh salvos of shells hit home.

With no anti-aircraft fire to contend with, Rossheim was stunned to witness a machine of his squadron tumble out of the air and crash in flames. Like the dawning sky, the realisation broke over him. The unfortunate Stuka had probably, by a thousand-to-one chance, managed to get into the direct trajectory of an artillery shell and in all probability had received a direct hit from its own artillery. Rossheim dwelt briefly on the bad luck of the crew but it was now necessary to make a run back to the field as fast as possible to rearm and refuel. This was going to be a long day.

Little more than half an hour had elapsed before Rossheim's dive-bomber formation reappeared and once again pulverized the islet of resistance.

CHAPTER 4

Tod durch die Himmel

OVER THE noise of the tank engine Dimitri Korsak had heard the commotion and from the open hatch of the driver's position he had seen the horizon light up with the myriad gun flashes that heralded the most titanic conflict the world had yet witnessed. Puzzled by this unexpected phenomenon he brought the T-26 to a halt and climbed out of the tank and stood upon the engine deck. Over to the west the sky was now lit up like daylight by the ceaseless explosions as millions of projectiles were hurtled towards the territory of the Soviet Union. From the huge fires and towering clouds of smoke it was clear that the fortress he had so recently left behind was now on the receiving end of the most ferocious barrage he had ever witnessed.

"What is happening here?" thought Korsak, who had not the faintest inkling that anything so major was about to happen. *"Have the fascists attacked? Or have those idiots in the fortress provoked some kind of response?"*

The sheer scale of the bombardment and the fact that the gun flashes were visible from horizon to horizon ruled out the possibility that this was merely some border skirmish. Clearly, this was not a local action.

This realisation immediately raised the question in Korsak's mind as to whether or not he should cancel the mission. *"The timing can't be a coincidence? Moscow must have expected this, so I had better carry on,"* he reasoned. After a further minutes' pause to take in the astonishing and truly awesome sight he climbed back into the driver's seat and pushed the starter button. The rapidly lightening sky to the east showed the way ahead. He was bound for a point 20 kilometres to the north-east of the fortress. It was here that he was due to meet with the mysterious bandsman and deliver his own package of death in return.

Moscow certainly issued some strange and perfunctory commands, but this was without doubt one of the strangest missions he had undertaken. *"Why a parachutist? Why a bandsman?"* mused Korsak. *"What's in the package... a Stradivarius?"*

These and other thoughts occupied the mind of Dimitri Korsak as he carved his way in a north-easterly direction, taking the most direct route regardless of the damage to crops, livestock or fencing. He was on official business from Moscow and he was enjoying his licence to misbehave. Clearly something huge was afoot and it was unlikely that a few broken fences or the lost crops of a Polish collective would cause any comment compared to the unbelievable spectacle which was unfolding to the west.

* * * * *

Ten kilometres to the north-east the 'bandsman' was

having problems of his own. Karl Wendorff had landed safely enough and his compass reading told him that he was almost at the spot where he was to rendezvous with Cobra and hand over the documents which filled the pouch of his special document belt securely fastened around his waist. By a million-to-one chance Wendorff had successfully completed his night-time descent. As he regained his breath and gingerly got to his feet he was thankful to discover that there were no broken bones and that he appeared to be in one piece.

"So, what next," he thought to himself. *"Well, get rid of the chute for a start! Then find the radio and start transmitting. Then what? Then what indeed?"*

All Wendorff had been told was that events would transpire which would be helpful to him. With that small crumb of comfort Wendorff collected up his parachute and opened his portable entrenching tool. He then busied himself for the next hour digging a hole big enough to take the parachute.

With the evidence of his clandestine descent disposed of Wendorff set off in search of the canister containing the radio he was to use to contact Cobra. It had been thrown out of the plane at the right time and he had seen the chute open beneath his. It must be nearby. *"But where?"* was the question that now presented itself. The answer to the question was soon apparent. Wendorff presently discovered a dirt highway lined by tall birch trees and as he began to make his way along he was stopped in his tracks by a sight that caused him great consternation.

There, hanging from the highest branches of a mature roadside birch, was the limp parachute, its harness tangled among the summer leaves. The canister that housed the radio transmitter could be clearly discerned. It was hanging down like an overgrown cocoon from the topmost bough, a full fifteen metres above the ground.

"Oh shit," thought Wendorff to himself, *"how am I going to get that down on my own?"*

Former SS-Oberkannonier and *funkmeister* turned reluctant Brandenburger, Karl Wendorff, possessed a quick and agile mind and he quickly ran through a number of possible solutions.

"Could he saw down the tree?" That was possible, but for the fact that he didn't possess a saw. *"Could he could blast down the tree using grenades?"* Again, that was possible, but for the lack of grenades. He certainly couldn't climb the tree and there was nothing around that he could use to poke the canister to the ground. *"Well, this is a conundrum and no mistake,"* he thought, but before he could pursue his line of thought any further the clock reached 04:15 Moscow time and the horizon exploded into life.

Even at this distance Wendorff could feel the ground tremor and shake as the barrage opened up and the first shells began to fall upon the fortress of Brest-Litovsk. He stood aghast and open-mouthed as the whole of the western sky for as far as the eye could see was suddenly lit by thousands of flashes. It took a few seconds for the sound to reach him but when it did Wendorff was left under no illusion. Something huge was happening. It looked as if Germany had declared war on Russia; and he was now on the wrong side of the line.

* * * * *

Rossheim's squadron was quick to rearm and refuel for take-off and soon they were back in the skies over the fortress of Brest-Litovsk. The fortress was already a mass of fire and the smoke was now so intense that individual targets on the ground could no longer be discerned.

"It's no use. Mission cancelled," called Rossheim.

"Do we head for home?" asked Küchler.

"There's too much danger of hitting our own men down there. I can't see orange smoke or any recognition signs."

As aerial observation was now impossible, the Stukas were clearly in danger of becoming a headache for their own men.

"Don't run for home loaded. Follow me."

Rossheim and his men knew that in the event that their main mission was thwarted they were to widen their operation in order to attack enemy reinforcement columns on the roads leading to the fortress. However, from the air there was not a thing to be seen. The roads were bare of traffic. Flying at an altitude of about 3,000 metres the squadron arrived at the point where they expected to find rich targets. Meanwhile, the morning had developed in to the forerunner of what looked set to be a brilliant summer's day. The empty road which led to Moscow from Brest stretched into the distance far below the wings of the dive-bombers and Oberleutnant Rossheim dropped to 2,000 metres and then to 1,500 metres in order to search the road and its immediate vicinity.

The skies were equally empty and the squadron flew further without the escort of fighter planes until finally Oberleutnant Rossheim spotted a lone vehicle making its way across country, leaving the unmistakeable signs of tank tracks. He swooped down to 1,000 metres. There was no question that the vehicle was a Russian light tank of the T-26 type. Why it was ploughing this lonely furrow across the landscape was unclear. Judging from the long tracks through the fields of ripening corn, it had worked its way from the fortress to this isolated spot. Whatever the reason for this strange excursion, Rossheim resolved that this would be the last journey this particular tank would ever undertake.

The noise of the not so distant barrage disguised the approach of the aero-engines as the first of the Stukas lined up for its bombing run. Oblivious to the threat from above, Korsak remained focused on the pleasant task of driving the light tank through the glowing dawn directly towards the rendezvous point. *"Nearly there,"* thought Korsak to himself. *"I'll complete the mission and then find out what the hell is going on."*

From high above, Rossheim circled and watched as Küchler lined up for a run on the tank.

"Good morning, Ivan. Here is your early morning post!" said Küchler sarcastically as he pressed the bomb release and gave the tank a burst of machine-gun fire for good measure.

"Your aim was quite good, but not perfect," observed Rossheim as the heavy bomb exploded a few metres from the light tank and the trail of bullets kicked up dust ahead of the machine which now began a series of sudden twists and turns in anticipation of further attacks.

Küchler's attempt was swiftly followed by two more approaches.

Down below, Korsak was now fighting for his life as two more bomb blasts rocked the T-26 and shards of shrapnel penetrated the thin armour of the fighting compartment. He threw the tank into a series of crazy manoeuvres, abruptly snaking left and right in an attempt to evade what now appeared likely to be sudden death from the skies. Nine aircraft still waited to deliver their payloads and as Korsak stole a glance skywards he realised it would only be a matter of time. There was nothing else for it. He slammed the driver's hatch down tightly and continued his wild series of moves, making for a tree-lined road which might provide some small measure of cover, but he had to reckon with Oberleutnant Rossheim who now lined up the tank and, coming in as slowly as possible, released his 800 kg bomb which sailed underneath the tank and exploded, hurling the vehicle into the air.

"That's how it should be done," Rossheim announced

immodestly. He watched with satisfaction as the tank came to rest on its side, the tracks now stationary. There was no sign of life from the crew and the next bomb would transform the vehicle into a pile of scrap metal. Suddenly a warning cry was raised over the air.

"Interceptors approaching from the east. Four o'clock high."

The warning cry, heard for the first time in the campaign in Russia, acted like a trumpet call, but it was trumpet call which came too late as first one Stuka then a second suddenly belched black smoke and tumbled earthwards.

The Stuka crews had met with hostile planes in the west and they knew full well that the cumbersome dive-bombers could easily fall prey to interceptors, which were now revealed to be a pair of Russian *Rata* fighters. There was not much time for contemplation, because the phosphorus filaments were already hissing through the squadron. The air was filled with the babble of voices and air-gunners as each of the Stukas began blazing away for all they were worth.

"Rata on our tail boss," advised rear gunner Köhler. The *Rata* (rat) was the German nickname for the Polikarpov I-16, a fighter which Rossheim had encountered in his days in Spain as a member of the Legion Condor. It was considered obsolete even before the present war had begun, yet it obviously plodded along as the Soviet Union's first line fighter.

"Well, I trust you'll make him feel welcome to join the

party," said Rossheim, placing the aircraft into a dive as he did so.

By applying the air brakes Rossheim was able to slow the Stuka's descent and the pursuing Rata was quickly engaged, first by Köhler in the gunner's seat of Rossheim's aircraft and then, as it overshot the slowing Stuka, by the fixed-wing machine guns controlled by Rossheim. Under the vicious stream of bullets the Soviet plane fell apart and crashed into the ground with a huge explosion, at which howls of delight were heard in the headphones. It was impossible to say whether the fate of his companion had a bearing on his decision or whether he suddenly realised that his fuel was close to exhausted, but in any event the squadron witnessed the joyful fact that the survivor thereupon showed the large red stars on the lower surfaces of the wings and veered off, heading east as fast as his aircraft would go.

As he re-joined his command, Oberleutnant Rossheim found time to count his squadron and found that two machines were now missing. That was unfortunately only a bitter confirmation of what he had already seen. During the air fight a Ju-87 had withdrawn with a trail of smoke behind it and looked like it might limp home. The other had crashed beneath them. He soon retraced his path and as he let the squadron pass was able to ascertain by the marks of the various machines that it must have been Leutnant Spiegel. Rossheim observed the tall pillar of smoke rising from the ground. He accordingly flew lower, and sure enough, a Ju-87 was ablaze there.

In spite of the severe damage to the plane he had after all succeeded in bringing it to earth under some form of control. Rossheim dropped to a low height above the ground and saw Spiegel, with his face blackened by smoke, frantically waving. Spiegel appeared to be uninjured, but his gunner was lying motionless beside a tree. Help was evidently urgently needed. By a lucky coincidence Rossheim spotted the welcome sight of a cloud of orange smoke from a canister lit by a German infantry battalion on the march on a small road not far from where the emergency landing had taken place. Rossheim climbed a little and wrote a note, with his left hand on the control column: "Wounded airman 300 metres west of the road beside burning plane. Needs help."

Placing the note in a message-bag he dived down again over the infantry, who were now frantically waving yellow cloths and dislocating their necks while watching the pilot doing his peculiar stunts just overhead. Rossheim let the message bag with its long coloured streamer flutter down and he watched in gratitude as a number of infantrymen ran to pick it up. If the wounded man could still be helped at all, his chances were now enhanced, as a surgeon always accompanied an infantry battalion.

Russian defence by fighter planes had now ceased to exist, so Rossheim and his dive-bomber crews were able to take liberties that would have been prohibitive had enemy fighter planes been about. Conditions were once again as in Poland, where everything that had a propeller had been smashed within a few days.

During the third attack of the day the Rossheim squadron pulled off a great coup. The sun had just risen and was breaking through the nocturnal veil of haze that still hung over the ground. Oberleutnant Rossheim was flying in the direction of Brest-Litovsk at an altitude of 800 metres when he spotted a long column of enemy trucks driving towards the fortress. Rossheim broke up the squadron to crack that nut. There was merry hell down below on that road as the vehicles crashed into trees, bucked into the ditch, or exploded under machine-gun fire and a hail of bombs. Oberleutnant Rossheim was just climbing a little higher in order to get a better view of the effect when suddenly he saw a gigantic spurt of flame from a group of trucks that stood for a few seconds over the column and finally reached a height of over 1,000 metres. That had obviously been an ammunition column!

* * * * *

The chaos of smoke and flames provided cover as number 1 gun rolled back from the Terespol gate to the relative calm of the jumping off point on the other side of the bridge, where SS-Hauptscharführer Fritz Rubbal and his repair team immediately made themselves busy. The guns were soon refuelled and restocked with fresh ammunition. With their work done the crews at last drew breath. Each man had his own way of dealing with the reaction to the stressful experience he had just engaged in. Some threw themselves down and slept where they fell, while others wrote letters or talked about the tumultuous events of the day. Officers and NCOs held debriefings.

Otto Wohl took the opportunity to turn to his favourite pastime and grabbed a pencil and sketchbook. He began to sketch the engineers going about their work, but his mind wasn't completely on his beloved pastime. He kept one eye on the small group gathered beneath a tree. The loss of number 2 gun so early in the campaign had come as a shock. SS-Hauptscharführer Becker and his crew had been popular with the battalion. They had come out unscathed from the campaign in France and had sailed through Yugoslavia and Greece and now they were gone. It cast a gloomy pall over the battalion. For Wohl there was also a layer of additional anxiety. He could see that von Schroif was angry and there was clearly an issue beyond the loss of the gun and crew. Knispel was clearly on the receiving end of one of von Schroif's infamous dressing downs. Wohl had a feeling that his failure with the radio was on the agenda and his fears were confirmed as Knispel left the group with a thunderous face.

"The boss doesn't look too amused," offered Wohl.

"That's an understatement," said Knispel. "Do you know the losses the grenadiers suffered in the assault?"

"No, I don't, SS-Hauptscharführer."

"They were over fifty per cent in some units."

"That's terrible, SS-Hauptscharführer," replied Wohl.

"Well, next time it could be you. The boss has decided

that you either master the radio duties or you transfer to the infantry."

"You wouldn't do that to me, SS-Hauptscharführer."

"It's not my decision. His mind is made up."

"So what do I have to do?"

"Report to Obersturmführer Sanger every day this week and pay attention."

Wohl's heart sank to his boots. Sanger was a former university lecturer who was responsible for educating the battalion in the mysteries of radio communication, but he was unable to distinguish between post-graduate students and the landsers who manned the StuGs. He was either unable or unwilling to simplify his already difficult subject in order to make it accessible to his charges. Bemused incomprehension was the most frequent reaction to a session with the enthusiastic but impenetrable Sanger.

In von Schroif's eyes rest after combat was essential. There was little as vulnerable as an exhausted crew, but training had also to be maintained. Much of it was repetition and reiteration but today the task was much more demanding and novel; getting SS-Kannonier Otto Wohl up to speed on the radio. The man charged with that task was a cliché of the academic prototype. He was tall and thin with round Himmler style glasses. His uniform seemed to have been purposefully tailored to ensure the worst possible fit. His thin neck did not give the impression that it actually touched his shirt collar. His narrow shoulders drooped inwards and, had regulations

143

permitted, he would have worn a wispy beard and bow tie to complete the archetypal look.

SS-Obersturmführer Sanger was a man in a hurry. He felt that all he had to do was to relay the vast store of knowledge in his own head and somehow the student would be magically transformed into an expert. No sooner had Wohl sat down than he was into his stride.

"There are two forms of radio communication: clear speech and radio telegraphy or Morse. We have two components here, see? Now, this is the cable that connects them."

"Yes, Obersturmführer."

"This is the receiver. This is the transmitter. In order to send and receive, they must be connected. That is why the cable is so important."

"Yes, Obersturmführer."

"Now, each vehicle may have a different set of components, in which case each set is given a different designation, usually the letters 'Fu' followed by a number. Now what does Fu stand for?"

"*Funk*," answered Otto Wohl.

"Correct," replied SS-Obersturmführer Sanger, barely managing to conceal his exasperation. "Now, you may also come across the designation FuG, which is short for?"

"*Funksprech Gerate*, sir."

"Well done, SS-Kannonier. Please try to maintain that level of concentration for the rest of this lesson. Now, I think we can dispense with the FuG designation as it mostly applies to aircraft radio sets. However, I think it is important that we cover only those radio sets found in our armoured vehicles. Why would that be, SS-Kannonier?"

"It may happen that we have to go to the aid of stricken comrades or in the event of breakdown or — God forbid — being hit. We may find ourselves having to commandeer another vehicle."

"Excellent. Now, luckily enough for us, the set we have is the Fu.8. This is the set used by most of the Panzers too. So, here we have the 10 watt transmitter — designated 10 W.S.c. Here we have the ultra-shortwave receiver — designated UKw.Ee. Here are the two power transformers. Then, of course, there are the accessories — headphones, microphones and a key pad for Morse, which I shall return to in a minute. You have been refreshing your knowledge with the Morse code book as proscribed by the regulations?"

Otto Wohl nodded, but in a manner which even Sanger could only ever interpret as 'unconvincing'.

"Now," Sanger continued, "as I said, for all intents and purposes the Fu.8 is the only set we really need concern ourselves with at the moment. However, for the sake of completeness, it is only fair to mention the one major exception to this general rule."

Sanger could see Wohl's eyes squinting in pain, but he felt he did have to cover all the ground. In war, one never knew.

"The one major exception to these designations is the

voice transmitter used in many combat support vehicles — generally armoured cars. Now you only have to remember this once. The Fu.Spr.f."

"The Fu.Spr.f, SS-Obersturmführer."

"Well done, SS-Kannonier. Now, our Fu.8 set is capable of transmitting both '*Telegraphie*', also known as CW or Morse code, and '*Telefonie*' — voice amplitude-modulated signals. If we were stationary and were equipped with a frame roof aerial, the 30 W.S.a. transmitter would have a voice range of over 15 kilometres. This could be doubled with the use of a big 9-meter winch mast with a star aerial on top.

"Now," Obersturmführer Sanger continued, pointing at the front of the unit, "the side-tone speaker cable is connected to the upper left corner post mount, while the two receptacles on the left of the face are for the receiver antenna binding post and ground. The two bottom-left receptacles are for the key and microphone leads and you can see that they are both connected. At the upper right of the radio face is the post for the antenna attachment, while the bottom-right connection is for power input from the dynamotor. Now, if we remove the cover from the transformer, what does it say on this decal here, SS-Kannonier?"

"*Deckel nicht im Fahrzeug offnen*," replied Wohl.

"And why would we want to keep the covers on?" asked Sanger.

"To keep air from getting in?"

Obersturmführer Sanger looked incredulously at Otto

Wohl. "No.... To keep you from getting electrocuted! This thing supplies 12 volts at 2.7 amps for the filaments and 400 volts for the plate supply!" Sanger rolled his eyes in frustration. Getting angry would have been too easy though. He had to get this information across to Wohl and he knew that shouting at him would only make things worse. He decided to change the subject slightly. He could always return for reiteration later that evening.

"Please don't tell me about it," thought Otto Wohl to himself, his mind distracted by the sound of renewed heavy shelling in the fortress.

"Wohl, over here, now," yelled Knispel.

There was the sound of revving engines. He saw the boss's halftrack take its place at the head of the column. Clearly the decision had been taken that they would have another crack at the fortress.

Despite his extreme weariness and the impending sense of danger, Wohl felt relieved to be away from the tedious Sanger. To his surprise as he slipped into the vehicle he saw that the place of the late lieutenant in command of number 1 gun had been taken by von Schroif himself.

The StuGs followed the now familiar path from that morning's first assault. As they rattled towards the fortress von Schroif filled in the tactical details.

"The situation has become somewhat confused. It looks as if the Reds have managed to take the Terespol gate back from our grenadiers and that has cut off our men who are in the citadel. There is also fighting going on at the other gates but the situation remains fluid. Our mission is to help the grenadiers seize the Terespol gate. We are expecting air support from a squadron of *Sturzkampfflugzeug.*"

Wohl was pleased to hear that the Stukas would be there to lend their weight to the attack. The psychological impact was immense; it heartened the German attackers and dampened the will of the defenders. Wohl was familiar with the powerful shriek of the sirens as the aircraft dived into the attack. *"That's good news. They terrify me, so God knows the effect they must have on the enemy!"*

* * * * *

"Third-class ticket for Brest-Litovsk, without changing!"

As Oberleutnant Rossheim and his crews made their way to their aircraft and his squadron took off, the last remark from the ground personnel brought a smile to his face. As the front swiftly crumbled and collapsed on that June morning the entire Russian army had either retreated or been captured. From the air it was abundantly clear that the last frontier strong point left to the Russian forces was now the fortress of Brest-Litovsk, which had become an island left behind by the greatest outflanking battle hitherto fought in the history of war.

As the Germans advanced everywhere along the front the surprised Russian forces were pushed further and further back, and the prospects for the fortress grew dimmer. The aerial bombardment of Brest-Litovsk represented one of the dramatic climaxes of the opening day of Barbarossa. As Rossheim guided his squadron back to the fortress for the third sortie of the morning all hell seemed to have broken loose there. Furthermore, it was clear that this time he and his men were not alone. A large formation of conventional He-111 bombers was approaching the target just ahead of the Stukas. The bombers dropped their deadly loads on the doomed fortress. For them it was hardly necessary to take accurate aim over the fortress and it was anyhow practically impossible to do so, owing to the dense pall of smoke in which the fortress was continually enveloped. The crews of the Heinkels simply carried out their instructions to the letter.

To the consternation of the Stuka pilots, they simply discharged their full payload and began to turn for home. The Heinkel crews obviously reasoned that every bomb was certain to score a hit because, in theory, the Russians were still in control of the fortress.

The reality on the ground, according to the latest intelligence coming from Leutnant Vogel, who was performing in a liaison role with the German forces attacking the fortress, was that the Ivans were indeed being confined into smaller and smaller areas under the relentless weight of the German attack and that the free space at their disposal was steadily growing less. From Vogel's reports Rossheim understood that the surviving Red Army troops were now all crowded together into three main islands in the narrow space of the fortress. Every defensible position in those islands was crammed full of soldiers and the streets and parkland were congested with troops and vehicles, but now the problem from the air was to ensure that all bombs fell only on the surviving defenders. According to Vogel, both sides were now hopelessly intermingled as men fought to the death with bullets, grenades, bayonets and their bare hands.

In light of this information the dive-bomber crews therefore made a careful observation over the fortress of Brest-Litovsk. The blazing oil tanks which had serviced the many tanks and vehicles were the chief source of the enormous clouds of dense black smoke which billowed into the sky and fell back to form the impenetrable pall of smoke lying over the fortress. When Rossheim and his squadron appeared back over the target, everything was at first black with smoke. Nothing was to be seen at all, visibility simply did not exist. Potential targets could only be made out dimly after having pierced the top layer of smoke and descending to the lowest levels, where the smoke from ground fires, explosions and gunfire was sometimes possible to see through, but it was impossible to tell from the fleeting glimpses whether the figures on the ground were German or Russian. There was a complete absence of ground recognition signs. No orange smoke, no yellow cloths, no swastika flags.

Despite the fact that the situation on the ground was so unclear, fresh waves of He-111 bombers kept on coming. It seemed as if the full might of Luftflotte 2 had been focused on the fortress and once the machine had been switched on there seemed to be no way of switching it off. The bombardment of the fortress of Brest-Litovsk from the air was now so concentrated that the Stuka pilots searching for targets beneath the conventional bombers had literally to be on guard to ensure that they did not get a bomb in the neck from a Heinkel flying above them.

The approach to that last bulwark had long since ceased to be a problem. Even hidden by banks of smoke the fortress of Brest-Litovsk could not be missed. Hostile aircraft were no longer to be observed over the fortress, only German planes were now to be seen. More groups of Heinkel horizontal bombers of the He-111 type passed above the dive-bombers and the pilots and gunners of the latter could then only watch and call out in frustration at the bombs indiscriminately dropping from all the bomb-wells of these formations.

* * * * *

On the ground it was the StuG battalion that bore the brunt of the indiscriminate bombing. As they approached the Terespol gate the first flurry of death from the bombers flying high above hit Kampfgruppe von Schroif. A stick of bombs landed with devastating force and the number 4 gun from the First Abteilung was thrown into the air by the force of the blast from a direct hit which blew the gun to pieces and left a huge crater. Just in the very nick of time von Schroif threw himself down into the interior of number 1 gun.

"Get on to Vogel and stop those idiots… can't he see what's happening?"

Vogel could indeed see what was happening. He was up with the action and was crammed, along with his own radio equipment, into the Beobachtungskraftwagen which von Schroif had vacated to join number 1 gun. Wohl was about to reach for the radio set and pass on his superiors grievance when there was the report of another huge series of explosions as a further stick of bombs landed nearby. The blasts rocked the vehicle and splinters could be heard rattling on the armour. Miraculously, none penetrated the thin armour of the roof and sides of number 1 gun. Number 5 gun of the third abteilung was not so lucky. A large shard of metal cut through the side of the fighting compartment, instantly killing the gunner and commander and forcing the two surviving crew members of the damaged gun to radio that it was falling out of the action.

Through his driver's vision port Junge could see that, from the force of the explosions, the command half-track had been pushed off the road and rammed up against a building. The machine wasn't altogether destroyed, but smoke was now issuing from the engine compartment. The crew began to scramble out and Junge could just about make out the figure of Leutnant Vogel who seemed to be unsteady on his feet as he staggered into cover behind a brickwork chimney breast, all that remained of a vanished wooden building. As he did so, a bullet ricocheted off the brickwork. Vogel made himself as small a target as possible and cowered behind the masonry.

"It's no use, the Beobachtungskraftwagen has been hit. They are bailing out," announced Junge, who was keeping the stricken vehicle under close observation.

The next to follow Vogel was SS-Oberkannonier Schultz. As he reached the ground a single shot rang out from the same direction as the bullet which had so nearly claimed Leutnant Vogel. This time there was no mistake. Schultz was spun around by the terrific force of the round and fell lifeless to the ground.

"Sniper!" called Junge. "He got Schultz. He's after Vogel."

"I see him," von Schroif said with a calm voice. He had traced the trajectory of the first bullet and had spotted the tell-tale wisp of smoke from behind an impossibly small pile of rubble.

"He's lying prone, behind those bricks at ten o' clock, two hundred metres."

Without waiting to be asked, Wohl loaded a high-explosive round, the *granatpatrone 34*. As he did so, Junge swung the StuG around to the appropriate facing and Knispel lined up the shot. By his own calculation he made the range one hundred and eighty metres. Rather than ask for a correction, he took the adjustment on his own initiative. He had to be quick, the lives of three men depended on his speed and accuracy. Just as he was about to fire he was distracted by an almighty explosion. The number 4 gun from the Second Abteilung had attempted to fire a round at the same target but what the crew hadn't known was that a shard of shrapnel had smashed into the short barrel of the main gun. It triggered the premature explosion of the round as it left the barrel. The untimely blast had completely destroyed the gun.

Despite the shock of the blast from the number 4 gun, Knispel had already acquired his target. He calmly pressed the firing button and the round flew towards its target. As the spent cartridge was ejected the fighting compartment filled with a cloud of choking acrid smoke and fumes from the propellant charge. With so many bullets and shell splinters flying around there was no prospect of opening any of the hatches so the StuG had to remain buttoned up and the fierce heat of the explosion only added to the unbearable atmosphere inside the StuG.

"It's a hit!" came the welcome confirmation from von Schroif.

It was almost destined to be his last utterance. As he spoke there was a crack like thunder and a piece of the wall of the fighting compartment next to von Schroif's head, the size of a man's fist, was dislodged and flew across the inside of the vehicle, missing Knispel by millimetres. A shaft of daylight flooded into the dim interior and von Schroif was instantly aware of what had happened. By shifting their direction to fire at the sniper, number 1 gun had presented itself side-on to a lurking anti-tank gun.

"Anti-tank gun, nine o' clock," called von Schroif.

Responding instantly, Junge threw the vehicle through a sharp turn. He was only just in time, as a second round struck the StuG, but this time in the thicker frontal armour. The deafening bang, the sudden rise in temperature, and the tiny shards of metal which sprayed over Junge and Wohl confirmed how close they had come to destruction.

"It's no use, the grenadiers are nowhere to be seen," shouted von Schroif above the din. "Order the battalion to withdraw back to their original positions."

Once again the battalion was forced to disengage from the fighting. As they rolled back towards the assembly area von Schroif reflected on the grim lessons that had been learned that morning. In these two brief exchanges five StuGs had been either destroyed or damaged. Eighteen irreplaceable crewmen had lost their lives, more were probably wounded and others would certainly have lost their nerve. The reality was that, without the firm intervention of determined ground troops, there was simply no way that armoured fighting vehicles could make any progress in the claustrophobic environs of the Terespol fortification. As Voss had prophesised, the Sturmgeschütze were simply too vulnerable to anti-tank weapons at close ranges and should not have been committed to fight in what was essentially an urban environment.

- CHAPTER 5 -

Die Planning und Verwirrung

DIMITRI KORSAK had slowly regained consciousness. Through the pain of his throbbing brain he was dimly aware of the detonation of distant explosions. As his recollection began to take form he scrambled out of the driver's hatch and gazed at the capsized T-26. The wrecked machine lay on a small rise in the centre of a cornfield and Korsak could see that it was surrounded by bomb craters. He was lucky to be alive. He couldn't understand why the Germans had abandoned their attack, he could only thank his lucky stars that they had. Turning his gaze to the south-west, in the direction of Brest-Litovsk, he could see a huge pall of black smoke which rose towering into the sky. He reached for his binoculars.

Even at this distance it was possible to feel the ground swell from the distant explosions, the largest of which could be seen rising high into the sky. Large formations of aircraft were circling the fortress while others could be seen flying deeper into Soviet territory. Another formation flew overhead and his aircraft recognition training told him that these were Dornier bombers, flying without a fighter escort. This was not good news. If the Germans could come and go at will, there must be a problem with the Red Air Force. Korsak formed the view that there must have been some kind of counter-revolution with German intervention.

Scanning the main Moscow highway he could discern a stream of German tanks and trucks moving east. Overhead, more German aircraft streamed eastwards. Peering into the wrecked tank, Korsak noted the massive jagged piece of shrapnel which had completely destroyed the radio set.

Slowly the details of his mission filtered back into his aching head. There was no way of knowing whether the mysterious bandsman was transmitting or not. Korsak decided that the only thing he could do was to make for the obvious centre of resistance. The fortress of Brest-Litovsk was only fifteen kilometres distant. He decided to abandon the rendezvous and follow his tracks to strike across country. His right hip ached, but it was the pistol in the holster hanging at his side that now attracted his attention. It seemed unnaturally heavy and the reason soon became apparent. Another large piece of shrapnel had crashed into the holster, splitting the pistol almost in two and depriving him of his only weapon. He unbuckled the worthless object, dumped it, and set off for the fortress.

* * * * *

It was not just Korsak who found himself in a predicament. The bandsman too was bemused and uncertain. Karl Wendorff stood on the tree-lined avenue and looked up helplessly at the canister containing the radio transceiver. He had tried a number of impractical approaches without success. He tried throwing stones, shaking the trunk of the tree, and had even made a couple of forlorn attempts to climb the damn thing, but nothing looked vaguely likely to succeed. *"Think man, there must be a way around this!"*

As he paused for thought he turned his gaze away to the south-east. There was a continuing rumble of explosions and he could clearly see aircraft in action above the huge smoke clouds which he knew to be coming from the direction of Brest-Litovsk. "Events will unfold to your advantage", was what he had been told, but standing in the middle of nowhere, dressed as a Russian bandsman, did not have the feeling of an event which could possibly unfold to anything other than his extreme disadvantage. For once, Wendorff was to be proved entirely correct. The noise from the bombardment combined with the low flying German aircraft passing to and fro overhead was intense but Wendorff now paid little attention to his surroundings. He was so intent on solving the conundrum with the radio canister that he failed to spot the approaching Red Army truck that flew up in a cloud of dust and screamed to a halt behind him.

"What are you doing, comrade?" called an NCO from the passenger seat of the ammunition truck.

Wendorff turned around in shocked amazement. He had to think fast, and he had to think in his second language. Although his father's family were generations old from Nuremberg, his mother's people were mixed *Volksdeutsche* of Belorussian extraction. They hailed from Volhaynia, near the Soviet frontier and, as expected, German supporters had been driven out of Poland by the awful events which had followed the end of the last war. At home he had grown up hearing a mixture of German and occasional Russian. He hoped his Russian would be good enough.

"I am not certain, comrade… I lost my unit."

"Where are you based?"

"Err… Brest-Litovsk," replied Wendorff, remembering his cover story.

"Well, you're in luck, that's where we are headed. Jump in."

Wendorff squeezed himself into the cab beside the obliging NCO and the driver roared off down the dusty lane.

"What is happening, comrade?" Wendorff asked in an attempt to cover his unexplained appearance on a country road.

"Don't you know anything? The fascists have stabbed us in the back. They invaded at four o' clock this morning. The fortress is still holding out though. They need ammunition. That's what we have in the back there. So, let's hope our fascist friends above don't drop a bomb on us or it will be the biggest fireworks display since the revolution!"

There was nothing in the Sergeant's short speech that gave Wendorff any form of comfort. He thought briefly about the possibility of plunging his knife into the man's chest but he would still have to overcome the driver and where would that get him? Wendorff decided to continue on the journey. The nearer to Brest-Litovsk he got, the nearer he would be to German forces.

"Keep your eyes peeled on the skies. I'll watch for fascists on the road."

"Yes, comrade," replied Wendorff, now in self-preservation mode.

* * * * *

The German forces attacking the fortress on that auspicious summer's morning continually attempted to exploit the advantages of their unexpected attack. The guns continued to pound away while the advance assault detachments of submachine-gunners made further fresh assaults, still hoping to capture the fortress in one energetic thrust. However, by mid-morning it was clear that the attempt to take the fortress in one fell swoop had failed. The German planners had expected their bombardment to reduce the fortress to defenceless rubble. They were wrong. The Russian soldiers were now fully awakened from their disorientation and, under the leadership of Captain Zubachyov, Commissar Fomin and others whom history has overlooked, they recovered very quickly, grouped themselves, and began a desperate, stubborn, and well-organised defence.

The grounds of the Volhyn fortification, which the

assault troops had tried to capture in the first hours of the war, contained border-guard formations, a regimental school, whose cadets unfortunately were absent on exercises, and the large military hospital where Bettina Ostermann had worked.

On that Sunday morning when the unheralded bombardment fell, the military hospital serving the 4th Army was actually in the process of being moved out of the fortress. A large portion of the patients and medical personnel had opportunely been moved out. They were indeed fortunate, because the first enemy shells and bombs fell on the hospital's forty or so wooden hospital buildings which instantly took fire. As she groggily rose to her feet from the Nebelwerfer storm, Bettina instantly realised that the most seriously ill patients were beyond help. Those who could save themselves did and Bettina watched in terror as fugitives emerged from the flames. Many were hideously burned, while others exhibited terrible wounds. Bettina now pulled herself together as she recognised the familiar figure of Dr Stepan Babkin.

"Nurse Ostermann, help me to get these patients to the casemates of the earthworks."

"Yes, Doctor," replied Bettina and her professional training took over. She was able to escort and guide the patients into the tunnel that led to the casemate where they would be safe from the bombs and bullets that now flew in all directions.

The strongest patients and the few uninjured soldiers who had been on duty now took up arms and rushed back over to the surviving hospital buildings to beat off the attack. The defence was organized by Commissar Nikolai Bogateyev and Dr Stepan Babkin. Weapons and ammunition were issued to those who felt they could handle a weapon. Bettina was not one of those who felt she could be of any service in this respect. She watched as many of the doctors, nurses, orderlies, and patients also took up weapons. However willing they may have been, they could not hope to withstand the crack infantry troops for long.

The German assault forces soon penetrated the hospital grounds and the survivors fled back to the tunnel to await their fate. They brought with them horrific tales of what they had witnessed as the invaders surged through the hospital buildings, shooting, tossing grenades and bayonetting patients and medical staff alike.

* * * * *

With the morning sun behind him, Dimitri Korsak headed back to the fortress. Behind him the dust trails obscured the horizon, the rear units of the German advance kicking up clouds, some 25km long. He briefly calculated where the front line was now. *"If it was Kobrin this morning, then how many kilometres further east was it now?"* Occasionally he would wish for the sight and sound of Soviet planes passing overhead, the first sign of a Soviet counterattack, but none came. The only planes over Belorussia were headed in the opposite direction.

The Luftwaffe constantly flew overhead, passing into the east unopposed. The sun was already hot and his mouth was parched. Normally he would have gone looking for water, but, suspecting that the German reserves may not be far off, he kept as straight a line as possible for the fortress, hoping the defenders were still holding out. He briefly entertained the notion that the citadel may be the furthest point west in a new rolling Soviet offensive, but reason and reality forced him to dismiss this hope as unsupported fantasy.

"Live in the present moment, deal with the observed facts, and do not get distracted by daydreams."

Then, in front of him, he made out the unmistakeable sight of dust clouds coming towards him. Quickly calculating their direction and factoring in the knowledge that the column would travel across the open terrain of the grain fields he himself was in, Korsak decided to detour for a mile and head for the oak trees to his right.

"Bastards!" he thought to himself. *"How could it be so easy? Why was there no warning? Where were the opposing forces?"*

He consoled himself with the further thought that this state of affairs could surely only be temporary. The distances were so vast. How many times had he flown over them himself? Surely Stalin was setting a trap at this very moment? Draw them in, draw them in, wait until the supply lines are stretched. Yes, we are strong in the south. Maybe some grand pincer movement was already under way, a giant outflanking. Striding on through the huge field of ripening wheat Korsak cursed the decision not to take a crew. As he moved through the endless wheat Korsak again reprimanded himself. There were now no grand plans or strategies. *"Just keep your eyes and ears open, concentrate on the here and now."*

Before long he was amongst the oaks, which gave good protection, cover from the air, and shade from the endless sun while he considered what to do next.

Up ahead he saw a road leading to the entrance of the abandoned quarry which he had passed on the way out. Unfamiliar trucks were now parked there and above the rumble of explosions and roar of aircraft he could discern a new and disturbing sound, the sound of female voices, then shots and screams.

Korsak skirted up the rise to see if he could find out who was firing at whom. As he reached the top of the rise and looked down into the old quarry his blood froze. It wasn't the screams of the women and children that chilled his soul but the laughter of the German soldiers. He didn't recognise the unit or their markings, not at that moment, but he would never forget the faces, especially one in particular, an almost rat-faced creature who seemed to be the leader, the centre of attention, the ringmaster in the circus of horrors. Later Korsak would find out that this was SS-Sonderkommando Dirlewanger and that the beast who was in charge was one Oskar Dirlewanger. But this was information that would not come to the man who perched on top of an old quarry. This information would come to a different man, another

Dimitri Korsak, because what Korsak was about to witness would change him forever.

Looking down from his vantage point Korsak could see that a group of civilians had been herded into the quarry, where a large pit had been excavated. The men and women, all locals by the look of it, had been separated out. Some men were kneeling before a recently dug trench. A number of lifeless bodies already occupied the pit. A member of the unit was at the side of the trench, viciously stabbing his bayonet into the inert mangled mass of dead forms, checking, it seemed, for signs of life.

"SS-Untersturmführer Dirlewanger," he shouted, "one of our animals is still breathing!"

"Well, let's think what Hauptsturmführer von Schroif would say? Is he bolshevised?" shouted Dirlewanger.

"I think he is, SS-Untersturmführer," replied the man, prodding the prone figure with his boot.

"Good, then Hauptsturmführer von Schroif would expect you to obey the order and summarily execute him."

"It is done," said the man, thrusting his bayonet into the prone figure.

The name von Schroif was well known to Korsak but hearing it again came as a rude shock.

"SS troops under his command? It must be him? So he is still involved? It comes as no surprise that these fascist animals would condone a scene like this."

"We try and show these objectionable pieces of inbred shit some mercy by putting a bullet in the back of their

165

heads and this ungrateful *schwein* throws it back in our faces by staying alive!" said Dirlewanger, at which his men laughed loudly.

Behind him, one woman tried to escape from her guards and tried to run towards the trench, before being kicked to the ground. One of the soldiers raised his rifle to shoot, but Dirlewanger indicated to him not to fire.

"Let her live. I may have a role for her in a show I am thinking of putting on. I am an impresario, am I not? And we need entertainment, do we not? How else are we to find release from the repetitive drudgery of the slaughterhouse? Pick your favourites, men. You can have them after my little entertainment has worked up our appetites."

Hearing this degrading pronouncement his men laughed and cheered in their sickening manner.

To Korsak it seemed as if this ringmaster from hell was orchestrating his animals towards some inhuman, sadistic finale. It was obvious that the women and children had no idea what was to happen next — nor did Dimitri Korsak, who at least understood German — but by the looks on their faces, the sobs and the hellish low moaning, they looked only too well aware that some kind of unimaginable depravity was about to be unleashed upon them.

"Come here, sweet Frau." Dirlewanger motioned to the woman who had been kicked to the ground, opening his arms and smiling. "Please forgive my men. It has not been easy for them. Please do not be scared. Come to father. Please, I am begging you. Daddy is not going to hurt you."

The woman tentatively, still shaking, rose to her feet, but then the sniggers and cackling of Dirlewanger's men made her stop and freeze with fear.

"Comrades!" Dirlewanger shouted, his seriousness masking a grin he knew his men could see. "Please show some respect! Silence! Please, for this lady's sake!" He then returned his attention to the woman. "Come on, it's not all bad. Please come here." Again he opened his arms, looking for all the world like a long-lost uncle. "That's it. I'm not going to hurt you."

The woman looked terrified but, realizing she had no choice, she stepped slowly towards him. Dimitri Korsak felt sick.

"Now, my pretty young Madam," Dirlewanger continued as the woman grew closer, "do you speak German? Speaky Deutsch?"

The woman, still petrified, shook her head.

Dirlewanger continued in the fake long-lost uncle tone, talking down to the woman as if she were a small child or pet. Realizing that she did not understand a word, he changed the content of what he was saying.

"I am sorry. It was my mistake, all my fault. You are not a pretty young maiden at all. You are a fat, stinking piece of cow shit. But, having said that, please do not feel you will not give one of my fine German boys some pleasure before you die. This will be your final privilege, to stare into ecstatic German eyes at the moment you are thankfully expunged from this world. Now, it may be that more than one of these studs might want to share his pleasure with you, but that is a problem easily solved — we just use our knives to carve out a few more holes to add to the two you already have — new ones, but this time, clean ones. Please consider this an honour — and an unexpected joy. The more the merrier. The pig likes to be stuck, doesn't she?"

The woman looked on blankly.

"Now, my dear, what we need for this show is some atmosphere. It helps galvanise the male leads. Look, clappy, clappy!" Dirlewanger made clapping movements with his hands.

The woman looked on in disbelief.

Then, raising his hands above his head and clapping, he turned to the other women.

"Look, everyone — clappy, clappy!"

None responded. Dirlewanger, however, did not shout or lose his temper. He was enjoying himself too much. He smiled some more, raised his voice, and spoke in demented pidgin Russian.

"Da! Clappy, Clappy, then happy, happy, dancey, dancey, free to, to — go freee... free to go! But nyet, clappy, clappy," he continued, lowering his voice and pointing to the children, "then bangy, bangy, deady, deady!"

The message was clear, unequivocal and understood by all.

"Excellent!" exclaimed Dirlewanger. "I am glad we are all clear on this.... Now, after me, clappy! Clappy!" He put his hands back over his head and started jumping up and down. "Clappy! Clappy!"

Slowly the women started to clap — what choice did they have? Louder and louder it grew, this madness, this demonic dance. Korsak felt like shutting his eyes to try keeping the nausea at bay.

"Good. Good. Very good, good women, good women!" He then stopped clapping and motioned the first woman over to the trench. "Loew, come here!" he shouted to one of his men. "I think we need an interpreter — just so there are no misunderstandings here!"

Locw almost skipped across to do his master's bidding.

"Now, Loew, please speak to this bitch — and don't worry, you don't have to stand too close — and find out if she knows the scum in there who is still alive."

Loew then spoke to the woman in Russian.

"Commander, this is her husband."

"Perfect! Right, let's get him out!" Dirlewanger turned to the women, whose clapping was starting to wane. "Keepy clappy, clappy! Keepy clappy!" Then he turned to his men who were pulling the poor woman's husband from the trench. "Careful with him boys — we don't want him dying before the show is over!"

Dirlewanger then addressed Leow. "Can you find out if she has any other relatives here? Tell her…. tell her… tell her that… Ok, I've got it! Tell her that, under German military tradition, any man who survives a firing squad is free to go with all his family."

Leow then relayed this sickening lie to the woman

who, after a slight hesitation, pointed to a teenage boy, a young girl and an old man.

"My friends! Come here. Come here! Frau, Frau! Call your family across and give them the good news!" He then spoke again to Loew. "Tell her this, tell her to call her family and that they are now free to go."

Leow spoke to the woman, who then called her family across. Korsak had to fight every impulse in his body to prevent shouting out, but he knew he had to get back to the fortress. Unarmed, his death here would be futile. If only he had a weapon!

Once the family were together Dirlewanger strode across to the other women. "Clappy, clappy! Da, da! Or Bangy, bangy!" He once more pointed to the children.

Sickeningly, the women clapped louder.

"Good. Very good!" smiled Dirlewanger as he strutted back to the woman and her family. Then he addressed everyone assembled, like some crazed choreographer in the seventh circle of hell. "Ladies and gentlemen, boys and girls…" The last word was uttered with an inhuman roll of the eyes heavenward. "Please be upstanding for today's matinee. Let the show begin!"

Korsak looked on unbelievingly as the old man was instructed to undo the buttons on his daughter's blouse, a gun held to his grandson's head…

What followed was to scar Dimitri Korsak for the rest of his life. His life was now split in two. The life he had before what he was about to witness and his life after. He was about to become two different men.

The first was born in Germany as Wilhelm Stenner, with a love for the German people. Even after his political differences with the Nazis over their shift to the right, their cuddling up to big business, their betrayal of socialism and the murder of Gregor Strasser, even after all of that he still had some fond memory, some residual warmth for notions of the innate goodness of the German people and, in particular, the moral fibre of the German fighting man.

That would end this afternoon. Any fondness for his former countrymen was about to be eviscerated. He had never seen greater evil, nor could he even have imagined it. As he considered how he could make his way back through the German lines and into the fortress, where he could make sure the world got to know about the horrors he had witnessed, he realised that he was so shocked that he could not even remember how he had got there. So populated and polluted was his memory of what he had just seen, the sickening horror and sadism. The bloodlust, the joy — indeed, joy was the only word for it — of these troops as they spat and trampled on every accepted norm known to man. These men weren't subhuman, they were sub-animal. The vision of hell on earth burned in his mind.

The look on Dirlewanger's face as he had ordered the woman's father, then son, then daughter, to touch her breasts, all the time making the husband watch. This all accompanied by the unholy cheering and clapping from howling, crying, screaming women…

"Make him hard! Make him hard!" Dirlewanger had shrieked at the mother. "Come on boy, get it up. You are the son of a whore. Now treat her like a whore!"

Korsak shut his eyes and tried to block out what had happened next, but the husband's face kept coming back to him, the tears and shame of the grandfather… and then the butchery, the pack of wolves descending on the other women. The slaughter, the raping… the laughing….

"For every boy you kill, take a girl!" screamed Dirlewanger.

From his vantage point Korsak could only watch in horror as Dirlewanger's own lust was sated upon a young girl, maybe 9 or 10 years old. Her screams of terror were sounds Korsak would never forget. He wasn't Wilhelm Stenner anymore, he was now and forever Dimitri Korsak and the screams of the innocent deserved to be avenged.

Leow now dragged a teenage girl up the slope and stopped no more than ten metres from where Korsak lay in hiding. Had Korsak still had his pistol, he would have used it. As it was, he resolved to batter this man's brains from his evil skull. As Korsak felt for a rock to use for a weapon Leow threw himself on top of the girl. Just as the tawdry proceedings were reaching their climax, a procession of vehicles roared into the quarry. There were shouts of command. Leow immediately got to his feet, buttoned his fly, and sprinted down the hill. The sobbing girl was left behind, curled up in the foetal position.

Unable to help, Korsak left her to sob for the moment and peered over the lip of the quarry.

A number of bodyguards had leapt from the vehicles and formed a cordon. They were no sooner in position than they were followed by two senior SS officers. The first was in his thirties. Tall and well-built, with aquiline features, he wore an immaculately tailored uniform.

As the second stepped out of his Mercedes staff car Korsak gasped in disbelief. The identity of the man with the Asiatic features, small round glasses and toothbrush moustache was unmistakeable. The man was Heinrich Himmler.

"Reichsführer! This is indeed an honour!" gasped Dirlewanger, rushing up to his master. "We had not expected your visit so soon."

"I do not see why that would be the case," replied Himmler. "I informed you by telegram that I would like to see you shoot a hundred bolshevists in order that I could observe the actual liquidation. You appear to have begun your work already."

"We have over two hundred still waiting. Jews and Bolshevists," countered Dirlewanger.

The command was quickly reorganised and a further group of men and women were brought forward and lined up on the lip of the pit. As the firing squad raised rifles, Himmler stopped the proceedings. His gaze had fallen upon a handsome young man who was about to go to his doom.

"I notice that this young man is blonde and blue-eyed.

These are the hallmarks of the true Teuton. Surely he does not belong in this group?" said Himmler. "This cannot be right. Where is the interpreter?"

Leow stepped forward.

"Ask him if he is a Jew," said Himmler peremptorily.

Leow quickly translated the short question and received a reply.

"He says he is, Reichsführer," said Leow.

"Both parents?" asked Himmler.

"Yes, Reichsführer," came the reply.

"Does he have any antecedents who are not Jewish?"

Leow translated the question which again elicited a negative reply.

"No, Reichsführer, none at all."

Himmler theatrically stamped his foot. "Then I cannot help him." He gave the signal to continue to Dirlewanger, who in turn nodded to Leow.

"Fire!" came the call. The squad fired and the victims tumbled into the pit.

Despite the horror of the scene unfolding before him, Korsak couldn't help noticing that Himmler — who had ostensibly come to watch — stared at the ground. He shuffled nervously. Then there came a second volley. Again Himmler promptly averted his eyes. Glancing up, he saw that two women still writhed. "Don't torture these women!" he shouted. "Get on with it, shoot quickly!"

Seizing his opportunity, one of the SS officers directly addressed Himmler.

"Reichsführer, can you kindly note how deeply shaken

some of the men of the firing squad are? Some of these men are finished for the rest of their lives!" the SS man beseeched him. "What kind of followers are we creating by doing these things? Either neurotics or brutes!"

Dirlewanger moved forward. "I order you to be silent, Becker! How dare you address the Reichsführer? You will answer to me later."

But Himmler raised his arm. Acting on impulse, he ordered the command to gather around and began to make an impromptu speech.

"Regrettably, ours is a disgusting task," he said, "but, as good Germans, we should not enjoy doing it. Your conscience, however, should be in no way affected, because you are soldiers who must carry out every order, however distasteful, without question. I alone, before God and the Führer, bare the terrible responsibility for what must now be done. Surely you must have noticed that this bloody work is just as odious to me? The horror of it has moved me to the depths of my soul. But I, too, am obeying the highest law by doing his terrible duty."

With his short address now concluded, Himmler and his entourage re-entered their vehicles and sped off in the direction of Brest-Litovsk. The SS squad in the quarry despatched the remaining victims and also got ready to leave.

All this time the traumatised young girl had been overlooked and Korsak now moved over to her. She recoiled in terror.

"Don't worry, I am a friend. Come with me."

The bewildered girl got to her feet and they moved off together in the direction of the tree-lined road leading to Brest-Litovsk. As they reached the lane Korsak and his newfound companion crouched down behind the bank while he considered what to do next. Fortunately, he didn't have long to deliberate as events were about to overtake him.

- CHAPTER 6 -

In den Mund der Hölle

THE SOVIET ammunition truck screamed along the minor road as fast as the straining engine would allow. On the ridge over to his left Wendorff could see the main Moscow highway which was crammed with German tanks, vehicles and horse-drawn transport, all heading east.

Although the skies buzzed with aircraft, unbeknown to Wendorff and his new colleagues, the focus of the battle had already shifted far to the east. The Soviet city of Minsk was the new target.

The city of Brest had been quickly seized, as expected, and Kobrin, the following objective, had also been seized by the Panzers, who were already approaching Minsk. The single vehicle barrelling along the secondary road therefore attracted no attention from the air, but on the ground matters took a turn for the worse. The truck suddenly found its route back to the fortress blocked by a German staff car heading in the same direction.

"What do you want me to do, Sergeant?" asked the driver.

"Clear him off the road!" replied the sergeant.

Wendorff braced himself as the driver hit the accelerator. The truck leapt forward and slammed into the back of the staff car which slewed round through ninety degrees and hit a tree. The passenger smashed into the dashboard and slumped motionless in his seat. The German driver didn't wait and leapt from the car, running as fast as his legs would carry him. The Soviet driver didn't so much as pause and, with a roar of triumph, the truck sped on.

From his hiding position next to the road, Dimitri Korsak could hardly believe his luck. As the truck roared off, he sprinted from his hiding place and quickly established that the car wasn't too badly damaged and could still be driven. He dragged the unconscious figure of the airman and threw him aside. He ushered the shocked figure of the girl into the passenger seat. He could still see the dust cloud of the ammunition truck as it sped down the lane towards the fortress. *"They must know something about the situation,"* thought Korsak to himself and, revving the engine to its maximum, he resolved to follow the truck. He drove fast and was soon hard on the tail of the speeding truck.

The bizarre combination of the speeding ammunition truck with a German staff car close on its heels passing in a cloud of dust was something of an unexpected conundrum and caused such confusion in the few groups of German soldiers they passed that none sought to impede their rapid progress. Most of the scattered groups of German soldiers were focussed on their own missions and gave no consideration to the pair of vehicles which flashed by in a cloud of dust. As a result of the combination of misperception, indifference and surprise in the small groups they passed, they were able to reach the outskirts of Brest undetected and unchallenged.

The streets of the city were deserted. Rubble was strewn everywhere and fires raged unchecked. The larger formations of German infantry were bypassing the city and heading east. No one expected traffic from the direction of their advance and the clouds of smoke soon engulfed the speeding vehicles. Sergeant Yashin knew the streets like the back of his hand and was able to direct the driver towards the fortress. Korsak stuck to them like glue. It looked as though they would reach the safety of the fortress as they approached the Kobrin gate. Here, their progress was finally interrupted by a stream of bullets from a startled sentry that shattered the windscreen and shot through the roof of the cab. Reacting like lightning, the driver jammed his foot on the accelerator and scattered the small German squad which had attempted to prevent their progress. To Wendorff's immense relief, this was the only obstacle in their way and the truck soon screamed over the bridge and onto the island of Kobrin.

The situation around them on the large northern island was fluid as groups of Russian defenders wrestled for control with the German attackers. Both were equally bemused by the sudden appearance of the pair of speeding vehicles emerging from the smoke and chaos. The uniforms that flashed by Wendorff's window now changed from grey to brown, but rather than halt at the first Russian outpost, the driver, like a man possessed, hurtled through the parkland and clattered over the bridge to the citadel island. Once more there was no stopping. Despite the mortar rounds, artillery shells and small-arms fire from both sides all around them, both vehicles hurtled on and flashed over the southern bridge linking the citadel to Cholmsker Island.

With the destination now in sight, the driver finally slowed and drew up beside the casemate of the Volhyn fortification where a stunned group of Red Army soldiers waved both vehicles to a halt. There was no time to think. Sergeant Yashin was as bemused as anyone to see the German staff car pull up behind him. He was about to speak when, with mortar bombs falling all around, he thought better of it and called out to the assembled defenders, "Here, comrades, help us unload the ammunition before we all get blown sky high!"

Willing hands rushed to the back of the truck and the precious cargo was soon being unloaded and rushed into the comparative safety of the casemate. A young commissar rushed up to the German staff car and stopped in his tracks as Korsak emerged from the vehicle, helping the traumatised figure of a young girl to her unsteady feet.

"Comrade Korsak!" said the startled young commissar.

"Comrade Fomin, what is happening here? Is it a counter-revolution?"

"No, comrade, the fascists attacked us by surprise last night, but we are holding out. Why do you have the fascist staff car?"

"I took it from them. I was on a mission for Moscow that was interrupted by all this," Korsak replied, gesticulating at the explosions falling nearby, "and now I am at your disposal, but, please, first help me to get the girl to safety."

"Of course I will, Comrade Korsak," replied Fomin.

"She needs care. Her family were the victims of a massacre ordered by a certain Hauptsturmführer Hans von Schroif. Remember that name."

Wendorff stood stock still in shock, his ears now tuned for a further mention of his former commander.

"When he is not ordering mass murder and rape, he is likely to be in command of an armoured unit," continued Korsak contemptuously. "We know he is in the vicinity and I have a very personal score to settle with him."

"Well, your guess is good. The first prisoners have confirmed that he is the leader of Kampfgruppe von Schroif. The main force is a battalion of assault guns. We have seen them off at the Terespol gate and we suspect they are getting ready to attack again, so your expertise in armoured warfare will be very welcome indeed."

"I am at your disposal, comrade," replied Korsak.

"The situation is under control here, but I understand that Major Gavrilov is getting ready to defend the Kobrin fortification. We expect them to strike there next. Elements of the 98th Anti-tank Battalion are trying to make their way over to him, so it should be a very warm welcome."

"If that's where you feel I can best be of service, then I'll attempt to make my way over to him straight away," said Korsak. He concluded by gesturing towards Wendorff, who seemed to be doing nothing in particular. "Take care of the girl, she has had a terribly traumatic time," he said with a nod towards the girl.

Wendorff still made no move as he looked around in vain for an opportunity to make himself scarce, but he was intercepted by Commissar Fomin.

"Bandsman, are you listening? Where is your weapon?"

"I don't have one, Comrade Commissar," stammered Wendorff.

"Well, get yourself in there," Fomin said, pointing towards the entrance to a tunnel. "They will issue you with one. And take this young girl to safety. There are nurses in the tunnel."

There was no option but to obey and Wendorff soon found himself with a Soviet rifle thrust into his arms and the bulky ammunition stuffed into his pockets.

"You are to report to Corporal Balovsky," said the man who issued the rifle and then pointed down the tunnel.

As he walked down the badly lit tunnel a nurse appeared and took the young girl from him. Wendorff walked on in confusion. As he did so, he could dimly make out the shapes of injured men, women and, worst of all, children. The cries and moans were heart-breaking. Many were maimed or horribly burned and the word *voda* was repeated again and again. The surviving nurses from the hospital moved among the suffering, offering what they could in the way of aid, but there was obviously no water to be found anywhere.

The Soviet soldiers did not waste energy in conversation. There was the odd low mumble, but the overall impression was one of silent stoicism. It appeared as if the Russians possessed vast reserves of inner strength and courage. Wendorff began to form the conviction that this was a foe to be reckoned with, the opposite of any mental picture he had been fed before being parachuted behind enemy lines. How empty, two-dimensional and utterly wrong was the propaganda that had been pumped into him! If this small border outpost was anything to go by, then God only knew what awaited them in the vast interior.

Nor was this resistance homogenous. Many of the troops were from far-flung parts of the Soviet Empire. There were Tatars, Kazakhs, Georgians, Uzbeks, Armenians, Ukrainians and what seemed like countless others augmenting the solid core of Russians. But this was no rag-tag collection of warring tribes. They were as one when it came to fighting spirit and resolve. How many different peoples had they taken on? One aspect of these national differences did work in Wendorff's favour however. The many languages and dialects spoken meant that any discrepancies in his grammar, annunciation or general fluency were hopefully likely to pass unnoticed.

Eventually Wendorff came across a group of soldiers who were being marshalled together by a harassed corporal. The universal impulse common to every army that results in NCOs ordering subordinates to both hurry up and also to wait was present in the flustered corporal's confusing flurry of instructions.

"Fall in, bandsman. We are going to need every man… even musicians! We have to hold out here until we are relieved. It's going to get interesting later, so grab some rest now."

Wendorff obediently took a seat on a step next to one of his new colleagues. There was no conversation. The atmosphere was heavy with the palpable air of shock. His attention wandered to the pretty young nurse who was tending to a bullet wound on the shoulder of a stoic Red Army guardsman. She finished her work and slumped down beside him.

"You look exhausted," he said.

"We all are," replied the nurse, who was obviously not in the mood for further conversation.

"Is there anything I can do to help?"

"Yes, of course there is. You can find us some water. The mains don't work and no one seems to know what to do to get some."

"If the corporal will permit me, I will try my best," said Wendorff, looking over at the corporal. He didn't expect to receive permission, but he was looking for an excuse to leave this hellish environment.

"Sure, why not?" said the corporal. "We won't attack until nightfall. If you succeed, the wounded will thank you forever, as I'm sure Nurse Ostermann will."

The mention of his mother's maiden name came

184

with a shock like a lightning bolt to Karl Wendorff. His mother's side of the family were *Volksdeutsche* from Volhynia who had been driven out of the new Polish state following the last war. They had settled in Nuremberg, where she had met his father. Hearing the name was a heart-stopping moment. His first thought was that this was some twisted trick — that his true identity had obviously been discovered — and that a swift bullet in the back of the head was the best he could hope for now. However, nothing else was said and Wendorff began to breathe again. He must have misheard. His tired brain must have been playing tricks.

"If you can find water, we'll all be in your debt," she said, with a gesture towards those suffering the agonies of pain and thirst. "You can hear them, can't you?" said the nurse.

"I can, and I will do my best, nurse…?"

"For what it's worth, it's Ostermann… Bettina Ostermann," she said with an air of weary resignation.

Wendorff looked back at her open-mouthed in shock and unable to speak.

"I know, I know, it's a German name," she said, holding up a hand as if to ward off the inevitable question, "and yes, I have German blood in my veins. I'm from Volhynia, on the Soviet side of the border. If they want to kill me for it, they will." She gestured towards her own soldiers. "Or perhaps the Germans will. Either way, I'm dead, so I may as well do what I can for them in the time I have left."

"I'm sure that won't happen," said Wendorff, getting to his feet.

"Who are you to make promises? It didn't save my uncles during the last war and it won't save me this time."

"I won't let it happen," said Wendorff, who was desperate to reveal his true self to her. He wanted to blurt out, "My mother is from Volhynia. Her maiden name is Ostermann. We could be related! Maybe we are distant cousins!" But even in his confused and terrified state he had sufficient sense to know that he must keep his deadly secret.

* * * * *

As he returned to the target, Rossheim sensed that the conventional bombers had again been at work on the Brest-Litovsk fortress. The stronghold was ablaze everywhere. Many burning vehicles lay in the parkland and on the roads, but the enemy was evidently not bolting from its lair. Dense clouds of black smoke were being driven by the freshening wind towards the west, which meant that the squadron was unable to approach from the German side. They had to go out to the east, where rogue Red fighters who had somehow avoided the destruction of the Soviet airbases might still lie in wait for their prey. As a result of his sobering experiences earlier in the day Oberleutnant Rossheim was aware of that danger and had previously informed his pilots and wireless operators of the possibility of attack from that quarter.

While flying over the north-east sector of the burning fortress at an altitude of some 3,500 metres, he first looked around for hostile planes. It was a mistake to think of the devil. Like a shot from a gun, evidently swooping down from a great height, a familiar shape whizzed past Rossheim and made an elegant curve to get behind him. The Soviet pilot of the Rata executed the manoeuvre so neatly that he was now directly beneath and behind the tail unit of the squadron leader's machine after having flown out of the curve. It was annoying and unnecessary for half the squadron to yell out, "Rata behind you, boss!" Rossheim had already observed the fact with all desirable clarity. Repeating his manoeuvre from earlier in the day, Rossheim now depressed the nose of his ship and thundered earthwards with the expectation that the Soviet pilot would immediately follow suit. Having dived a short distance, Rossheim ran out the nose-dive brakes to lessen the speed of the dive and the Soviet pilot, unable to brake his descent, promptly whizzed past him on one side.

"See you again, comrade," cried Rossheim sarcastically. "Some other time, perhaps."

But the Russian was destined to never have the chance to meet German dive-bombers again. Rossheim had hardly called his sociable parting greeting after him when another aircraft shot past him like a shadow, heading in the same direction, after the Soviet plane. Rossheim just had time to recognise the black crosses in a hazy way and realised that there was no need for anxiety. He pulled his machine out of its dive and looked down, where the German Messerschmitt 109 was now shooting down the Russian fighter. The whole occurrence, from the appearance of the Rata until he was shot down by the Emil, was over in a few seconds.

"Choose your targets carefully. Be alert for ground recognition markers. There's some anti-aircraft fire, so be vigilant," Rossheim told his squadron and the bombs of the Ju-87 formation were soon raining down on the identifiable targets far below in the fortress. It was almost impossible to observe the details of the hits, everything being instantly wreathed in dense clouds of smoke.

As Rossheim had warned, there was some desultory anti-aircraft fire and, needless to say, it was one of those rounds which registered a hit on the oxygen bottle in Rossheim's Stuka. The oxygen bottle promptly exploded. Fortunately, the explosion left both crewmen uninjured, but it had a catastrophic effect on the aircraft, which seemed close to disintegration. Simply everything on that machine now wobbled and shook, but somehow it remained in the air, despite the fact that everything seemed to have been torn apart.

"We have some problems with the aircraft," Rossheim radioed — a masterful understatement.

He glanced back and saw to his dismay that the tail unit was practically severed, hanging by the operating rods of the controls alone. Accordingly, he slowed down to the slowest possible airspeed and made a long turn for home. He was praying that the machine would stay in the air. Somehow, it held together. He knew from his long experience which stretched all the way back to Spain that the Ju-87 could take an enormous amount of punishment, but this particular machine couldn't go on forever. It dissolved into its component parts as it landed on the temporary field near Terespol, but by a miracle neither Rossheim nor his gunner were injured.

As he disentangled himself from the wreckage and slowly began the long walk back across the grass Rossheim was staggered to witness the welcome sight of Leutnant Spiegel, who simultaneously arrived by horse-drawn cart. Judging from the bloodied bandage around his head, Spiegel seemed to have been badly wounded. Rossheim was delighted to see him back, but from the look of him it appeared that he had endured a more than adventurous journey.

"Welcome back to the squadron," said Rossheim, greeting the wounded man as he stepped down from the cart which deposited the airman on home turf. "We thought we'd lost you... Are you badly hurt?"

"It's nothing serious... just a gashed forehead."

"That's good news. Was it a bullet?" enquired Rossheim.

"Fortunately, no, it was not. It actually happened to me later in the day. When the Rata got me I had to make an emergency landing with numerous hits in the engine. It's so embarrassing for me. That fight with the Soviet fighter must have been the very first engagement of the campaign and I went straight down."

"Well, it's fame of a sort. The good thing is that you're back in one piece. Did your gunner make it?"

"Sadly, no, Oberleutnant, he did not. He was too badly wounded and, unfortunately, he died soon after our landing. I had no idea where he had come down and I didn't know whether the territory had already been occupied by German troops, or whether it was still in Russian hands. Fortunately, the infantry battalion you spotted was on the march nearby. When they got to me I expressed rather... err... *forcefully* how important our air support mission was and I had the barefaced cheek to demand a car at once!"

"Looks like it failed," said Rossheim with a nod to the departing cart.

"It didn't actually, Herr Oberleutnant. To my immense surprise, a car and driver were immediately placed at my disposal and then off we went, heading slowly down the side road to Brest-Litovsk. The chauffeur was terrified and was keen to drive me to the German jumping off lines, so we slowly bowled along, aiming for the airfield here at Terespol."

"You must have been glad of an uneventful journey. No contact with any lurking Soviet remnants, I take it?"

"Well, it wasn't entirely uneventful. We did, in fact, have a brush with Ivan. A Soviet ammunition truck came hurtling along behind us and ran us off the road, into a tree. That's where I think I got my injuries. I must have blacked out because the next thing I knew I was in the cart. Fortunately, it feels like nothing too serious and it was then no great distance here. So here I am."

* * * * *

Fierce fighting continued in the fortress throughout that fateful morning. By noon on the 22nd of June the Germans had captured most of the surviving buildings in the hospital grounds. In a surge of bloodlust fuelled by their own losses, they killed the few remaining patients and all of the wounded officers and men. Under the cloud of smoke, savage fighting continued throughout the immense fortification. The defence that was mounted at the southern Cholmsker gates and on the outer earthworks was especially fierce.

All the while the surviving nurses did their best to treat the patients and wounded men who were now hidden in the casemates. Nurse Bettina Ostermann took a brief break and recorded the names and addresses of those who were there that day on her trade-union membership card. She sorrowfully recorded how she had been told the tale of how a nineteen-year-old nurse, Vera Khoretskaya, had died a heroine's death while shielding a wounded soldier as the enemy infantry closed in.

By the end of the 22nd of June the Germans had made further gains and had managed to occupy the barracks between the Cholmsker and Terespol gates, but the spirit of the defenders was strong and the prospect of renewed struggle on the morrow remained.

* * * * *

As the battered StuG battalion rolled back into the assembly area Fritz Rubbal and his maintenance team went to work. Fresh ammunition was loaded aboard from the plentiful stocks and fuel cans were dragged to the thirsty vehicles. As he dismounted from the assault gun, von Schroif recognised the familiar figure of SS-Sturmbannführer Voss, who patiently awaited von Schroif's report after each engagement, eager to understand the course of events. With him on this occasion however was General Schlieper, commander of the 45th Infantry Division. This required some formality and von Schroif sprang to attention.

"Hauptsturmführer von Schroif reporting, General. I regret to inform you of the loss of four vehicles and that another is severely damaged. I regret also to inform you, Sturmbannführer, that you were correct yesterday when you warned us about the reality of fighting Ivan. It is impossible to advance here. The infantry can't make any headway because the highly-organised rifle and machine-gun fire from the deep gun emplacements and horseshoe-shaped yard cut down anyone who approaches."

"Well, we are both aware that the Sturmgeschütze should not advance without infantry support," Voss replied. "From my experience, there may be only one solution — to force the Russians to capitulate through hunger and thirst."

"We too have sustained very heavy casualties," said

General Schlieper, "and we are ready to use any means available to exhaust them... Our offers to them to surrender have been unsuccessful..."

"I fear that this is only the beginning," said Voss. "These are not men who will simply give up the fight. I recall that, during the hard winter of 1916, a Russian regiment was surrounded in the woods by my command and had to be starved out. According to the prisoners, the Russians subsisted during those weeks on a few pieces of frozen bread, leaves and pine needles which they chewed, and some cigarettes. It had never occurred to anyone to throw in the sponge because of hunger, and the cold, which reached minus thirty, had not affected them. The kinship with nature, which the Russians have retained to a greater degree than the other peoples of Europe, contributes to the ability of the Russian soldier to adapt to terrain features, and to actually merge with them."

"You have experience with the Soviets?" asked Schlieper. He was not happy with the idea of having to cooperate with these political soldiers, but one never knew who they were connected to, so he wisely allowed Voss the floor.

"Yes, I fought them in the last war for three years. I know Ivan. He is a master of camouflage, entrenchment, and defence construction. With great speed he disappears into the earth, digging in with unfailing instinct so as to utilize the terrain to make his fortifications very difficult to discover. When the Russian has dug himself into his native soil and has moulded himself into the terrain, he is a doubly dangerous opponent. The bombardment may just have created a new type of fortification."

"Is there any tactical advice that you can offer, Sturmbannführer?" asked von Schroif.

"I could talk all day on the subject, but time is moving on. So I'll just say that, as a soldier, the Russian is primitive and unassuming, innately brave but morosely passive when in a group. These traits make him in many respects a superior adversary to the self-confident and more demanding soldiers of other armies. In attack, the Russian fights to the death. Despite our most thorough defensive measures in the last war, he would continue to go forward, completely disregarding losses. He is generally not subject to panic. For example, in fortifications which had long since been bypassed and which for days lay far behind the front, they continued to fight, even when every hope of relief had vanished. Often, following our advances, fortifications which had originally been cleared of the enemy were reoccupied a few days later by groups of Russian stragglers and had to be painstakingly retaken by a division which followed in the rear. The sum of these most diverse characteristics makes the Russian a superior soldier who, under the direction of understanding leadership, becomes a dangerous opponent. It would be a serious error to underestimate the Russian soldier, even though he does not quite fit the pattern of modern warfare and the educated fighting man."

"I hear what you say," said General Schlieper, "but we will give one more heave. This time we have a detachment of combat engineers, ready to assault." He pointed to a large group of men standing nearby. The men were loaded with equipment and half a dozen were loaded down with flamethrowers. Von Schroif noted them with particular interest. Schlieper's eye was drawn to one of the assault engineers who had scrawled the word *Fafnir* across the flamethrower strapped to his back. Although it was strictly against regulations, here in the frontlines many otherwise punishable offences were overlooked and even encouraged.

"Perhaps the flame of the legendary dragon might help to winkle out the enemy from his lair," said Schlieper hopefully. "We will swing in from the east this time. Ivan is unlikely to expect an attack from that direction. Be ready to move out in two hours."

* * * * *

Wendorff returned empty handed from his expedition to find water. It had been a short trip. No sooner had he emerged from the entrance to the casemate than a veritable storm of machine-gun and mortar fire had broken out, forcing him to return to the relative safety of the tunnel. Once more he trooped past the long line of wounded until, head down, he re-joined Bettina Ostermann. She looked briefly hopeful then downcast and resigned to her fate.

Embarrassed and frustrated, he gazed disconsolately around him. Men suffering in silence were staring at the ground in grim determination, except for one. The young boy sat opposite Bettina and Wendorff. Why had he not noticed him before? Had he been there long? The boy had an almost unnatural aura about him, as if he was beyond the suffering of all those around him. He was sitting cross-legged, motionless, serene-looking, a tiny beacon of peace in this tunnel of war. Looking by his side Wendorff was astonished to see a battered old violin case. Wendorff couldn't help but stare at it, the incongruity almost too much to bear. Then Bettina spoke.

"You play the violin, bandsman?"

"I do, Nurse Ostermann," he replied truthfully.

Wendorff immediately regretted his honesty. He sensed where the conversation was leading and instantly looked away, not wishing to become the centre of attention.

"It would help," said the nurse, now sitting next to him, giving him a gentle nudge in the ribs.

"Why not play something soothing and German?" said another. "It might calm the animals down."

"Anything but Handel's *Water Music*," another joked, to some derisive amusement.

That was the last thing Wendorff wanted to hear. He felt himself squirm and sweat a little more. The young boy then started to speak, sparing Wendorff.

"My teacher once played with the great Magyar,

Joseph Joachim, and Joachim told him that the Germans have four violin concertos. The greatest, most uncompromising, is Beethoven's. The one by Brahms vies with it in seriousness. The richest, the most seductive, was written by Max Bruch. But the most inward, the heart's jewel, is Mendelssohn's."

Karl Wendorff could not believe what he was hearing. It was almost heart-breaking. He daren't imagine the second movement for fear of breaking down.

"I love that work," Said Nurse Wendorff, "it reminds me of so many happy times, but the andante is so sad, it's painful."

"You know the andante from Mendelssohn's violin concerto in D?" continued the boy, looking at Wendorff.

Of course he did! This was his solace, the place where his soul went for repose! But he could not admit it, not here, not now. So he motioned toward the young boy using his hand and a slight bow to indicate 'After you.'

Sadly the boy looked back at him and lifted his arm, revealing a bloody bandage over his right forearm. He had lost his hand.

"I'm so sorry," said Wendorff, feeling the young man's loss with all his heart.

"It is not the greatest loss," the boy replied with equanimity beyond his years or situation. "At least I still have my voice. I did play violin, but it is my voice that gave me entrance to the study of music. Shall I start singing the part of the bassoon? You can come in when you are ready?"

Wendorff almost mechanically accepted the offer. What choice did he have? But one half of him could not believe what he was doing. He was about to play perhaps the most hauntingly beautiful piece in the entire German repertoire to an audience of wounded and dying Soviet soldiers, whilst above them his own countrymen were shelling, bombing and machine-gunning everything that moved. German countrymen, the same country of Beethoven, Brahms, Bruch and Mendelssohn…

Taking the violin from its case, Wendorff applied rosin to the bow and expertly tuned the strings. His heart almost broke into pieces when the young boy began to sing the opening notes of the slow movement. Wendorff was immediately struck by the tone and sweetness of his voice. Who knows, when he matures he could perhaps sing baritone? What a voice! He threw himself into the piece. Not physically, but emotionally, drawing out its aching core. Nurse Wendorff began to weep, borders dissolved, and the power of music conquered all.

On finishing, Karl Wendorff felt shattered. The quiet applause and murmurs of approval only added to his pain. The music had posed a question. How, in a world where music could talk to any man, all men, could men still turn on each other like animals?

"That was beautiful, bandsman. I don't even know your name," said the young nurse.

"It's, err…" Wendorff was now in a blind funk. He could no longer remember his cover story. He knew he was a bandsman sent to augment the garrison orchestra, but his false name eluded him. "...Oistrakh, Ivan Oistrakh," he blurted, grasping at the first name that came to mind.

"That's wonderful," said Bettina, "are you related to the maestro?"

"No... No," said Wendorff, panicking inside. "It's just coincidence."

* * * * *

Dimitri Korsak considered whether to utilise the staff car for his return trip to Kobrin but then thought better of it. Instead, he utilised the network of tunnels that ran under the fortress. The intermediate trips across open ground proved eventful, with bullets flying from both sides and constant shellfire adding spice to the adventure. He eventually arrived at the Kobrin fortification and found Major Gavrilov.

"Commissar Korsak, armoured warfare specialist, reporting for duty," said the breathless Korsak. "I bring greetings from Commissar Fomin."

"Glad to have you here, Comrade Korsak," said Gavrilov. "You are just in time. I fear we will soon need your expertise. We anticipate attack by enemy armour. I'm in the process of forming tank-hunting teams. I was about to brief the men. Now that you are here, you can give the men the benefit of your experience."

"Of course, comrade," said Korsak. He immediately stepped forward to address the small group of assorted cooks, orderlies and store-men who formed the small group of tank-hunters.

"Comrades, I have just come from the Cholmsker gate and I can inform you that anti-tank guns of the 98th Anti-tank Regiment have survived the bombardment and are on their way to us, so take heart from that, but in the meantime there is a great deal that we can accomplish with the weapons at our disposal." Despite their lack of knowledge or training Korsak was delighted to see that the men looked determined to do their duty. "We are likely to be fighting at very close range and that works to our advantage. Improvised firebombs will also work, so we should commence filling bottles with petrol and making sure we have rags to create the wicks."

Nodding heads and the faintest flicker of a smile from the most enthusiastic recruit confirmed that the men were paying attention. Korsak continued with his briefing.

"Humble weapons like the anti-tank rifle are highly effective at close range. In conducting fire against enemy tanks and other fighting vehicles, it is vital to observe the results of hits carefully, and to continue to fire until we see definite signs of a hit. A burning tank is the most obvious sign, but also be alert for signs of the crew leaving the tank, and the shattering of the armour or the turret. Watch enemy tanks which have halted but do not show any of these signs constantly, even though they show no other signs of life. While firing at the active tanks of the enemy, one should be in full readiness to renew the battle against those that are apparently knocked out."

The grim yet positive expressions on the faces of his audience indicated that they were following his every word and Korsak was able to move on with the briefing.

"In the current action, our comrades at the Terespol fortification have already been faced with a new type of fighting vehicle, the armoured assault gun which the Germans call the Sturmgeschütz. You will also hear it called by its contraction, the StuG. For determined tank-hunting teams there is very little to fear when encountering this vehicle. It is built on the chassis of the enemy's Panzer III tank, but without the benefit of either a turret or a machine gun. It has a reduced crew of four which means that the men inside have more to do and less time to concentrate on our tank-hunting teams. You could not have asked for a better introduction, comrades. This will be like a beginner's training course. Your grandmothers could defeat these machines!"

Smiles and faint laughter greeted this last statement as Korsak carried his audience with him.

"Now, if you find yourself pitted against the self-propelled assault gun, advancing towards you from the front, you should direct your fire at the driver's port, and below the tube of the gun. However, if possible, you should try to attack from the side, particularly against the armour protecting the engine. And remember, the roof is particularly weak. The attack from behind is best of all, the vehicle is blind and particularly vulnerable to attacks against the exhaust vent."

Korsak's words were timely. Within the hour, and for the third time that morning, the dwindling ranks of the StuG battalion rolled into combat once more. Only ten machines now remained in action, but they still presented a menacing array of firepower that the beleaguered defenders could not hope to match. Hoping to take the defenders by surprise this time, at Schlieper's command the objective had been switched to the eastern Kobrin fortification set in the parkland of the northernmost island.

The assault guns made a wide circuit to the north then curved round to attack from the east, which, it was hoped, would be an unexpected direction. Although they were unaware of the fact, the reality of the situation was that the battalion commanded by von Schroif was once more about to be pitched into action against the men of the 98th Independent Anti-Tank Artillery Battalion, who came rushing up just as the guns were being readied for their renewed assault. The anti-tank gunners had already been rewarded that morning with the sight of two of the guns burning after having been hit by their anti-tank shells, and two other burned-out carcasses were now obstructing the possibility of further advance towards the Terespol gate.

The loss of one of their precious anti-tank guns to accurate fire from the lead StuG had not disheartened the anti-tank gunners. They felt they were winning the personal struggle between the StuGs and the anti-tank battalion. With only one prime mover remaining in action, they had not been downhearted, and had manfully dragged their guns through the maelstrom of explosions, ready for the next encounter.

As von Schroif and his battalion deployed at the Kobrin fortification, the initial signs were more auspicious.

"There is no evidence of any anti-tank presence," reported the lieutenant in charge of the assault detachment. "We have carried out a reconnaissance in force up to the edge of the fortification, as ordered."

There was no question that the lieutenant's words were true regarding the situation just twenty minutes previously. However, in the intervening period, and in the very nick of time, the anti-tank guns of the 98th Independent Anti-tank Artillery Battalion were rushed in to take up defensive positions. Exhausted by their alarming journey through the war-torn fortress, the worn-out Soviet gunners had just about enough energy to deploy the extra guns on the eastern- facing earthworks. Lieutenant Ivan Akimochkin, the battalion's chief of staff, and Senior Political Instructor Nikolai Nesterchuk took charge of the defence.

Their presence remained completely unknown to Hans von Schroif, who had not the faintest inkling that they were there. "This is an improvement on the Terespol side," he commented to Knispel from his uncovered position in the open commander's hatch of gun number 1. He then raised his binoculars and turned to survey the surrounding parkland. "We have more space to operate as a battalion here," he said, indicating his qualified satisfaction to the commander of the advancing grenadiers.

There was certainly more room to deploy the assault guns on a wider front, but as the guns rolled forward the anti-tank detachments sprang into action. Fortunately, the first shells struck the heavily armoured fronts of the advancing Sturmgeschütze and there were no immediate casualties, but it was enough to halt the advance.

"Find cover, lay down smoke!" commanded von Schroif.

The guns responded by rolling to a halt and firing the smoke shells carried by all of them. The anti-tank gunners, from their concealed positions, fought off all attacks by the Sturmgeschütze. A series of difficult skirmishes along the entire line of the defence were fought between the assault guns and the anti-tank guns.

There were no further casualties on either side, but the supply of anti-tank shells was running out for the Russians. An ammunition supply depot was nearby — only a few dozen metres away in no man's land — but it was impossible to reach because of a solid wall of high-explosive fire that the Sturmgeschütze were able to bring down. Finally, as the rate of fire slackened dangerously, Private Levsky took the initiative. He was the driver of the last intact towing vehicle remaining. Despite the best efforts of those ranged against him, he succeeded in making several runs to the depot and brought hundreds of shells back to the fighting positions.

Several hours passed. An anti-tank gun, commanded by Volokitin, that occupied an all-round defence position in the rubble stopped and burned another Sturmgeschütz. Number 2 gun from the third abteilung was the fifth gun to be completely destroyed that morning. Worse still, the gun crew dispersed the supporting enemy infantry column and their accurate stream of high-explosive shells eliminated the possibility of all further infantry attacks.

Eventually von Schroif decided that the only solution was to deploy a pair of assault guns to deal with the troublesome anti-tank gun. He ordered the rest of the battalion to give supporting fire while his own number 1 gun, with number 3 gun in support, moved against the troublesome nest of resistance.

Volokitin was alert to the danger. Despite the flurry of shells from the supporting Sturmgeschütze, he managed a direct hit on the side of number 3 gun which penetrated the fuel tank and set the Sturmgeschütz on fire. To Volokitin's discomfiture the remaining assault guns continued to advance. The deadly accurate eye of Michael Knispel guided the high-explosive rounds home and the entire Russian gun crew died in this unequal battle.

The remaining anti-tank gunners remained resolute and continued to beat off the enemy attacks from the direction of the Moscow highway and the Volhyn fortification in their position at the crest of the earthworks.

Assault guns advanced on the embankment from several sides and the last of the grenadiers approached on foot. From up on top of the crest bursts of machine-gun fire and solitary shell-bursts rang out. Grigory Derevyanko, the assistant political officer, met the enemy assault units with machine-gun fire.

Wohl was quick to relay the message and immediately the engines of the other guns could be heard, revving up as their crews took them backwards, out of the action. However, there was no corresponding movement from number 1 gun.

"We've thrown a track," Junge stated calmly.

"Oh, no, shit, no... not here, not now," thought Wohl to himself, but he wisely kept his own counsel.

The mishap that had befallen number 1 gun was exactly the type of opportunity Commissar Korsak and Private Borodin had been waiting for. "Now's your time, Comrade Borodin," exhorted Korsak. Borodin held a bottle full of petrol in one hand. A length of fuel-soaked cloth protruded from the neck of the bottle. Korsak put down his anti-tank rifle and held his lighter under the cloth, which immediately took flame.

"Death to the fascists!" Private Borodin shouted as he began to sprint towards the stranded vehicle. At the same time as Borodin made his move, a second group of defenders attempted to rush the vehicle from the side.

"Enemy infantry approaching the vehicle, eight o' clock, 150 metres!" screamed von Schroif, who was now firing his machine pistol through the pistol port.

"Watch out! Enemy with fire bomb, 11 o' clock, 100 metres," called Junge. "Why is there no damn MG on this thing?"

Across the rubble-strewn street brown-clad figures could be seen rushing from the gate.

"Bale out, abandon the vehicle," von Schroif ordered, but as Wohl threw open the first of the hatches a stream of machine gun bullets forced him to close it just as quickly.

"*So this is it… we die here*," thought Junge as Borodin closed in on his target.

Just when it appeared as if all was lost the noise of an aircraft siren pierced the noise of battle. A huge explosion engulfed Borodin and his Molotov cocktail was consumed by the blast.

Leutnant Rossheim pulled his aircraft out of its dive and swooped back over the stranded StuG, machine-gunning the advancing Russians. When the first bodies fell the others made their way back to the fortification. The other aircraft in the squadron joined in and the attacking Soviets scattered in all directions.

Seizing the opportunity, Knispel and Wohl leapt out of the StuG and began the terrifying task of replacing the track while the Stukas circled menacingly overhead.

CHAPTER 7

Gefoltert durch den Durst

FORTUNATELY FOR Wohl and Knispel, the Soviet machine-gunners kept their heads low and sought to conserve their precious stocks of ammunition. Nonetheless, it was a nerve-wracking and frantic experience and Wohl was delighted when Knispel finally declared the job done and both men hopped back into the vehicle in record time.

"Take us home Junge," came the welcome command and the StuG began to reverse once more out of the danger zone. The crew were elated to be alive but also deflated by a sense of defeat. This certainly did not feel like a battle that would be won anytime soon. Some other intervention would obviously be required.

* * * * *

Wendorff threw himself down among his erstwhile comrades. His brain was becoming addled through lack of water and his thoughts travelled down strange paths. He was not a religious man. Nietzsche was his mentor, his tutor, his guiding light. For some arbitrary reason it was these thoughts of the great philosopher that now flooded his dehydrated brain.

"*I teach you the overman. Man is something that*

shall be overcome. What have you done to overcome him?

"All beings so far have created something beyond themselves; and do you want to be the ebb of this great flood and even go back to the beasts rather than overcome man? What is the ape to man? A laughingstock or a painful embarrassment. And man shall be just that for the overman: a laughingstock or a painful embarrassment...

"Behold, I teach you the overman. The overman is the meaning of the earth. Let your will say: the overman shall be the meaning of the earth! Man is a rope, tied between beast and overman, a rope over an abyss... What is great in man is that he is a bridge and not an end: what can be loved in man is that he is an overture and a going under..."

Was he, Wendorff, an overman? Were these Soviets the beast? Was this conflict the bridge over the abyss, the meaning of the earth?

His crazed thought process could take him no further on the road to madness as just then the earth shook and he ducked as flying bricks, mortar and dust filled the cellar. Looking up, he could hear voices, German voices — "Raus! Raus!" — and see light pouring in from a hole in the outside wall.

His first impulse was to rush to this newly-formed breach, to greet his comrades, to go home... But then he considered the men he would have to run past. Would they then know? He decided it would be better to follow the crowd out into the sunlight.

"Bring out the sick and wounded. We will take care of

them," continued the German officer. "You have nothing to fear."

Wendorff looked back along the tunnel. Heated discussions were taking place amongst the soldiers as to what to do.

"Fight!"

"With what?"

"The wounded cannot last much longer."

Looking across from him, Wendorff's eye was caught by the young boy. "Is it safe, do you think?" he asked. "Can we trust the Germans?"

Wendorff did not want to be seen to reply too quickly or enthusiastically so he deliberately looked around and wore a look of confusion, as if he was waiting for orders. Then he entertained the romantic idea that he may be able to use his influence to get this young musician back to Germany. The world deserved to hear this natural-born talent, this voice. He knew a surgeon. Perhaps he could even find him a place in a conservatory…

"Is it safe?" repeated the boy.

Wendorff looked at him, saw his wide, innocent eyes, looked straight into them, gave him the most discrete of affirmations, and handed him his violin back. The boy silently thanked him with a trusting smile, put his violin back in its case, and rose to walk up the tunnel. Wendorff was just about to join him when a familiar female voice shouted from the back of the tunnel.

"We need help to get these wounded out!"

Without even thinking he turned and walked back up

the tunnel to help Nurse Ostermann. Kneeling to help lift one soldier who had lost both of his legs, Wendorff looked back up the tunnel and saw the young boy approach the hole in the wall, his tiny frame silhouetted by the sunlight pouring in from outside. Then he heard a chilling voice.

"So, the rats are crawling out of the sewers. What do we do to rats, boys? We *burn* them."

Outside the tunnel the engineer stood ready, the 11.8 litres of *Flammöl 19* mixed with tar (to give it weight and distance) weighing on his shoulders. Knowing this should allow him a distance of twenty-five metres, he rechecked his aim to make sure the deadly flaming jet would go right down the tunnel. On the order, he released the fuel and immediately ignited it with the hydrogen torch. Holding for the designated ten seconds he felt the power course through him. He knew the temperature of the flame discharged by his inhuman weapon would reach 4,000 degrees centigrade. The engineer was therefore surprised when the first powerful blast hit the figure of the young boy who emerged from the tunnel entrance and this slight figure remained stock still and upright. Usually the victim fell straight to the ground, or ran briefly before falling to the ground, but each case was different. As the oxygen was completely used up all around the target, most died instantly, but some victims could survive for a few agonising seconds before collapsing. This boy took the full blast and just stood there, on fire, not even screaming.

Inside the tunnel, Wendorff felt the searing heat of the first burst and instinctively threw himself to the ground. His life had been saved by the fateful decision to return to help the wounded, placing him out of range. Looking up, he was horrified to see a scene from hell as flaming victims ran screaming back into the tunnel or just burned to death where they lay with their hair, clothes and bodies on fire. All that he and the others could do was to take off their jackets and try to put the fire out, but this inevitably made things worse as skin and cloth stuck to each other. If only there was water!

Then, looking further down the tunnel, Wendorff was appalled to see a small figure walk slowly back into the tunnel, completely aflame. Astonishingly, he made no sound as walked back. Wendorff gathered his jacket and rushed towards him. Just as he arrived he realized the reason for the silence. It had nothing to do with that otherworldly aura the young boy had carried with him, nothing to do with serenity. It was stomach-churning. The flesh on the boy's face had melted and sealed his lips together. This great beautiful voice had been so reduced, so deformed, that now it was unable even to scream. But his eyes were screaming, what was left of them, before they too melted over and the boy slumped to the ground. Karl Wendorff fell to the ground with him, passing out and falling in such a manner that it looked as though he may never recover.

* * * * *

Despite all of the losses so far incurred, on the morning of the 24th of June General Schlieper announced the surprise decision that the 45th Infantry Division was to intensify its attack on the citadel and to commit its reserve troops into the fight. As a result, a fierce battle now erupted at the Brest gate. The citadel was protected on the north and east by the Kobrin fortification, the largest in the entire fortress complex. Up to a thousand officers and men from various units were still fit enough to take part in its defence. However, the defence of the entire fortress was impossible. There were simply not enough troops for that. Three pockets of resistance were therefore formed and the defenders had to act independently. The commanders were eventually able to meet when Regimental Commissar Yefim Fomin transferred his command post to the citadel and it was here that he made contact with Captain Ivan Zubachyov, assistant commander of the 44th Rifle Regiment, and who was commanding the defence in the citadel's northwest sector.

Fomin and Zubachyov immediately decided to create a joint command for the defence of the central island and sought the advice of Major Gavrilov.

"Comrades, you have seen more of the fascists than I. What is your analysis of the current situation?" asked Fomin.

Zubachyov and Gavrilov looked at each other in silence as they each attempted to defer to the other. Who could possibly want to voice such grim and hopeless tidings? Gavrilov finally took a deep breath and chose to speak first. His tone was measured and without accent or inflection.

"The Cholmsker gate still holds. The others we have only intermittent contact with. Water shortages are acute. Ammunition is low. Medicine is almost non-existent."

"Any radio contact?"

"No, comrade, we have neither equipment nor power," said Zubyachov.

"Do we have any idea what is happening along the front? In fact, do we even know if we are part of a front?" asked Fomin.

Zubachyov and Gavrilov shook their heads.

"Do we have any idea how much longer we can hold on without ammunition or supplies..."

There was no need for Fomin to wait for an answer. He could tell by the faces of his fellow commanders just how critical the situation was. He had seen it with his own eyes. Women and children — those that were left — loading machine guns and scurrying about the ruins and remnants of the fortress scavenging for food, water and ammunition. He struggled to formulate a plan. The wounded — how much more pitiful could their condition get? Water — was there any hope? Radio communications — was there nothing that could be done? Were there any alternatives? Surely there must be alternatives?

At this moment of crisis, unbidden, his Grandfather Abram's favourite saying came to his mind. *"Yefim, my boy, please remember this Jewish wisdom from your ancestors — if life only offers you two choices, always take the third!"*

So what was the third choice? Surrender? The thought chilled him, but surely it must be considered?

Then Major Gavrilov spoke, capturing a thought or a notion which was in the air but as yet unexpressed. "Sometimes, in war, it is best to postpone victory to a future day, to leave and return when the tide has turned."

"We've discussed this before!" snapped Captain Zubachyov. "All exit routes are cut off — there is no possibility of retreat!"

Pyotr Gavrilov lowered his voice even further.

"Comrade, it was not retreat that I was referring to... it was..."

"Surrender!" thundered Zubachyov, his voice so loud that Commissar Fomin had to gesticulate to him to modulate his insubordinate tone.

"I am not making the coward's case," replied Major Gavrilov. "I am more than prepared to fight and die for every last inch of the Motherland. But if we all spill our blood here then where shall we be if she needs us at a more critical time? How many prisoners are there already? For the sake of the women and children we should at least consider a strategy of a breakout, to regroup and come back at the fascists."

"You are right," said a voice off to Fomin's right, though he was not yet able to determine who it belonged to until the speaker stepped forward out of the shade and into the light. It was Dimitri Korsak.

"That strategy should now be fully considered. Don't be afraid. Please tell them what you saw, Rivka," said Korsak as he gently ushered a young girl into the cellar.

"They are... I saw... I..." she stuttered, ashen and shocked.

"Go on, Rivka, do not be afraid. Tell the officers what we saw that day."

"First it was Jewish people," said the reticent young girl. "They shot some in the streets and then... they took them in trucks... I was at my grandfather's farm... They made them undress... old people... they made them take their clothes off. My friend Rosa... her father did not want to undress... he did not want to stand naked. They tore the clothing off the old man and he was shot. Then they shot her mother... then her grandmother, who was already eighty years old... she was holding two children... and then her father's sister. She also had children in her arms and she was shot... with babies in her arms. Then her sister... she went up to the Germans with one of her friends, they were hugging each other, and she asked to be spared, standing there with no clothes on... A German looked into her eyes and shot the two of them... the Germans then shot Rosa's second sister, and then Rosa's... I saw the German take the child from her arms. The child cried out and was shot immediately. And then he aimed at her. He aimed the revolver at her and ordered her to watch and then... then he shot her. Then she fell to the ground, into the pit, amongst the... bodies... Then they took everyone, they said we were bolshevists, to the quarry… It was awful, too awful…" The girl could speak no more and dissolved into tears.

"Thank you, Rivka," said Korsak gently.

"I'm sorry, truly sorry," said a shocked Zubachyov to the young girl.

"The Jews should be used to hard times by now," said Gavrilov.

Yefim Fomin could not believe what he was hearing. Words failed him.

"We are all Jews now," said Zubachyov.

"Comrade Zubachyov is correct," said Korsak. "The fascists have a phrase which we will all have to come to terms with. The German word is *untermensch*. It's not just a term reserved for Jews, they use it for gypsies, for undesirables and, of course, Slavs. What shocked me was the scope, the scale, the planning, the inhumanity. It was burned into my soul. It has destroyed young Rivka's life and it is only the beginning."

Korsak was usually a man of calm consideration, he liked to think of himself as a soldier, a tough man, but today he was no longer the assured political operator he had once been. A volcano of raw emotion boiled up beneath the surface.

"I have looked into the face of pure evil. It has marked me forever. See, this is what a single exposure did to me." Korsak swept off his officer's cap, revealing a shock of pure white hair which contrasted starkly with his jet black eyebrows. "It happened to me instantly on that spot. I left the fortress on the morning of the 22nd of

June with fine black hair. I returned on the 23rd of June like this," he said, pointing to his pure white hair. "It was so horrifying, so base and so inhuman, that it aged me instantly. I'm an old man now and, whatever time I have left, I shall dedicate every second of it to fighting these fascist beasts."

"Surrender is no longer to be discussed or considered," said Zubachyov. "No one surrenders to absolute evil. Certainly not soldiers of the Red Army."

"Comrades, I have made my decision," announced Gavrilov. "We will break out of the encirclement."

*　*　*　*　*

Following the decision to break out, the garrison continued to fight on from a patchwork of ruined buildings, casemates and tunnels. Soon afterwards it became clear to even the most optimistic defender that the front had moved far eastwards and that, in reality, no help could be expected from that direction.

The officers of the citadel therefore decided that the time had come to form a strike force to break out of the fortress. If this attempt succeeded, it was mooted that Captain Zubachyov would then lead the main contingent of the besieged troops in the citadel to break out after the first group.

The breakout attempt was timed for noon on the 26th of June, the fourth day of the siege. Following a short mortar barrage that had used up the last of the precious mortar rounds, and with a passionate shout of "Hoorah!", an advance unit of one hundred and twenty desperate men rushed out of the Brest gate in the direction of the bridge.

However, as a result of prisoner interrogations the breakout had been expected and the assault guns were waiting. They had assumed covered positions and each was loaded with high-explosive.

"Rapid fire!" barked von Schroif over the radio as the Soviet infantry rushed towards their goal. "Don't let any escape."

The storm of steel from the guns was accurate and unremitting. The attackers were simply blown to pieces by the vicious rain of high-explosive shells which projected ferocious pieces of jagged metal, tearing off limbs and inflicting gruesome injuries to the soft human forms. Within seconds the breakout attack was reduced to a debacle and von Schroif in particular was determined to end the resistance and avenge the dead crewmembers and lost guns. The Soviet machine-gunners used up a great deal of their dwindling supply of ammunition in giving cover to the attacking troops, but the precious bullets rebounded harmlessly from the dug in StuGs. It immediately became apparent that this was a brave but hopeless endeavour.

"Reload with HE only, rapid fire," ordered von Schroif and the battalion barked out their messages of death.

Despite the curtain of high-explosive and the unremitting rattle of small-arms fire, a few small groups of Soviet attackers actually succeeded in fighting their way through the solid ring of German troops. The vast majority were not so lucky. One hundred maimed and mangled bodies soon lay strewn across the grass leading to the Brest gate.

The attack was soon on the verge of petering out and von Schroif was about to order the guns to cease fire when suddenly there was a deafening crack on the side of the StuG and a plug of metal flew into the gun. Almost instantly, a small hole was blown in the other side of the vehicle. Pulling himself together from the shock of the unexpected, von Schroif quickly surmised that an anti-tank round had penetrated from one side of the fighting compartment and passed straight through and gone out the other. Luckily, the ammunition was not hit. Otherwise, they would have all been blown to kingdom come.

"Anti-tank team at 2 o' clock," said Knispel, now alert to the danger. "Looks like an anti-tank rifle."

Although he had no way of ascertaining the truth for certain, Korsak sensed he had been spotted. He was certain that his first shot had hit and penetrated the vehicle. Despite the temptation to finish the job, it was time to change position. Fortunately, he was armed with the portable PTRD-41 anti-tank rifle. He was an expert in handling this light and highly effective weapon and the mobility it brought was an advantage in the deadly game of cat and mouse which now unfolded.

Despite his inexperience, Private Alexi Pushkin, a cook

turned anti-tank rifle loader, was alert and responsive to Korsak's brief commands. At long range the PTRD-41 was effectively useless against any reasonably thick armour, but in a close up contest it had the necessary penetrative power to punch through the armour on just about any part of the Sturmgeschütz, except for the heavily armoured front of the vehicle.

"Remember, the fuel tank is vulnerable," said Korsak by way of encouragement, "so is the engine and the driver's vision port. There are almost too many targets to choose from. All we have to do, Comrade Pushkin, is to stay alive long enough to claim ourselves a fascist trophy."

With that, Korsak scuttled from behind the pile of rubble which had sheltered the two man team and sprinted to a shell-hole. Pushkin was hard on his heels and threw himself down beside him. At the same time, the loader grabbed one of the bulky shells from the rapidly diminishing supply in the ammunition box. Korsak gingerly peered over the lip of the shell-hole then swiftly withdrew as a high-explosive shell screamed towards them and exploded just three metres from their hiding place. Korsak's cap was blown off his head by the force of the blast and earth and shell fragments rattled against Pushkin's metal helmet. They were not to know it, but they were up against a crack marksman in Michael Knispel, and he had their range.

Inside the smoke-ridden atmosphere of the StuG, Otto Wohl selected another high-explosive round and rammed it into the breach. Never taking his eyes from the viewer for a moment, Knispel tracked his quarry, alert for the next move.

Korsak instantly realised the danger and was again first to move. His shock of white hair made him a noticeable target.

"I'll get that white devil with the anti-tank rifle," barked Knispel, but Korsak was again too quick for him. Once more he and Pushkin sprinted to their next position. Lying prone, Korsak took careful aim and fired just as Junge swung the StuG around to present its strongest armour. The projectile produced another jagged crack on the steel plate covering the side of the vehicle, then ricocheted skywards.

The second warning was enough for von Schroif. He was brave, but not foolhardy. There was no sense in sacrificing the vehicle for the sake of stubbornness.

"Pull back," he ordered, "the next one could finish us. Leave it to the grenadiers to finish them off. We've done enough here. Tell Grunewald to bring a barrage down on them."

Knispel sent one last round hurtling towards Korsak and Pushkin, but the shell failed to find its target and the guns swiftly withdrew, leaving the grenadiers to deal with the survivors.

Seeing the Sturmgeschütze pull back, Korsak too decided that discretion was the better part of valour and he rapidly exited the scene of the encounter which had been so fiercely contested. Knispel watched in frustration as the figure with the unmistakeable shock of white hair and disconcertingly dark eyebrows dodged from cover to cover.

"Looks like your white devil will live to fight another day," said Junge as he watched the Soviet duo dart into the shelter of a burned-out building.

Korsak was just in time as just then all hell broke loose. With a howling surge of fury, thirty-six high-explosive warheads crashed into the former battlefield. The effect was overwhelming. The explosions, in close succession, ripped the air from the lungs of anyone in the blast area and killed by concussion. As the smoke cleared it was clear that the *Nebelwerfers* had succeeded in their deadly work. Nothing was left alive in the cluster of shell-holes that marked their target zone. Two kilometres away Grunewald ordered his teams to reload, but there was clearly no need for a second barrage.

The small victory wrought by Korsak and Pushkin in forcing the withdrawal of the Sturmgeschütze was the only shaft of light in an otherwise unrelenting tide of dismal events. The abortive breakout now brought the truth home. There was no prospect of escape. For the defenders of Brest-Litovsk, this could only be a slow fight to the death with no prospect of relief.

CHAPTER 8

Wie eine Ratte in einer Falle

IN THE tunnels of the east fortress Karl Wendorff felt like a rat in a trap. He did not know what was worst — the heat, the thirst, the smells, or the persistent feeling that each moment might be his last. Furtively he looked around the brick-lined tunnel. He saw a man to his left grimacing as one of his comrades tried to dig a bullet out of his shoulder with a bayonet. Further down the line he saw a nurse in her last moments, a sheet being readied. He'd already overheard the conversation.

"We found her tied to a stake. The bastards used her for bayonet practice... and then they…" Wendorff noticed the blood smeared between her thighs and did not have to hear the rest as a blanket was laid over her.

The tunnel they were in was stifling, its red brick walls featureless. The stench from putrefying wounds was overwhelming, the heat almost unbearable. Strangely though, his own personal fear had vanished, the fear of being exposed as a soldier of the Reich, the fear of being torn limb from limb — perhaps justifiably so, if these men were to identify him as one of those who had inflicted this pain, this suffering and this carnage.

However, these logical thoughts were fleeting. The overriding mental preoccupation, never more than a heartbeat away, always there, always insistent, was thirst

— choking, relentless, agonizing thirst. The combined effects of the baking sun, the airlessness, the unwashed uniforms and the heat from these packed bodies had turned the cellar into a fetid, noxious cauldron. Every part of Wendorff was soaked in sweat. *"How could this be?"* he wondered to himself. *"Where was it coming from? When was the last time that water had passed his dry, parched throat?"*

But that was a mistake. To even think of water or drinking was to open the door and invite the demons in. He couldn't try to take his mind away from the torture. The most mundane memories would turn and torture him, memories of rain, of waterfalls, rivers and springs. *"How we take things for granted!"* To think that he had once complained because the weather was too wet! If he could only run in that rain now, or dive into a river or even drink from a shower!

"No, Karl, don't think about these luxuries. Banish them from your mind. Ignore these demons. Concentrate on the here and now. Think about how you are going to get out of here without being killed or cooked alive."

Wendorff's brain somehow wrenched itself away from thoughts of water. *"How can I get a message to von Schroif? Fire-beacons, semaphore, reflected light... smoke?"* As each thought presented itself to Karl Wendorff it was instantly dismissed. Thinking about smoke signals reminded him of the American frontier novels of Karl May he had read as a child. It made him smile, but he was clever enough to know that even the most laughable of potential solutions to problems should never be dismissed offhand. In fact, in his experience, sometimes the most ridiculous suggestions provided mental starting off points which might eventually bear fruit. However none of these means of communication offered any immediate prospect of practical satisfaction — they were all too detectable, too imprecise. This was not to say they should be dismissed out of hand. No, he would store them on a mental shelf, ready to return to one — or perhaps a combination of more than one — if he could come up with no productive further lines of thought.

If only he had a damn radio! He had to get a message to von Schroif.

Perhaps he could build one himself — with what though? What about a primitive Morse transmitter? He would need a capacitor — and where would he find one of those? And then an inductive coil — ridiculous idea... *"Stop thinking about it,"* he told himself. *"Relax. Think about something else and then it may come to you."*

As always at times like these, Karl Wendorff's mind turned to music and to better days. He had been at his happiest in Berlin, when he got his first job at Vox Radio at number 4 Potsdamer Strasse. It was here, at Vox-Haus, that he and the other engineers had made history by working on Germany's first broadcast station.

For some reason the schedule of that ground-breaking broadcast popped into his head. It started at 10:00 in the morning with a report about prices of all things. That was followed by a news report and then, at lunchtime, the regular stock market update. Then a time signal, then at 13:05 more news and more stock reports. And then, from 17:30 to 19:00, his favourite, music — often from the wonderful Berliner Funk-Kapelle. Then a language programme, often German/English, followed by a lecture from some acclaimed academic or expert. In fact, Karl Wendorff recollected with pride, he had even suggested the subject matter for one of these lectures. A broadcast about Ewald von Kleist, a German pioneer in the study of electricity, inventor of the Leyden Jar, the earliest... capacitor....

That was it! Wendorff didn't need a capacitor! He only needed a glass jar and some metal foil! Why hadn't he thought of that before! That was it! He still had his Morse key secreted away in the pocket of his battledress. He was halfway there! Now he only needed some copper wire which he could use for an inductive coil — and an antenna!

* * * * *

While the rest of the crew saw to rearming and refuelling the gun before turning in for a well-earned rest, Otto Wohl despondently made his way over to where SS-Obersturmführer Sanger waited with the latest instalment of radio revision torture. Wohl craved rest with every sinew of his tired body, but orders were orders and he had no option but to obey.

"Ah, Wohl, take a seat. Today, we will turn our attention to Morse."

Wohl felt his heart sink into his boots.

"Now, why, in this day and age, would we consider using Morse code, SS-Kannonier?"

Sanger knew he should have expected nothing more than a blank stare. Drawing a deep breath and feeling his patience run thinner, he chose to provide the answer himself, rather than waiting for Wohl to provide some ludicrous approximation. "Not only does a signal sent in Morse code require *less* power, but, *for the same power*, a signal can be sent further and with more clarity. What do I mean by *clarity*?" Sanger was now fully committed to the practice of only asking rhetorical questions of Otto Wohl. "When I say *clarity*, I mean in a situation where there is a lot of pre-existing signal noise, or when jamming is in use. Do I make myself clear, SS-Kannonier?"

"Yes, SS-Obersturmführer," nodded Wohl.

"One dash equals… how many dots, SS-Kannonier?" enquired Obersturmführer Sanger.

"Err… three?" replied Otto Wohl hesitantly.

"Well done, SS-Kannonier. Now, the space between letters equals how many dots?"

"Err… is it… four?"

"No, Wohl! In action, your life may depend on you knowing this! For God's sake, man!"

After a prolonged pause, Otto Wohl was forced to give up. Better to admit he didn't know, he thought, than to guess again. "I am sorry, SS-Obersturmführer."

"Well then, let's try a different approach. Was the dichotomic search tree any more helpful?"

Otto Wohl stared at his instructor blankly.

"This resource, here," replied von Sanger sternly, pointing to a sheet of paper. "From the start position we go left and right to the only two letters with one dot and one dash and then move to I and M, the next two letters, which have only two dots and two dashes. Now, which letters have only one dot and one dash?"

The interview was clearly going nowhere. Wohl was getting more and more frustrated, and Sanger's patience more and more worn.

"The two letters at the top of the tree are the letter E, with one dot, and the letter T, with one dash. Will you *ever* grasp this? It's the very basis of your craft!"

* * * * *

Unlike the hapless Otto Wohl, the principles of radio communication came very easily to Karl Wendorff. He was now determined to get a message back to von Schroif and his team. Slipping away from the corporal had been easy. He now kept his head low and tried to make it look as if he was following some urgent order. As he wandered the tunnels beneath the casemate in the unlikely hope of finding exactly what he was looking for he could still feel the tremors of exploding shells. As he stumbled along he tortured his brain as to where he could find some copper wire. *"Old radio equipment? Shell casings?"*

He came to a staircase leading to the building above and hesitated. In an ideal world, he would have been able to wander around the fortress cannibalising every burnt-out hulk for the precious metal he needed, but to stand close to a window or stepping through a room could mean certain death. Despite the danger, he would have to explore the building above. Wendorff quickly ascended the staircase. It was to prove a fortuitous decision.

He slowly advanced along the first floor corridor. To his left were the rooms which faced over the courtyard. He avoided these, flashing past the empty doorframes to make sure he presented only the briefest target to any lurking sniper. On his right, on the inside of the building, were occasional storerooms and cupboards. All had been ransacked, either by the defenders or attackers, he couldn't be sure. He glanced at the contents as he passed. There was nothing of any use. It was then that he discovered the last of the ransacked stores. The door was slightly open, but it was worth a try. Another huge barrage shook the building to its very foundations, forcing him to cower in the dust for what seemed like an eternity. With the barrage over, he felt ready to move again. Almost blinded by the clouds of red dust and with his parched throat clogged with dirt, he slowly made his way across the corridor to the storeroom door.

He slowly pushed the door open, alert for any sound of movement. He listened intently but heard nothing beyond the sound of distant small arms. He pushed the door a little more and squeezed his head through the gap. The storeroom was empty. Looking over his shoulder, he reassured himself that no one was following him and slipped through the door, pulling it quietly closed behind him.

Taking a minute to calm his breathing, he let his eyes adjust to the low light as he squinted through the dusty gloom. By the dim light of his flickering hand lamp he made out a wooden floor strewn with rubbish and old crates. Then he noticed some crude shelving. Walking slowly, careful to avoid stepping on any broken glass, he made his way over to the shelving. The store seemed to have been recently ransacked. Empty boxes, presumably once used to hold food, drink and perishables, had been thrown against one of the walls. Looking down, he noticed that the floor was strewn with tin cans and bottles, all empty. Stepping gingerly around them he approached the wall and quickly scanned the shelving for anything resembling copper wire or a glass jar. He noticed some tins of paint, what looked like a pair of gardening shears, some hand brushes, a fishing rod and an old lamp. There was nothing of any value.

He then got to his knees and started searching along the bottom shelf. It really looked like the place had been stripped of everything of any value. Then he noticed a large glass jar, lying on its side, empty. Perfect! Running his finger along the edge and then smelling it and tasting it, Wendorff was able to identify it as having once contained formaldehyde. Now all he needed was some tinfoil for the Leyden Jar and then he could concentrate on finding the copper wire. It was then that he noticed an empty box with some foil in it. Sniffing it, he determined that it had obviously contained tea. Stuffing the foil in his pocket and emptying the remaining formaldehyde out of the glass jar, Wendorff now resumed his hunt for copper wire.

Looking further afield he found nothing. Surely any mechanical parts would be in a workshop, not on the first floor of a building? *"I need to find a workshop,"* he thought to himself. *"Which objects might contain copper wire?"* He ran his eyes back over the shelves and then his attention was drawn to the fishing rod. Perhaps, just perhaps… He then walked quickly over to the fishing rod and picked it up. To his intense delight, he discovered a reel of copper fishing line. He couldn't believe his luck! He felt like letting out a little whoop of joy.

There was no time to loose. He undid his fly and, through great force of will, was able to force his protesting body to produce half a litre of dehydrated urine which he passed into the jar which was then covered in foil.

Within the hour he had his amateur transmitter and immediately began to send the message VSWEN-DORFFINEASTFORTRESS. He then transmitted his simple message again and again. VSWENDORFFINE-ASTFORTRESS, VSWENDORFFINEASTFORTRESS. He had no way of knowing if his message was being received and his plight had unhinged his normally calm manner. Over and over again, in a frenzy which bordered on madness, Wendorff sent and resent his message. All he could do now was hope against hope that someone would receive it and understood what it meant.

✱ ✱ ✱ ✱ ✱

Day by day the grind of the fighting continued. German troops eventually captured the main body of the Volhyn fortification, but only after three days of intense and unremitting close combat. Only eighteen of its original detachment of three hundred defenders remained alive. The bitter fight for the Volhyn fortification mirrored the fight for the Terespol gate, which had flared up at the outset of the German offensive.

As he sat hunched in his headquarters, desperately attempting to find a solution to the increasing mass of issues, Fomin was vaguely aware that the last of the Terespol fighters had staged a breakout. The bedraggled band of survivors was brought in to give their report of the fighting to Commissar Fomin.

"Comrades, you've been through a great deal. No need for formality, just tell me what happened," said Fomin, turning his attention to the grime-encrusted corporal whom he assumed to be the leader of the small band of survivors.

"I will try, comrade," said Corporal Vadim. "When the attack came there were about three hundred officers and men inside the Terespol fortification."

The shell-shocked corporal had just led the small

band through hell on earth to reach this new position and he was still breathing hard.

"We were unprepared to repel the enemy's surprise attack, so they gained a foothold. However, within a few hours we had managed to rally ourselves and drove the German troops from the fortification. We later learned that this had cut off communication with the German force that had managed to get beyond us and infiltrate the citadel. Under the direction of two border-guard officers, Fyodor Melnikov and Akim Cherny, who rallied round and led the organization of the defence, we were able to mount a coherent defence for some days. However, we were always too few in number and we did not have sufficient ammunition, provisions or water.

"We therefore fought our way through — on the night of the 24th of June — to the Kobrin fortification, and then, today, here to the citadel. The steadfastness of the defenders of the Terespol fortification is best illustrated by one heroic example. During the breakthrough, we found a border-guard with a light machine gun in the bushes. There were a great many spent cartridge cases on the ground around him, along with reserve disks for his machine gun, and there were dozens of dead Nazis lying nearby. He was apparently on duty at one of the border posts when war found him, and he remained at his post all these days, carrying on an unequal battle with the enemy.

"When we found him, he looked terrible. His eyes

were bloodshot and his face was grey and pinched. His bony hands were still clutching the machine gun grip. He had obviously not eaten or slept for several days. He seemed to be unconscious. Suddenly he raised his head and looked at us. We suggested that he should join us in the breakout, but he parted his cracked lips with difficulty and said firmly: "I will never leave this spot."

"That is the kind of spirit we will all need to demonstrate if we are to hold out until we are relieved," said Fomin. "We are in need of reinforcements here. How many are left of your group?"

"I regret to inform you that our numbers are few," replied Vadim. "Only fifteen men remain alive out of the three hundred who defended the Terespol fortification. The enemy suffered heavy losses too. I dutifully report that we effectively stopped their advance, although all of our officers were killed. I am privileged to report that we held on persistently, but our situation was becoming markedly worse. The lack of adequate ammunition and food supplies was obvious. More seriously though, we had no water, and the wounded needed medical attention. Nikolai Nesterchuk was wounded by an enemy grenade during one of the attacks, but he unfurled a red flag above the casemate. It was struck down by shells and machine-gun fire, yet each time he raised it again.

"After repeated attacks, the fascists succeeded in breaking into the casemates. After hand-to-hand combat, they captured Lieutenant Akimochkin, who was wounded and shell-shocked. As I retreated towards the citadel I looked back and saw Lieutenant Akimochkin executed."

* * * * *

"Today, we will deal with the theory and practice of Morse," began SS-Obersturmführer Sanger.

His unwilling pupil again felt his heart sink to the soles of his boots. Wohl craved sleep. All he could think about was the need to rest his tired brain and yet here he was, again faced by this relentless tormentor.

"Now the British, who invented the system, have their own systems for learning Morse, but they cannot compete with German ingenuity! We do our research, do we not?" It was a rhetorical question and one to which Wohl could not have given an answer in any event. "Ludwig Koch! That is the man we owe this debt to. Koch was a psychologist at Die Technische Hochschule in Braunschweig. The Koch method — named after the great man, obviously — was his pronounced contribution to the field. And his goal was?"

Again Wohl could do no more than to stare blankly at the thin academic who sat opposite him.

"To discover the most efficient way to teach Morse code to young men like yourself — prospective radiotelegraph operators — in order that you might meet international standards in the shortest time possible," Sanger continued. "So, what are these standards? The operator must send 100 words in five minutes. They must copy a 100 word telegram, also in five minutes, and copy 125 words of ordinary text in five minutes — one word being reckoned as five letters. So, how did he set about achieving this?"

Otto Wohl felt like his eyes were glazing over, but he thought he should contribute something by way of reply. "I do not know, SS-Obersturmführer."

"You need to research, SS-Kannonier! Research! Find out what the best are doing, examine current teaching methods, test them, and then, when you have done your research and have your results, devise something better! Koch ran three series of tests to determine how the code is comprehended and for this purpose used four competent, actively-practicing, radio telegraphers. Three of these operators had learned the code solely by sound, while the fourth was self-taught from printed code charts."

Sanger was now immersed in his own world and it no longer mattered whether Wohl was following or not.

"For the first test, each operator was to send, by regular hand-key, the series of ten letters — b, c, v, q, f, l, h, y, z, and x — at various speeds while monitoring his transmission with a pair of headphones to satisfy himself as to its quality. Out of his sight and hearing, a recording system made an accurate timed graphical record of his transmission so that the actual timing of signal and space durations could be examined in detail. Below about ten words per minute the only operator who closely conformed to standard timing was the one who had visually learned the code. The other three deviated considerably from 'standard' timing. At five words per minute these deviations were appreciable. The *dits* were too short, the *dahs* tended to be longer than three times *dit* length, and the spaces between characters were too long." Sanger paused briefly. "Are you following me?"

Wohl thought briefly about telling the truth, but rather than an honest "*No, I'm not getting a fucking word of this,*" he meekly offered up a weak nod of affirmation.

"Good. However, spacing between the components of a letter was almost perfectly equal to their *dit* lengths. At successively higher speeds this situation changed slowly and somewhat irregularly until a rate of about ten words per minute was reached, when all four operators were forming fairly accurate patterns of sound. Nearly up to the international standard, in fact.

"The three operators who had learned by sound obviously showed no real sense of sound patterning at these very low speeds, no sense of unity, but rather just a series of separate elements strung together. Only by about ten words per minute were the code characters now felt to be entities of sound in themselves, patterns which were clear-cut in each operator's mind and no longer shattered elements, disjointed parts."

Otto Wohl had long since given up trying to make sense of this. The effect of his stressful morning was now beginning to catch up with him. He was struggling to stay awake and was beginning to get resentful. Oblivious to all, Sanger droned on.

"Test One," continued Sanger. "Each operator was to copy the thirty German Morse characters sent by a machine in perfect 'standard' timing at each of four different speeds over the same speed range as before. At about five words per minute these experienced operators hardly recognized a single character correctly! At seven words per minute only forty per cent to sixty per cent of the letters were correctly identified. At ten words per minute all operators were getting about ninety-five per cent correct. By twelve words per minute all of them correctly identified every character. Fascinating! I'm sure you'll agree?" Sanger paused briefly again. "Are you sure you are paying full attention, SS-Kannonier?"

"Yes, but we were up all night and in action this morning. I'm really feeling the effects."

"Well, you might be back in action soon and, under the circumstances, it is essential that you are up to speed on the basics of radiotelegraphy. Koch observed that, in the early stages of learning, the beginner has to concentrate intensely to catch the letter rhythm-patterns. Was there anything that could be done make this easier for him?

"He observed that some teachers were speaking, or even almost singing, the sound patterns of code characters using the syllables *dit* and *dah*, whose vowel qualities and lengths make sound patterns stand out somewhat like little melodies. This helps accentuate the differences between sound patterns and simultaneously promotes an immediate sense of meaningful unity of the acoustic patterns. Could the use of two different pitches, one for *dits* and the other for *dahs*, make it easier for the new student to recognize the wholeness of the rhythmic pattern — the 'melody' — of a code character, and make it easier to learn? Could it help reduce the stress caused by the intensity of his concentration in the early learning stages, while he is being introduced to the rhythms and trying to get accustomed to them? It looked worth a try."

"Please make it a nutshell," Wohl thought to himself.

"The Koch Method provides us with a proven method for learning the character set with a minimum amount of frustration. In this way, you learn the characters at full speed, from the start, and you only have to learn one new character at a time. The characters become reflex with a minimum amount of effort." The scrawny academic finally paused for breath and prepared for the next stage of the lesson. "So, I will now go into the radio truck and transmit, while you write down. When you have finished, bring the message to me."

Sanger went into the truck and Wohl put on the headphones. Immediately a stream of letters began to fill his headphones. "Hold on, you arsehole, give me a damn chance," Wohl muttered to himself as he grabbed the pencil and began to transcribe the stream of letters as fast as he could.

FORTRESSVSWENDORFFINEASTFORTRESSVS-
WENDORFFINEASTFORTRESSVSWENDORFFINE-
ASTFORTRESS.

Satisfied that the message was simply being repeated,

Wohl moved over to the truck and opened the door to find Sanger fiddling with the transmitter and swearing roundly.

"I've got a message for Hauptsturmführer von Schroif: Wendorff is in the east fortress."

"You can't have. I haven't started transmitting yet."

"Well, I'm receiving this repeated message: VSWENDORFFINEASTFORTRESS."

* * * * *

Still in the wrecked storeroom, Wendorff continued to send his desperate message. He had managed to slip away from the living hell below every day so that he could continue to transmit his despairing communication. It had become part of a demented routine, but his world stopped when he heard the crunch of glass behind him and felt the cold steel of a pistol on the back of his neck.

"Comrade, I think you have some explaining to do. Turn around."

Wendorff froze and could feel his face flush and sweat start to form. He knew he had to turn around, so he slowly started to move, his brain working furiously to come up with as believable and plausible a lie as possible. Having turned around, he was faced with two men. One, he recognised — the political commissar Yefim Fomin. The other, judging by his uniform, was a sergeant in the 84th Rifle Regiment. Both were staring hard. Wendorff needed something convincing, but he could think of nothing. As a last resort, he thought he'd better just start talking and see what came out.

"I, ah… some of the men, Sir… thought that, ah…"

"Thought what?" Fomin asked curtly.

"Water, sir. We thought we might be able to attach a jar… this jar… to some fishing line and fish for water from out of the second floor window, next to the river, for the wounded, sir."

Fomin looked through Wendorff like he wasn't even there. An age seemed to pass. Then his face broke out into a broad smile.

"Initiative. You are to be congratulated. But take these," he continued, picking up what Wendorff had thought earlier were a pair of gardening gloves. "Copper wire may be good for fishing for water, but it can also be used for garrotting fascists. Is that not so, Comrade Tarovsky?"

The sergeant smiled.

"Thank you, sir," said a grateful Wendorff.

"I will take you at face value, bandsman…?"

"Oistrakh," replied Wendorff.

"You show good initiative, Comrade Oistrakh. However, as we say in the NKVD, 'Trust, but verify'. The sergeant will accompany you. Dismissed."

* * * * *

As the assault guns returned, Rubbal counted them anxiously before he and his maintenance crews set about rearming and refuelling the precious machines. Sturmbannführer Voss waited for von Schroif and, with a cordial wave, summoned him into the farmhouse which served as the headquarters of Kampfgruppe von Schroif.

"Welcome back, Hauptsturmführer. Good to see that the whole command has returned safe."

"That is something to be thankful for, Sturmbannführer. Today, at least, we have achieved our mission."

"I was going to come to that. I have the latest orders. It would appear that we have all achieved our mission here. The Sturmgeschütze have done the best they possibly can. The fortress looks set to fall within the next few days. Victory is almost ours."

"I have no doubt about that, but it feels like a defeat to me. We have lost too many good comrades and half the machines."

"I understand your frustration, and your sadness, but we knew from the outset that this was the wrong assignment for the Sturmgeschütz. It was not designed to fight in a built up environment, but orders are orders and your command has progressed exceptionally well."

There was a knock on the door and Captain Grunewald entered, looking as dapper as ever. His immaculate uniform was perfectly creased and he had with him a bottle of schnapps.

"Forgive my intrusion, but, as the command is being split up, I thought I'd take the opportunity to present a small memento of our first action together. I hope it won't be the last."

"Well, news certainly travels fast around here," said von Schroif. "I've only just learned that the kampfgruppe is being disbanded and the wake is already in full swing."

"Do you know where your unit is headed, Captain?" asked Voss.

"We have been ordered to Smolensk," said the Captain. "It looks like we're headed for Moscow, and you?"

"It seems we're headed south. We're re-joining the division, it would appear."

"That will be welcome," said von Schroif with a smile, "but I suppose even you don't have the clout to get us a posting to Africa. I am not looking forward to a winter in Russia."

"We are certainly available and willing," said Grunewald.

"Sadly, I'm not a magician," said Voss. "Our destiny looks set in stone. It seems to me that Russia will be our mistress for some time to come."

CHAPTER 9

Die Endlösung

IN THE comfort of his grand office at Tirpitzufer 76/78 Canaris shook his head in sorrow.

"I am afraid the news is not good, Lehmann. It seems that all of our worst fears were true. Plan Ost is already in operation. My sources have confirmed that Himmler and Heydrich are in the rear of the battle zone. They have been observed at a number of execution sites. Our friend Dirlewanger is involved in the operation."

"That comes as no surprise to me," replied Lehmann.

"His Sonderkommando is composed of hardened criminals, but even they are reported to be finding the work unpalatable. Himmler's orders are to exterminate as *humanely* as possible," said Canaris with palpable contempt in his voice. "In addition to open-air shootings, they have also made use of 'gas vans'... they kill by carbon monoxide. Being mobile, they save the trouble of building permanent installations and having to transport the victims to a distant killing site.... They look like closed trucks and are so constructed that at the start of the motor the gas is conducted into the van, causing death in ten to fifteen minutes."

"And how big are these vans?" probed Lehmann.

"They vary in size, with capacities ranging from fifteen to twenty-five people. Dr August Becker, an SS lieutenant and the inventor of the vans, considers himself to be a humanitarian. In order to eliminate the victim's suffering, as well as the resultant filth as they evacuate their bowels, he has ordered a change in technique of administering the carbon monoxide. The valves are to be opened slowly, instead of all at once, so that 'prisoners fall asleep peacefully.'"

"Presumably the inventor is delighted with the results?" ventured Lehmann.

"No doubt he is, but the firing squads are posing the real problems. We understand that some of these men, as savage as they are, are having mental breakdowns. A number of officers have taken their own lives." The Admiral paused briefly, as if it was almost painful for him to continue. "It makes me sad to admit to being a member of the German nation, but, regrettably, there are some who have taken to their task with excess enthusiasm and sadistically maltreated the prisoners. There are also reports of a series of bestial acts of a sexual nature, but, as you say, that is only to be expected if Dirlewanger is anywhere in the vicinity."

"Can't these acts be dealt with by way of a formal complaint?" asked Lehmann.

"No, of course not. We are not dealing with the humdrum of the normal world here. The sad fact is that this is not some isolated incident of madness, but part of a considered plan, a general policy dictated by the most senior levels of our state."

"How widespread are these incidents?"

"You clearly didn't study Plan Ost in enough detail."

"That's certainly true, Admiral Canaris," replied Lehmann. "We could not take the risk of having a copy made, so you will have to refresh my memory, I'm afraid."

"The resources are substantial. Four SS *Einsatzgruppen*, of 3,000 men each, have been ordered to follow in the wake of the Wehrmacht. As you and I know, their mission is not just to ensure the security of the operational zone; that is, to prevent resistance by partisan groups and civilians. These are special police of a very singular nature. They have been given an additional task by Heydrich. Their chief task is to round up and to liquidate not only bolshevik leaders, but all Jews, as well as gypsies, 'Asiatic inferiors' and 'useless eaters', as they refer to the mentally disabled and incurably sick.

"We know that Heydrich himself has drafted new orders in accordance with Plan Ost stating that the Einsatzgruppen are to execute all Soviet officials of medium rank and above, members of the Comintern, 'extremist' Communist Party members; members of the central, provincial and district committees of the Communist Party, Red Army political commissars and all Communist Party members of Jewish origin.

"With regard to Jewish populations in general, no steps are to be taken to interfere with any purges that may be initiated by anti-Bolshevik or anti-Jewish elements in the newly occupied territories. On the contrary, these are to be secretly encouraged. Everything is clearly detailed in

Plan Ost and now the plan is being put into operation. It's a black day for Germany when these subhuman barbarians can do this in our name."

"We can only hope that Plan Ost is now in Moscow. I am still firmly of the opinion that its publication will be big enough to bring down the corporal's regime."

"I regret to inform you that Moscow has not received any plan. This message has been received. It is being transmitted from inside the east fort in the fortress of Brest-Litovsk. According to our monitoring posts, this message has been repeated daily: VSWENDORFFINEASTFORTRESS."

"I regret I'm not following you, Admiral," said Lehmann, who was genuinely confused.

"I'll spell it out for you. Our courier's name is Wendorff. His former commander is Hans von Schroif, who is in command of a StuG battalion attacking the fortress at Brest-Litovsk. It would appear from the context of this message that the only copy of Plan Ost is currently located inside a corner of the besieged fortress. If the courier survives the siege, which is rapidly coming to a successful conclusion, and this plan falls back into the hands of Obergruppenführer Heydrich, the man even Hitler calls 'the man with the iron heart', it won't take long for the SD to work out where it came from."

"Is there anything we can do?"

"Possibly, if we can intercept the courier and get the documents safely back to you... can you get them back into Heydrich's safe?"

"That's assuming that he hasn't missed them in the meantime," said Lehmann nervously.

"I don't think he will have had the opportunity to miss them. If there had been an investigation into a break-in, we'd have heard about it by now. We know for certain that he has been touring the rear areas with Himmler constantly since the beginning of Barbarossa. They are hell-bent on seeing their plans for genocide through. I think we can safely assume that his mind is not currently focussed on the paperwork."

"I think we can manage to get it back inside the safe, if you can get the plan back," replied Lehmann, although his manner was unconvincing.

"Good. It's a long shot, but, should we succeed, you must make sure that you do your bit. The consequences for our respective families would be too awful to contemplate. Fortunately, Abwehr still has some effective agents in the field. I know a man who might be able to make this happen. For the sake of everyone you know, you had better start praying that he does not let us down."

* * * * *

Exchanging few words, Wendorff and Sergeant Tarovsky made their way through the tunnels to the building where he had indicated he was going to fish for water. What small talk there was had revealed that the sergeant was from Orel. The sergeant had showed him a picture of his wife and small child by the Oka River. Wendorff had relayed his cover story, that he was brought up in eastern Volhynia on the Soviet side of the border and that his parents were *Volksdeutsche*, which explained his German accent. Suddenly this cover story had sounded alarmingly precarious.

It was after this that Wendorff started to think about what he would do when they reached the second floor of the building. Despite claiming that he had fished as a young man, the truth was that he had never fished in his life. Would he simply tie the copper wire around the neck of the jar and throw it in the water? He surreptitiously looked at the reel attached to the rod he was carrying, but decided that to attempt to know its workings would make him look foolish.

He then decided that the best way forward would be to offer the rod to the sergeant in a gesture of good faith with some kind words about the fame of Oka fishermen. But then he realized that these thoughts were peripheral and relatively unimportant. What he should really be thinking about was how he was going to be able to kill this sergeant from Orel. Would he do it when the man's back was turned? Would he use a knife or a rock or his rifle? If he was to knife him, should he cut his throat?

Wendorff felt uneasy thinking these thoughts. No one had told him that war was like this. War wasn't supposed to be like this. Wars were supposed to be fought at a distance, against a faceless inhuman enemy, not by meeting with your foe, getting to know him, seeing pictures of his wife and child and then, when his back was turned, pulling out a knife and slitting him open.

Wendorff's misgivings were suddenly interrupted as the sergeant, who had moved a step or two in front of him, raised his hand in a signal that could only mean one thing. At the same time, the sergeant hissed at him. "Quiet. Stop!"

Wendorff stopped immediately. Up ahead, off to their right, voices were coming from behind a door. The sergeant turned around and restated, with a finger to his mouth, the need for silence. He then approached the door slowly, readied his rifle and put his ear to the door and listened. Unexpectedly, he then turned around, grinned broadly at Wendorff, and pushed the door open, announcing in a loud voice, "Comrades!"

Part of Wendorff grimaced. This meant more lying, more deception and a greater chance of being found out. However, another part of him felt relief. His cover had held so far and the nightmare was not to be realized; the nightmare that those voices might have been German and that he would have been forced to fight for his life with men from his own side.

Wendorff stayed in the corridor, presuming that the sergeant would exchange some pleasantries with the men inside and then continue walking. Instead, to Wendorff's horror, he ushered him into the room. He began to feel claustrophobic. The room was small and chokingly hot. Half a dozen men sat there, obviously completely intoxicated, a crate of vodka in the middle of the room.

He wanted to tug the sergeant's sleeve and insist that they carry on with their journey to the second floor. That would have been preferable. But what he really wanted to do was walk — no, run — away from confined spaces, away from Russians, to fresh air… and German voices…

He had no choice, however, and, as he was steered into the room, to his horror, he saw the smiles vanish from the faces of the men inside. Did they know? Had they found out? Was this some kind of trap? Then, to his utter bewilderment, they all burst out laughing. One man, who seemed hopelessly drunk, actually fell over from his sitting position, still pointing at him. Was this some kind of sadistic ritual? Had they known all along and tricked him into entering this small windowless room before killing him?

Then the sergeant, sensing Wendorff's unease, put his arm around him and said, "Poor man. Thought he was going on a fishing trip and ended up in a war!"

This statement provoked even more hilarity. It was also at this point that Karl Wendorff realized the reason for all this mirth. Here he was, standing in a doorway, in the midst of the greatest military engagement of all time, with a fishing rod in one hand and an empty glass jar in the other. He permitted himself a wry smile before being encouraged to enter the room.

"Sit, comrades! Share a drink with us! It could be your last!"

Despite his craving for liquid of any description, Wendorff's first thought was to decline. That's what he usually did. He wasn't a drinker and his own personal code of conduct dictated that he say no. However, the decision to sit was made for him by the sergeant putting one arm around him and using the other to indicate where he should sit. As soon as the newcomers were seated, the largest of the seated Russian soldiers picked up a full bottle of vodka and offered it to him. His mind froze. What should he do? Russian drinking protocols! What were they? Could he refuse? If not, what was the correct procedure?

He racked his brains. He had been briefed about this very contingency during his training. Slowly it came back...

When you have alcohol in Russia, it must be drunk until it is gone. One should not put a glass with alcohol in it back on the table. Traditionally, alcohol is poured out to all the people present, though they are not required to drink. One should not make a long interruption between the first and second shots. The latecomer must drink a full bottle, called 'penal'. Outgoing guests must drink a last glass, called 'na pososhok'. It can be translated literally as 'On a small staff', meaning 'an easy or lucky journey'. Every portion of spirit should be accompanied by the touching of glasses and a toast, except for funerals and commemorations, where the touching of glasses is forbidden. It is not allowed to pour out by hand when holding a bottle from below. It is not allowed to fill a glass being held in the air. It is considered bad luck to make a toast with an empty glass. It is considered bad luck to put an empty bottle back on the table when it's finished.

With these thoughts running through his mind, Karl Wendorff prepared to drink his first full glass. He paused briefly, but his parched and dehydrated body, forgetting the habit of a lifetime, called for him to drink anything. He began to drink the glass offered to him. He had to stop halfway through, as he felt the vile spirit rise up from his gut and try to force itself back out his mouth. By an act of sheer will he managed to swallow it back down without throwing up. He then took a breath and downed the second half of the glass, fighting to keep his face from screwing up too much; trying to give the impression that he was an old hand at this game. The second glass followed quickly and went down a little easier. The sergeant was next, drinking the two glasses in quick succession without the flicker of an eye or even a facial muscle. Wendorff could feel his brain start to heat up.

"So, comrade, it is apparent that you were unlucky today. You did not make a single catch?" asked the burly Russian private, the one who was doing all the talking.

"It is not fish, but water, that he is trying to catch. For the wounded," said Sergeant Tarovsky, thankfully answering the question for Wendorff.

"This was your idea?" asked the private, looking at Wendorff.

Wendorff nodded, at which point he could feel an almost palpable outpouring of warmth and respect.

"It may be," said the private, "that in these conditions, water is as valuable as ammunition. One of the nurses described to me the agonies being undergone by patients. There is no water to boil, so not only are infections increasing, but amputations… amputations with a cold knife… this is not something we want to think about. So, thank you, comrade. This is a great service you do."

Wendorff found himself nodding in humility at the power of the compliment. All the time aware though that not only was he the one responsible for the water in the fortress being cut off in the first place, but that the whole fishing for water story was a lie. He began to feel uncomfortable.

"What is the current situation with the fortress?" the private asked Sergeant Tarovsky.

"The fascists have captured the Terespol gate and most of the western island. Cholmsker Island is gone, but under Captain Zubyachov and Commissar Fomin we are still holding out in the citadel. The defences there are strong and we still hold at the east fort."

Then there was silence as the group waited for the answer to the one great unspoken question.

"I regret, no," continued the sergeant, "there is no word yet of reinforcements."

The atmosphere in the room dropped palpably and Wendorff felt his own mood drop too. Why was that? Where did this sudden feeling of solidarity come from? The thought of possibly having to kill one or more of these men in the coming hours and days depressed him.

The need to get the message to von Schroif now seemed irrelevant. Perhaps he should just stay here with these men, his new pals, a group of skulking cowards selfishly consuming the last of the precious liquid which could be put to good use in the stinking hell of the tunnels beneath them. His addled brain told him he could stay with these equally hopeless men and let the world continue its fight outside. He could make sure they were treated well…

Suddenly there was the noise of footsteps in the corridor outside and the atmosphere in the room was transformed. The private grabbed his submachine gun and dashed out of the door. Most of the drinkers followed him. Wendorff remained sitting, looking in bemused terror at the equally confused figure of Sergeant Tarovsky. There was now the sound of shouting, screaming and machine-gun fire in the corridor outside. The last of the Russian soldiers who had occupied the room grabbed his rifle and ran to the door. Almost immediately, he fell back inside. He had been raked by machine-gun fire and his chest was a mass of bullet holes. He lay bleeding and dying, but Wendorff just sat there, stunned into immobility. It was then that he heard a clank and a grenade bounced off the inside of the open door and landed right in front of him.

Wendorff just stared at it, but the sergeant had more presence of mind. He hurriedly plucked it off the floor and threw it back into the corridor. Both men dived for the floor as the deafening explosion shrieked through the corridor. After that, all he could hear was the screaming in German of a young man who screamed for his mother. Wendorff stayed face-down on the floor, his only reaction to instinctively arm himself with his knife as the bold Sergeant Tarovsky picked himself up, fixed a bayonet to his rifle, and stepped outside.

The next sound Wendorff heard was the death rattle of the young German as his misery ended. Then came more shouts and the unmistakeable screams of hand to hand combat, grunts, shouts and the sounds of clubbing and stabbing; the noise of a fight to the death. The sounds came to an abrupt end and Wendorff hid behind the door, knife in hand. Then he heard the sound of footsteps and, turning slowly, was appalled to see the sight of Sergeant Tarovsky walking slowly back into the room, a young German on the end of his bayonet. The German took a series of agonising slow and faltering steps backward before Tarovsky twisted the bayonet and the German fell to his knees as he cried out for help. The man was beyond help and there was no prospect of mercy in this confined version of hell. The sergeant gave one final twist and pulled the bayonet out of the dead man.

"Out, before the next wave arrives," ordered Tarovsky.

Wendorff fell in obediently behind him. He and his quick thinking companion fled back down the staircase and reached the safety of the tunnels of the east fortress.

*   *   *   *   *

Von Schroif sat under the bough of a shady oak tree. He

was engaged in the task he hated more than any other, writing sad letters of condolence to bereaved parents. Many officers had a standard form that they harnessed for each fatality, but this practical approach offended von Schroif's sense of honour. He tried to write each one completely from scratch, adding personal details, but everything he wrote amounted to the same pack of lies, all attempting to conceal the awful details behind what was mostly a series of grisly traumas.

There was no such thing as a painless death in an armoured fighting vehicle. Vicious shards of metal tore soft bodies to pieces or, even worse, cruel flames immolated the crew. If he was honest, von Schroif could have scrapped all the nonsense about single bullets to the heart and peaceful last moments and simply written "Dear Madam, I regret to inform you that your son was trapped in his vehicle and burned alive. He died screaming for help, but received none. He took about three minutes to die. We are certain that he was tortured by the utmost agonies. Yours etc., Hans von Schroif, Officer Commanding."

He was not altogether sorry therefore to be interrupted by the sound of an approaching staff car. He was intrigued to see that it was a Luftwaffe vehicle. No sooner had the car drawn to a halt when there came a loud shout followed by a cheery word of greeting and there, springing from the car, was his old friend, Oberleutnant Rossheim.

On duty, Rossheim was the archetypal Prussian,

serious and business-like. Like von Schroif, Rossheim was one of those men who loved to get his hands dirty. He loved life at the front and felt that he could carry out no greater duty than when asked to put his experience and skill to any mission. Off duty, however, he was magically transformed into a garrulous and vocal reprobate who loved to drink, carouse and hang out in any bordello he could find. Rossheim was the type of character who made life bearable, and he was just the man to ease the growing feeling of defeat which now hung over von Schroif, despite the successful conclusion to the protracted siege that was now just days away.

"SS-Hauptsturmführer von Schroif, as I live and breathe, it's good to see you! How is the front treating you?"

"Badly, my friend, but it's always good to see you. Please, take a seat."

"Indeed I will. Now come, let us share a glass of this fine Polish vodka!" said Rossheim, producing a new bottle of the local spirit.

Glasses were soon produced and Hans von Schroif enthusiastically took up the offer. For his part, von Schroif treasured his occasional meetings with his old friend. Rossheim was amazingly well-connected and he was an amazing conduit to the bigger picture. He was the most reliable source of information that he had ever encountered and von Schroif trusted his friend to provide an accurate and comprehensive picture as to what was happening, not just on a day to day basis, but also at the larger strategic level. No sooner had he sat down than Rossheim was in his stride.

"Well, Hauptsturmführer! What a fine start we have made between us to this operation Barbarossa, eh? Three and a half million men working in harmony! Thousands of Soviet planes destroyed whilst still sitting on the ground, hundreds of thousands of Reds captured and the leading elements of this Army Group now at Smolensk! My sources tell me that Army Group North is making great headway. Things are a little slower than we'd hoped down south, but, so far, a dazzling advance!"

Von Schroif's expression betrayed a little disenchantment. Surprisingly, Rossheim appeared to know the reason for his downbeat mood.

"Don't worry, my old friend, assault guns were not designed for this type of work. A little bird tells me that you will soon be out of here. I have no doubt you will be back on the wide open spaces at the front, hopefully before we reach Moscow!"

"I'd like to think so. It's been hell here. We've lost more than half the battalion. So, Moscow is von Bock's target?" asked von Schroif, changing the subject.

"My sources tell me that is the case," replied Rossheim, pouring a generous couple of measures. Over the years, von Schroif had come to know that 'my sources' was Rossheim's code for his unexplained, but amazingly accurate, flow of information. It was a fact of life which von Schroif never once questioned. He had never even hinted that he might like to know who Rossheim's 'sources' were, perhaps that was why Rossheim continued to confide in him.

"However," added Rossheim, lowering his voice somewhat, "I am told there may be — how shall we say — differences of strategic emphasis at the very top."

"How so?" asked von Schroif.

"Well," said Rossheim, draining his glass, "as you know, the Führer has always been at the forefront, keeping himself informed of the role of technology — particularly motorization — in the waging of modern war. Plainly, he knows that energy is the key to modern warfare, particularly oil. Power does not just come from the barrel of a gun anymore; it also comes from a barrel of oil."

"I would not disagree with that," replied von Schroif, sipping appreciatively at his glass of vodka.

"Now, let us postulate, SS-Hauptsturmführer," continued Rossheim, "that there may be... err... let's say... *differences* of strategic emphasis at the very top. Let's perhaps suggest that these two camps may be crudely described as modern and.... old fashioned."

"Go on, my friend," said von Schroif.

"Whereas an old-fashioned commander might seek to win a war by the traditional means of decisively defeating the enemy on the battlefield, driving on to Moscow and fighting a traditional campaign, a more modern view would be to look to securing the source of power..."

"Would you by any chance be referring to the Soviet oil fields in the Caucasus?"

"Got it in one! I have always thought you one of our most perceptive commanders, SS-Hauptsturmführer! He who controls the oil controls the world!" At which both men clinked their glasses and drank heartily.

"So, what brings you here today, my old friend?" asked von Schroif, who was sufficiently astute to realise that Rossheim usually had a plan in mind; generally involving drink, debauchery, disputed bills and late night mayhem.

"I was invited along by our mutual friend, Captain Grunewald. I understand they are preparing to bring the Karl-Geräte into action today. I am told they are the biggest guns on the face of God's earth. I thought it would be fun to see them go off."

"You are remarkably well informed, as always. Everybody I have spoken to has been intrigued to see what happens."

The Karl-Gerät was a huge self-propelled piece of artillery which rolled along from the railhead on its own colossal self-propelled platform, the size of two railway carriages side by side. It was enormous and fired the biggest artillery shells on the planet. It was the ultimate siege weapon and it was now being readied for the closing stages of the siege. This was naturally a huge source of interest for bored soldiers. Everyone who was not on duty turned out to see the two guns which had been seconded to the siege of Brest-Litovsk. They watched in fascination as two of the gigantic self-propelled howitzers lumbered along the specially prepared road surface to take up their firing positions in the field behind the StuG battalion workshops.

"Ah, here comes the ever impressive Captain Grunewald," exclaimed Rossheim as the immaculate figure approached the table. "Welcome, Captain. Pull up a chair and have a drink. You are just in time to explain the mysteries of the Karl-Gerät to the Hauptsturmführer."

"Certainly, Oberleutnant, I've been following its progress for years," said Grunewald with obvious enthusiasm. "I'm addicted to technology. The Karl-Gerät is the biggest howitzer in the world. It has been constructed by German engineers on a monumental scale. It makes me so proud to be a German soldier."

"You have the advantage on us," replied von Schroif. "Please, do enlighten us further."

"Certainly, Hauptsturmführer," replied Grunewald, as eager to please as ever. "It all began in March 1936. I became aware that Rheinmetall had made a proposal for a super-heavy howitzer to attack the Maginot Line. Their initial concept was for a weapon that would be transported by several tracked vehicles and assembled on site, but the lengthy preparation time drove them to change it to a self-propelled weapon. I learned that extensive driving trials took place in 1938 and 1939 using the first *Neubaufahrzeug* tank prototype to investigate the extremely high ground pressure and steering of such an enormous vehicle. I was aware that firing trials had taken place in June 1939, although I was unable to gain access to the test.

"The full-scale driving trials were held at Unterlüss in May 1940. General Karl Becker of the artillery was involved in the development, from whom the huge weapon gained its nickname. In total, six Karl-Geräte howitzers have been manufactured. The nicknames give you a sense of the power they pack. They are known as Adam, Eva, Thor, Odin, Loki, and Ziu. In our sector, we are lucky to have Thor and Odin.

"The shells these guns fire are so massive that Panzer IV tank chassis have had to be modified as *munitionsschlepper* with a superstructure capable of carrying four shells replacing the turret and each has had to be fitted with a crane just to be able to lift the things! Amazing! Two or three of these *munitionsschlepper* are assigned to each weapon. You'll see them in action shortly."

Grunewald's enthusiasm was real, but not wholly infectious. During his long explanation, Rossheim's attention wandered to the radio truck, a door of which now opened. Obersturmführer Sanger emerged, followed by Otto Wohl.

"Ach! Here comes trouble!" said Rossheim to von Schroif, who was also thankful for the diversion. "I see Sanger is still with you. Is that your young Bavarian artist he is mentoring?"

"It's my attempt to instil some radio discipline before he gets us all killed. He is on fatigue. Obersturmführer Sanger is supposedly refreshing him on the rudiments of radio-telegraphy. He is an excellent loader, but he has virtually no conception of Morse code. It may be an unwinnable struggle."

"Greetings, Obersturmführer Sanger," called Rossheim cheerily. He had an uncanny ability to remember names and faces that never ceased to amaze von Schroif. "Still trying to achieve the impossible?" continued Rossheim in his characteristically friendly manner. "Why do you waste your wonderful tutoring skills on Bavarian idiots? Wouldn't it be easier to teach cows to do the polka?"

"I think you might have a point there, but I'm not really much of a dancer," said Sanger, who seemed to have got the point.

"Tell me, SS-Kannonier, do you like music?" asked Rossheim, turning his attention to Otto Wohl.

"Only if it's American!" replied Otto Wohl, much to von Schroif's consternation.

"I am in full agreement!" replied Rossheim before von Schroif could intercede. "If I am going to listen to St Louis Blues, it had better be Louis Armstrong and not Goebbels' ersatz monstrosity Charlie and his fucking Orchestra! Come over to the squadron one afternoon and I will explain to you how to listen to Morse. You must learn to feel the rhythm! It is an art — not a science!"

"I would be delighted to debate the relative merits of each in the art versus science debate, Oberleutnant," interjected Sanger, always ready for an academic discussion, "but we have received an urgent message for Hauptsturmführer von Schroif. It would appear that a good friend of ours is trapped inside the fortress."

"Tell me it's not the legendary SS-Hauptscharführer Knispel!" said Rossheim. "I don't think any fortress could hold that lunatic."

"No, Oberleutnant, it's Karl Wendorff, our former colleague and radio communications expert without equal," said Sanger. "It looks as if he is being held prisoner in the east fort. It's one of the last parts of the fortress that is still holding out."

"So what is the exact situation on the ground?" asked Rossheim. "How long can these lunatics seek to hold on?"

"I can answer that," volunteered Captain Grunewald. "I spent the whole of yesterday in the forward artillery observation post. It seems that after all of this fierce and continuous fighting we have now occupied most of the fortress of Brest-Litovsk. But the fighting goes on even though there are now only isolated centres of resistance. Despite the hopelessness of their plight, the Reds fight on even more stubbornly and ferociously. The basements of the White Palace of the Engineering Headquarters building and the barracks of the 333rd Rifle Regiment were some the last centres of resistance in the citadel. I watched the assault engineers dealing with them yesterday. I can assure you that they certainly put an end to the resistance there."

"Do enlighten us, Captain," said Rossheim, his interest once more kindled.

"The 81st Combat Engineer Battalion was given the task of blowing up this building on the central island in order to put an end to the Russian troops' flanking fire at the north island. I watched while explosives were lowered from the roof of the building towards the windows. Then the fuses were lit. When they exploded, we could hear the Russian soldiers screaming and groaning, but still they continued to fight. The engineers only gradually managed to take one defensive position after another as a result of stubborn fighting. The garrison of the so-called 'Officers' Corps' on the central island only ceased to exist with the building itself... the resistance continued until the walls of the building were destroyed and razed to the ground by more powerful explosions".

"So, is the citadel cleared?" asked Rossheim.

"Not quite, but we are getting there," replied Grunewald. "The emphasis has been switched to the east fort and the rumour is that the Karl-Geräte will be used to crack that nut."

"Well, why don't we go and see this marvel in operation?" said Rossheim in the manner of one who had just hit on a great idea for a picnic.

"Agreed," said von Schroif. "Let's hope our colleague survives to re-join us."

"Indeed," said Rossheim. "I'd like to meet Wendorff again."

The five of them trooped round to the field behind the battalion workshops just in time to see the mighty weapons being driven the last few hundred metres to the intended firing location. The sheer scale of these spectacular weapons had drawn a large crowd of hangers-on and spectators of all ranks. They watched in idle fascination as the preparations were made for firing. All the while, Captain Grunewald kept up a running commentary.

"Despite its extreme weight, somewhat surprisingly, the Karl-Gerät has proved to have no problems moving over normal soil, but under no circumstances must they be allowed to make turns on soft soil, in case they throw one of those mighty tracks. The chassis has to be backed into position to fire, and the firing position has to be precisely levelled and the approach route prepared ahead of time to fill in soft spots and any ditches and so forth."

Finally, all was in readiness. Under the interested gaze of the growing army of spectators, each chassis in turn was lowered to the ground to distribute the recoil forces more evenly. The huge barrels were then lowered.

"The howitzers can only be loaded at zero elevation," said Grunewald, who had taken over the role of tour guide.

"So it has to be re-aimed between every shot?" enquired Sanger, who was absolutely absorbed by the whole cumbersome process.

"I'm afraid so, yes," continued Grunewald.

"I'll bet they can give you a bit of a headache," said Wohl, looking at the monstrous guns in wonderment.

"They certainly can," continued Grunewald. "The heavy 60 cm concrete-piercing shells, the *schwere Betongranate*, make a crater up to fifteen metres wide and five metres deep. They contain three hundred kilograms of explosive. They are capable of penetrating three metres of concrete. This is the second battery. Here we have Thor and Odin, and they have been issued with thirty-six rounds."

Just at that moment two turretless tanks drove up to the guns and the sense of scale made the spectators realise the true size of these devastating weapons. The tanks, which were built on the Panzer IV chassis, then the heaviest Germany possessed, looked like children's toys beside the massive howitzers. These immense guns required a crane to hoist the huge shells into the maw of the beast and the onlookers were treated to the entertaining display as the cumbersome ammunition was hoisted and manhandled into position before the barrels were raised and the aiming procedure took place.

At last all was in readiness. After an infuriatingly long pause that elicited some heckling from the eager spectators, the first gun finally fired its massive shell. The explosive power was enormous, the noise of the detonation was huge, and the sound made by the projectile as it hurtled off towards the fortress was a sound to make the Gods tremble. Seconds later the round impacted on the nearby fortress and the earth shook and rippled with tremors. The enthusiastic spectators burst into cheers and applause and watched in rapt delight as the second gun was fired and a second massive shell rocketed into the summer sky.

* * * * *

The effect of the two massive explosions was indescribable. They had come out of the blue, completely unexpected. The defenders had felt the shock of sudden explosions of all calibres from grenades to heavy artillery shells, but this was unlike anything they had ever experienced. The sheer power of the blast shook every inch of the fortress, causing the vaulted ceilings of many of the cellars to collapse, burying their hapless occupants alive. The earthquake-like force of the blast was completely overpowering. It tortured eardrums and drew the air from the lungs of the survivors.

A few hapless individuals happened to have been tending to some wounded in the courtyard and had been enveloped by the fringe of the blast. Staring out over the courtyard, through the smoke and debris, Karl Wendorff tried his best not to linger too long on the lifeless forms and bloodied body parts that lay strewn across the ground and scattered about burnt-out cars and armour.

It was impossible, however, to avert his eyes. The sights were too grotesque and unimaginably dreadful. This was especially true for those blasted and mutilated frames which still contained some semblance of life. One woman in particular, just a few yards from his vantage point, was hauling herself inch by excruciating inch back towards the doorway beneath him. Something told Wendorff that she was a nurse — though how he could tell would have been beyond the ability of most observers. Whatever tunic or uniform she had been wearing was so blood-soaked and charred that it fell to one of those curious characteristics of the human mind — the ability to fill in the gaps between missing bits of information — to arrive at such a conclusion.

Wendorff looked on in revulsion as the stricken creature — for surely one could no longer apply the term nurse, woman or even human being — threw its one remaining hand repeatedly out in front of itself to grab at the very earth in an effort it to pull itself forward. 'It' was a torso with one arm remaining, the other cut off at the elbow. Blood poured from the stumps where her legs had been, three crimson trails marking her journey. To make things worse — as if they could get any worse — a still smouldering piece of shrapnel was lodged in the small of her back and Wendorff could hear the horrific sound of new blood spitting and boiling as it came into contact with the red hot metal.

Wendorff tried to look away but could not help but look at the woman's face. Mercifully, it was impossible to make out her face, just the back of her head, charred and hairless. The only clue that there was a face was the low grunting and gasping as she made the superhuman effort to claw herself back to safety. Safety? What possible meaning could the word possess in a situation like this? Back from where to what? It then crossed Wendorff's mind to help the woman. Would he carry her, lift her, offer her his hand? Almost immediately a spray of machine-gun fire raked across the ledge below him, forcing him to duck under the window, the dust burning into his eyes.

Leaning back against the wall, he felt like crying, he felt like he wanted to lie down, close his eyes, and never wake up. All the young life — all that was good and vital about him — felt like it had been hollowed out and rudely emptied on the ground around him. The young boy in flames, the look of betrayal in the eyes of the Russian soldier who had befriended him and confided in him, and now this pitiless creature on the ground beneath him, these visions all now seared into his brain with a power that suggested they would never ever leave him.

He, like all the young men in this war, had met the old soldiers of older wars and had listened to the stories, the stories of nightmares and cold sweats, waking up back in hell, but like all young men he had listened and forgotten, thinking it a weakness of particular old men. This could never happen to him surely?

However, in this moment, Karl Wendorff now realised and partook of a universal truth, one that affects all warriors of all ages. The truly shocking and indescribable can never be related or described. It cannot be discussed, talked or reasoned away. Once seen, it can never ever be forgotten. This realisation, that these ghosts would haunt him forever, that these brutalities would visit and revisit him, even in his sleep, was the last straw for Karl Wendorff. He curled himself into a ball and shook uncontrollably, an inner voice repeating itself over and over in the dark, *"Take me from here! Take me from here!"*

He was interrupted by the soft voice of Nurse Bettina Ostermann.

"Bandsman Oistrakh, can you help me? Surely the end is now here. We need someone to help the children to safety. We need to get them out." She carried with her a white flag made from her underskirt which had been crudely fastened to a pole.

"I agree, the time has come, there is no more to be done here," said Wendorff, accepting the makeshift banner from Bettina.

"Excellent. Now let's get moving. You have a sympathetic face. This may be the job for you, come."

They moved down the steps and soon arrived at a tunnel which led into a cellar, the occupants of which would have softened the heart of even the hardest and war-weariest soldier. In the dimly lit near-darkness, a group of children, the oldest of whom couldn't have been much older than seven or eight years old, stared back at Wendorff and Nurse Ostermann as they entered the cellar.

Despite all they had seen and suffered, their eyes were still bright, their spirits undimmed. Some wore bandages and splints, but the thing that impressed most upon Wendorff was the silence. There was no wailing, crying or pleading, just the wide-eyed trust that suggested they knew they were in safe hands and that everything was going to be all right. In all this violence and madness, these truly were the innocent.

"From the bottom of my heart, I thank you. These young eyes have seen enough already," said Bettina. "Who knows what future awaits them? But God knows, it has to be better than they have suffered in here. On behalf of them, their parents, and Mother Russia, I salute you."

Wendorff felt a welling-up in his soul, but remained silent and just nodded. Bettina Ostermann had hidden reserves of strength and she rose to the situation. "If you carry the flag, I will follow with the children. They will be fine. We have grown quite close."

This last statement was accompanied by such a gentle hint of a smile that Wendorff could not help but smile back. It was then that he noticed her beauty, a beauty that found its origin not just in her face or figure, but also in her spirit and heart. This became even more evident when she smiled, turned and kneeled before the children, explaining in soft clear tones what was about to happen. The children stared up at Wendorff wide-eyed, like true-believers to the one true Saviour.

The catastrophic force of the two colossal blasts in quick succession had sucked out the will to resist. In any conflict, there comes a moment that is the tipping point. It is that moment when rock-solid resolve suddenly evaporates and all that is left is hopelessness. The defenders of the east fort had now reached that point. Within minutes, a series of white flags had been waved along the walls and windows of the east fort.

With his hands above his head, Wendorff continued to wave the flag and stepped out into the courtyard. To Bettina's surprise, he also started shouting out in fluent German.

"Cease fire! Cease fire! We are coming out with the children! There are wounded, we are surrendering! Please don't shoot! We surrender!"

He had to keep waving the flag to obscure the fact that his arm was shaking uncontrollably. As he realised the danger of his predicament, a current of fear ran through him like electricity. Here he was, dressed as a Soviet soldier. Any idiot or avenger could cut him down, but no shots were fired and, when he judged that perhaps the truce was holding, he looked behind to motion to Bettina.

"Come now, my lambs. Don't be scared. The soldier will make sure you are safe," she said gently as she shepherded the children out from their hiding place. Walking with her back to Wendorff, still looking at the children, she continued with her soft words of encouragement. "Don't look at anything. Just look into my eyes. That's it. Just look into my eyes. The nice soldier will make sure you are safe. Come, my little lambs."

Despite his fear, Wendorff felt quite overcome. Who was this Bettina Ostermann? What kind of world would put them on opposing sides of these barbaric barricades? As he walked on, Wendorff's rich imagination could not help but construct a vision of himself and this angel Bettina perhaps setting up home in the new Germany, a family, children... His thoughts were immediately interrupted by an unexpected question.

"Anyone called Wendorff here? Calling Wendorff? Identify yourself."

"I am Wendorff," he said.

"Good. We've been expecting you. You speak German?"

It should have been the most welcome sound in the world, but there was something in the voice. It was unwholesome, reedy and almost reptilian. Wendorff had blindly assumed that he would fall with relief into the arms of the first German to greet him, but there was something about this particular character that was distasteful.

"I am Karl Wendorff, of the Abwehr Brandenburg battalion. I would like to report to Hauptsturmführer Hans von Schroif of the Sturmgeschütz battalion."

Bettina took her attention away from the children and looked at him in shock. Her eyes registered astonishment, betrayal and contempt.

"Get a move on then, Wendorff. Forget the untermenschen. We have been waiting long enough for you," replied the spectral figure. "My name is Oscar Dirlewanger, of Sonderkommando Dirlewanger. If you make your way to the command post, I will ensure that the children are looked after."

There was something about this man that sprinkled ice about Wendorff's soul, but what choice did he have? Anything too sudden and either side could open up.

"I will walk with the children and the nurse up to the command post," Wendorff bristled.

"You'll do what you are told. Double-time move and you can change out of those rags and into something more befitting a German soldier."

Wendorff, biting his tongue, turned and spoke to Bettina in Russian.

"They want me to go in here for five minutes. Don't worry, it's not too serious. If you just go with this officer, I will come and check on you as soon as I can."

He had expected a soft response, but from the way Bettina looked at him he knew that, if she had any saliva in her thirst-tortured body, she would have spat in his face.

"You fascist animal! You are no man. Do not speak to me, you slime."

- CHAPTER 10 -

Der Albtraum macht weiter

A S HE followed the signs leading to the battalion's headquarters, Wendorff was haunted by thoughts of Bettina Ostermann. He should have been the most joyous man on the planet, but he was as miserable as could be. He was free from a nightmare and he was still alive and in one piece. Once again in the uniform of an SS-Oberkannonier, he fitted in with the panorama of life: German lines, passing bivouacs, stores, mobile workshops and camouflaged artillery emplacements. He drew in a deep breath. Suddenly, his load seemed lighter. Perhaps there could be an end to this. Perhaps peace would come soon.

"SS-Oberkannonier Wendorff, I don't believe it! It really is you!"

The familiar voice had boomed out unexpectedly. Turning around, Wendorff could make out the unmistakeable figure of Otto Wohl running towards him.

"SS-Kannonier Otto Wohl! Of all the people! I was just thinking about you and the boss!"

"Ach, the boss is fine," replied Wohl, "as are Junge and Knispel and the others, but I warn you, he is in one of his moods. He's trying to train me on the radio, Morse and all that. Otherwise, it's a transfer to the infantry for me. Perhaps you could help me, I've..."

"I'm sorry, SS-Kannonier Wohl. I don't mean to be rude, but I've been through a lot and I'm not a teacher. I have a matter of the utmost importance to discuss with SS-Hauptsturmführer von Schroif."

"Yes, of course. That's his HQ by those trees over there. We're pulling out tomorrow and heading back to the division. You're back just in time. Perhaps you can join us?"

"I think I already have. Someone was kind enough to provide the uniforms," said Wendorff. "And, after what I have seen, it would be good to have some friends around me again."

"Indeed, SS-Oberkannonier. Allow me to escort you as guard of honour."

With that, the two comrades made their way briskly to von Schroif's position. They arrived just in time to see the last of the Polish vodka being splashed into the glasses of the four officers. Rossheim, von Schroif and Grunewald had been joined by SS-Sturmbannführer Voss, who had an uncanny knack of being able to show up at the point when a bottle was opened.

"Wendorff, so good to see you," said von Schroif with genuine warmth. "Please, take a seat. You must have much to tell us all."

For all its horrors, no soldier would deny that war has its elevated moments of great personal warmth and heightened camaraderie — none more so than the meeting of old friends — but in times of battle this is given greater power by the immediate knowledge that the participants have not gone the way of so many unfortunate souls and have indeed survived. So it was with these newly-reunited comrades, but, beneath all the handshaking and feeble jokes, Hans von Schroif could tell that there was some weight on Wendorff's mind, and therefore was not surprised when Wendorff asked if they might talk in private.

"That's alright, Wendorff, you are among friends here. Feel free to say anything," said Sturmbannführer Voss.

"As you wish, Sturmbannführer. It concerns my mission from Abwehr." Wendorff placed a sweat-stained document pouch on the table.

"I was supposed to deliver these documents to a contact behind Soviet lines, but everything fell apart and I ended up inside the fortress."

"Highly intriguing," said Voss. "What kind of documents are they?"

"I don't know, SS-Sturmbannführer," said Wendorff truthfully.

"You mean to say you haven't read them?" Rossheim asked, quickly leaning forward. He picked up the pouch and examined the seal.

"No, Oberleutnant, I have attempted to fulfil my mission, but, as you can see, the seal is unbroken."

"I have no reason to think it would be otherwise," said Rossheim.

"You have not told us enough about your role behind Soviet lines," said Voss, eager to learn more.

"I've said all I can," replied Wendorff, "without

compromising anyone else involved. Suffice to say, I must now ensure that these documents find their way back to Abwehr."

"Well, they are in good hands now," said Rossheim, abruptly rising from the table. "I happen to be on my way to Berlin this afternoon. I shall deliver them personally. You are certain that you have not opened or read the documents?"

"Absolutely certain, Oberleutnant," replied Wendorff earnestly.

"Good. Otherwise, I'd have been forced to kill you!"

The others burst out laughing, but there was something odd about Rossheim's reaction and the way he looked at him that stopped Wendorff from joining in the mirth.

Rossheim's demeanour now altered immediately. His formerly jovial exterior vanished as he snapped to attention and clicked his heels. "I'll make sure they are with Abwehr today." With that, he made his salutes and was gone.

The sound of Rossheim's departing car had hardly died down when it was replaced by the noise of shooting and then screaming in the forest off to their left. These were not the typical screams of war though, not the screams and shouts of men locked in mortal combat — these were screams of an entirely different order. These were the screams of women and young children…

"Partisans?" queried von Schroif, picking up his machine pistol. "Wohl, you stay and guard the StuGs." He turned to give an order to Wendorff, but he had already set off towards the woods himself, hoping that what he feared was happening was something else entirely.

On reaching the scene, Wendorff could not believe what he was seeing. A mass of young children, the very children for whom he had just secured safe passage, were now lying dead in the centre of a clearing. Some had obviously run for their lives and were being hunted like wild animals for sport, their executioners smiling and laughing as they targeted and hunted the terrified children. Where was Bettina?

Wendorff saw two soldiers emerge into the clearing, both laughing. One was brandishing a blood-stained broken bottle. Sickened by an awful sense of foreboding, Wendorff raced passed them. Then the awful sight met his eyes. At first, he was unable to take in the sheer horror of what he was seeing. He then reeled in disgust as the vision swamped his brain. Bettina's lifeless corpse was splayed out on the ground, her arms and legs spread and tied to four wooden stakes. Her skirt had been lifted and she had been mutilated...

Wendorff looked around and saw Oskar Dirlewanger emerge from behind a tree. He ran straight at him, screaming and repeatedly punching him.

"Bastard! Bastard!" screamed Wendorff, raining down the blows. He would have continued until the man had been reduced to a bloody pulp, but he felt a massive blow from behind and found himself grappled to the ground by two of Dirlewanger's command. Dirlewanger stood over him, smiling.

"You murdering bastard," screamed Wendorff.

"You *must* learn to moderate your language, Wendorff. I have clarified the orders with Hauptsturmführer von Schroif. Eliminate all bolshevised individuals. That's the standing order."

Wendorff couldn't believe what he was hearing. "She was a nurse, for God's sake!"

"Really?" replied Dirlewanger. "Well, what's this then?" He produced a Soviet document. "Unless I'm very much mistaken, this is a trade union membership card from a bolshevist trade union. You will note the name Bettina Ostermann... and furthermore, the bitch stole the gun of one of my men. It was all a Soviet trap. The scum are so low that they will even use their own children as weapons. They have no respect for the innocents, the poor loves, caught up in the crossfire like that. Now, I'm afraid I cannot possibly retain the trust of my unit if I allow the likes of you to escape unpunished for attacking an officer of the Reich.

"Leow, what shall we do with this traitor? We all saw him in Soviet uniform, trying to infiltrate the sow and her swine behind our lines. Summary execution followed by a bit of paperwork, or something a bit more delicious? On second thoughts, I think we have had our fun today. Summary execution it is then, Loew?"

Loew laughed and nodded. Dirlewanger pulled out his pistol and pointed it at Wendorff. Smiling and insouciant, he was just about to pull the trigger when he heard a voice behind him.

"Dirlewanger!"

It was Hans von Schroif and behind him stood a squad of armed men from the StuG battalion. At their head was Hauptscharführer Michael Knispel.

* * * * *

As Dirlewanger and his command made their way out of the clearing in the direction of the fortress, Hans von Schroif watched every move. He had a great deal on his mind and he showed complete contempt.

"You will have to take charge here, I'm afraid," he said to Knispel. "Give them the best burial you can. I'm going to make sure there's no repeat when the fortress falls."

The awful task of burying the bodies of the children now commenced. It was heartrending. The tiny remains signified innocent, prematurely destroyed lives. Knispel supervised the burial. He was a hard man, but even he was almost reduced to tears by the harrowing task.

He was glad when his attention was drawn to a figure hunched by the edge of the clearing. The man was part of Dirlewanger's unit. He had been unable to join the others and was left behind, still vomiting and shaking. Next to him was a powerful hunter's rifle. Knispel moved swiftly and soon stood over him. The man's arms were tightly folded, his hands concealed under his armpits as he continued to wretch.

"Can you stand up?" asked Knispel.

Eventually the man looked up. "I don't know. I don't

care anymore," he said weakly, his wandering gaze failing to focus on Knispel.

"Otto Frankl!" exclaimed Knispel. "'What are you doing here?"

"Michael Knispel? It's you? After all these years..."

"So what brings you into Dirlewanger's unit?"

"I was given a choice, stay in jail and rot or sign up as a marksman with Dirlewanger."

"Why were you locked up?"

"You know me, Knispel, once a poacher... always a poacher. I got caught plundering deer. I got five years."

"God almighty! How much did you poach?"

"It wasn't the amount, it was where... they caught me on Göring's estate."

"You idiot, even I wouldn't be that stupid!" said Knispel in astonishment.

"Well, I don't care anymore. I can't do this. They can shoot me for all I care. I won't go any further. I'm finished, Knispel. My life's over. The things I've seen, they haunt me day and night. I can't go on. Can you get me out of this, Knispel?"

"Well, Sturmbannführer Voss does have the right connections to Deitrich. We can sometimes arrange transfers... even for total idiots."

Knispel's gaze then fell longingly on the hunting rifle. "I see you've got yourself a Sauer."

Knispel knew that rifles with telescopic sights were only given to the best marksmen, irrespective of rank. They were looked upon as an honour, and changes were avoided as far as possible. This was not military issue. It also carried a fine telescopic sight of the sporting type, and one like this was not suitable for military purposes. In any event, it could not be manufactured within a short period in the large numbers required. The intention of the military was to issue as many serviceable telescopic sights as possible, and not to develop just a few high-grade optical instruments. The present army telescopic sight had a low magnification, but was practical and rugged. When properly handled, it was effective in the field.

Knispel was much more familiar with the sporting sight on the Sauer rifle which Frankl carried. It was a general rule that the greater the magnification of the telescopic sight, the smaller the field of vision. A telescopic sight like this with wide field of vision and high magnification was the poacher's stock in trade, but was not available for military service because of its size and its sensitivity. Sights were very delicate and had to be tested and, if necessary, corrected. This was nearly always the case when the sights had been transported for long periods.

"It's yours now. I'll never touch one again, as long as I live," said Frankl. "They can do to me what they like."

As he spoke there came the sharp report of a nearby explosion as Thor sent another huge shell hurtling towards the fortress. The siege was drawing to a close and the impact of the mighty gun was bringing it towards a swift conclusion.

Knispel now thought of von Schroif, who had followed Dirlewanger. He might need some help.

"You have an agreement, Frankl. Welcome to the Sturmgeschütz battalion. I'll take care of this."

Michael Knispel picked up the elegant Sauer rifle and made his way to the fortress.

* * * * *

The huge detonations were indeed draining the last will of the defenders to resist. They also caused further casualties. Yefim Fomin was one of those. Unlike the others crouched in the rubble of the citadel, Fomin did not pick himself up and try to dust himself down. The effects of a catastrophic explosive event like the detonation of a massive shell in close proximity cannot be easily subdivided into neat linear packages. The deadening of the senses, the all-pervasive shock, does not end cleanly and decisively. In some cases, it ever ends.

From his depressing experience, Captain Zubachyov knew this all too well. So, when he shook Fomin gently, he did not expect an immediate reply, or any kind of reply for that matter. It was just what had to be done, and what needed to be repeated, again and again.

"Comrade.... comrade..." he said, shaking the commissar, but Fomin lay still.

Despite the ferocity of the blast, the destructive capability of the howitzer was uneven. In the Kobrin fortification, Pyotr Gavrilov and Dimitri Korsak were

287

thrown to the ground, but were quickly back on their feet. As soon as they realised that they were personally unharmed they at once grabbed binoculars and took stock of the overall situation. From the nearest vantage point in the Kobrin fort, both were immediately apprised of the calamitous effect the huge bomb had had on the citadel's defenders.

They could see that German troops were now moving in from all directions and, despite the fitful crack of small-arms fire, resistance in the citadel seemed to have evaporated. Small groups of defenders, stunned into senselessness, had now started to stagger out into the courtyard, many waving white flags. Nearly all were wounded.

In the corner of the Kobrin fortification, which they still held, Gavrilov turned to Korsak.

"Comrade, the situation requires utter honesty. All is lost. I shall not leave, nor will those men who still stand with us. However — and this is an order my friend — a report has to be made. Not just for the purpose of intelligence, which is obviously vital, but... and I am not being sentimental here — far from it... but as a memoriam... that these lives that have been lost here have not been lost in vain... that their sacrifice shall remain long and honoured in the history of glorious Mother Russia and also that these brave men and women's fate should serve as a spur — a hellish reminder — for those who continue to fight.

"The entire nation should be awakened as to what

these animals have done here. This is a fight to the death and we owe those who will carry that fight the right to know what absolute evil they face. We cannot allow the people of this country to sleepwalk into annihilation. Your job is to waken the nation and rouse them on, to victory."

Korsak's look immediately betrayed the fact that he had no intention of leaving the fortress, but, before he could utter a word, Gavrilov continued.

"Time is short, comrade. I will not repeat myself again. That is an order. Now, change out of that commissar uniform and into this." A dusty private's uniform was produced. Gavrilov then turned to a soldier who waited with a notepad. "Take down what I say. When I have finished, Comrade Korsak will assume the heroic task of delivering our last despatch."

Gavrilov, speaking hesitantly at first, began to dictate his dispatch.

* * * * *

A few hundred metres away, in the ruins of the citadel, Zubachyov was still trying to rouse Yefim Fomin.

"Comrade! Comrade!"

When Fomin at last stirred, it is probable that it was the effect of this intervention by his commander, but whether it could be said that Fomin in any understandable way actually heard what Zubachyov was saying is doubtful. When all is gone, only reflex remains.

It was when Fomin turned slowly towards him that Zubachyov noticed his injuries. Blood was dripping from one of his ears and bone was protruding from his left arm. Zubachyov sighed and looked around. It was as if the explosion had expunged all life from the immediate area. What kind of devil's shell or bomb could wreak such havoc! Through the still-swirling dusk, all that he could make out was the staggering number of bodies, broken and without breath, littering the room. One man over in the far corner was trying to get to his feet, but how long would it take him, and for what purpose? Then he heard the shouts outside.

Dimitri Korsak woke as if from a nightmare. For once, the reality made him wish to go back. Three soldiers stood peering out of the wrecked mouth of the tunnel where Karl had done its deadly work. They held sharpened spades in their hands.

"Raus! Raus! It is over! Raus! Raus!"

Zubachyov tried to think clearly, but the notion had no meaning at a time like this. Worse, such an event not only destroys the body and the mind, it attacks the spirit. If there was no will to fight or resist, how could the mind respond with anything approaching clarity?

Such was the nature of Zubachyov's surrender. It was not a decision. It was the last step in a forced march. Coughing violently, he motioned to the struggling soldier to follow him out the door. He then helped Fomin to his feet.

"Jews! Commissars! Jews! Commissars!" shouted

Oscar Dirlewanger, strutting about the ground in front of the building. Prodding the wounded as they staggered out of the building, he continued shouting at the dazed and wounded Soviet troops. "Ivans, Ivans, bring me your Jews and commissars! Ivans, you shall be treated well. Extra rations and water if you point out the Jews and commissars!"

However, no man even looked at him. Then Dirlewanger took off his cap and started to pour water over himself. Tilting his head, he poured it down his throat, gargling and making exaggerated slurps of pleasure.

Just then a boy of about six ran up to him. He pulled at his trousers and begged, "Water, water, please." His lips were cracked and bleeding from thirst.

"Young man, you look as if you badly need to drink. Of course you can. I shall give you all the water you need. Enough to slake your thirst... enough even to shower!" He then knelt and put his arm around the young boy. "Yes, look. Water, mmmm... Smell the beautiful water... have a taste..." He wet his finger and ran it salaciously round the young boy's lips. He then moved his mouth right next to the boy's ear and started whispering.

"Now, young man, you can have this water, all of this water, all that you can drink, for only one tiny little favour in return. This is all yours. All you have to do is let me know who the commissar is, or any Jewish person. I need to talk to them in order to organize water for all the wounded men first. Please, for their sake, just one Jew or commissar."

Beyond himself with thirst and taken in by Dirlewanger's weasel words, the boy turned and pointed at Yefim Fomin.

"Him!" Dirlewanger shouted to his men. "Put him against that wall and shoot him!" He then turned to the young boy, gave him some water, and said, "That is enough for now, my brave young man. Stay by my side and you can have all the liquid you need."

Zubachyov looked on helplessly as Fomin was dragged in agony and forced at bayonet point by Dirlewanger's men to stand against the nearest wall.

"Form a line, men. Quickly. We do not have all day!"

* * * * *

Michael Knispel had reached the ruins of the citadel. He was still carrying the Sauer hunting rifle with the impressive sporting sight. He crawled among the ruins to the top of a wall overlooking the courtyard and settled into a firing position. He was content to wait for events to unfold and was prepared to wait as long as required, but it proved to be a short span of time as he soon saw the familiar figure Hans von Schroif, striding purposefully towards Dirlewanger.

"Dirlewanger, what is happening here?"

"Pest control," replied Dirlewanger airily, "just exterminating some vermin."

"Are you insane?" replied von Schroif. "This man is badly wounded. By the commonly agreed rules of engagement, I order you to see that this man gets immediate medical help."

"Order? You *order* me? Ha! This is not some training ground exercise, von Schroif." Turning to his men, he yelled, "Aim!"

Knispel lifted the rifle into a firing position. Through the high powered sight, Dirlewanger's head was magnified. The target was not one that he was likely to miss. He was about to pull the trigger, but then he hesitated as an infuriated Hans von Schroif pulled out his pistol and pointed it at Dirlewanger's head. His small movement blotted out Dirlewanger entirely and placed himself in the line of the shot. Knispel was forced to look away from his scope in order to understand what was happening in the courtyard.

"This is my last warning, Dirlewanger. Do not think I will not shoot. I am ordering you to desist. Now! That is an order!"

Dirlewanger turned slowly and smiled haughtily at von Schroif.

"Orders... Whose *orders* am I supposed to follow? Am I to follow the orders of the Führer himself, or those of my *former* commander? I will always — even unto death itself — follow the orders of the Führer. There is no higher authority. His will is my will."

"How dare you drag the Führer into it!" replied von Schroif.

"The order comes directly from the Führer. There is no question of *dragging the Führer into it*," retorted Dirlewanger.

"Which order?" shouted von Schroif, his patience running out.

"You may not be familiar with the Führer's decree of 14th May regarding military jurisdiction in the Barbarossa zone," replied Dirlewanger, a look of smugness in his eyes. "Order number 44822/41. When fighting bolshevism, one cannot count on the enemy acting in accordance with the principles of humanity or international law. In particular, it must be expected that the treatment of our prisoners by political commissars of all types, who are the true pillars of resistance, will be cruel, inhuman and dictated by hate."

From his perch amongst the rubble, Knispel could only look on in frustration. Unless the two men shifted their positions, he could not hope to get a shot in between them. Down below, in the courtyard, Dirlewanger paused to ensure the von Schroif was following him.

"The troops must realise firstly that, in this fight, it is wrong to trust such elements with clemency and consideration in accordance with international law. They are a menace to our own safety and to the rapid pacification of the conquered territories. Secondly, they must realise that the originators of the Asiatic barbaric methods of fighting are the political commissars. They must be dealt with promptly and with the utmost severity. Therefore, if taken while fighting or offering resistance, they must, on principle, be shot immediately."

"The Führer would never issue an order like that. Show me a copy or, by God, Dirlewanger, I *will* shoot!"

"Hauptsturmführer, I would not do that if I were you."

The words were softly spoken and came from behind him. Turning slowly, he could make out the elaborate uniform of an SS-Obergruppenführer. It was none other than Heydrich himself. And behind Heydrich, flanked by a bevy of staff officers and hangers-on, stood Reichsführer Heinrich Himmler.

"Obersturmführer Dirlewanger is correct in his assertion. Your misgivings are understandable, Hauptsturmführer. There were no circulated copies of that order. Warlimont himself limited its circulation. Written copies went to commanders in chief of armies or of air commands, respectively, with an instruction to inform the junior commanders by word of mouth," said the Reichsführer with complete composure. "But please trust me on this matter. This order, I can assure you, *does* come directly from the Führer himself. It is his will. He has a grasp, a clearer vision than any of us... And I am sure that you would agree that, if we cannot trust in this broader grasp, this forensic vision... then we are failing in our duties as Germans and as soldiers of the Reich. It is not our job to question the mind of the Führer — how futile would that be! It is our job to unswervingly follow his wishes. Do I make myself clear?"

"Yes, Reichsführer," replied Hans von Schroif, a

momentary delay betraying a less than enthusiastic assent.

"Good," replied Himmler. "I believe our work here is almost done. It has perhaps taken longer than we expected, but I am sure you will agree that, in the final analysis, we did prevail. Now, please return to the assembly point with your unit and prepare for the next stage in this glorious advance. Dismissed."

Hans von Schroif saluted, turned, and left.

Once out of earshot, Himmler turned to Dirlewanger.

"Now, Obersturmführer Dirlewanger," he said, motioning to the broken and still groaning half-conscious figure of Yefim Fomin, "please continue with your work."

* * * * *

Half a mile away, Pyotr Gavrilov, acutely aware of the encroaching enemy troops, drew a deep breath and continued with his final report. He sensed that this was now a balancing act with time, but he was determined that the full story be told. Again Gavrilov paused, but drew enough breath to continue the grisly roll call of the honoured and the dead.

"Thirst. Thirst and hunger. Not only were the fortress defenders threatened by the numerically superior enemy, but soon they also began to run out of food, because many of the food supply depots had been either destroyed or burnt. They collected whatever food and water there was left in the canteens and in the badly damaged warehouses. It was far too little though. Each passing day made their hunger pangs sharper. Medical supplies and bandages also quickly ran out. We sought fresh supplies in damaged warehouses and the dressing stations that were still intact. Undergarments were torn up and used as bandages, but wounds received in fighting were increasingly left un-bandaged.

"The worst hardship borne by the fortress defenders, however, was thirst. The enemy had bombarded the fortress with incendiary bombs, dropped petrol-filled barrels, and used shells that splattered burning liquids when they exploded. Some parts of the fortress were a solid sea of fire. Everything that could burn, did burn. The fires continued unabated in various spots. The hot summer air was even more unbearably hot and, together with the thick smoke and the dust from shattered bricks hanging constantly in clouds over the ruins, it made the people inside the fortress unbearably thirsty. There was no water though, with which to quench their thirst.

"The water tower located above the Terespol gate was destroyed early in the fighting and the water supply system was damaged in many places. There were no emergency reserves of water in the fortress, nor were there any wells inside it. The Mukhavets flowed only a few meters from its walls, but it was impossible to obtain water from it. The enemy installed machine-gunners in the bushes along the riverbanks who opened fire at anyone who tried to reach the river. Anyone who attempted to reach the river by day or night was immediately shot down. There were attempts to dig wells in the casemates, and sheets attached to ropes were thrown into the river then pulled back, and the dirty water was wrung out of them into mess-tins. People even put damp sand into their mouths. None of this, though, could replace a single drop of ordinary water."

Korsak had by now reluctantly reconciled himself to playing his part in Pyotr Gavrilov's scheme. He was now dressed as a humble private and he listened intently as Gavrilov moved on to the final part of his report.

"We are nearly there, comrade," he said to Korsak, "but I would like to finish by singling out the heroic behaviour of two men."

Korsak nodded in agreement and Gavrilov continued with his despatches.

"Several times during the day of the 23rd of June, Nazi loudspeakers urged the defenders of the fortress to surrender. Enemy artillery ringed the fortress, constantly firing on the citadel, and dive-bombers raided it. Commissar Fomin organized an attack by the soldiers of the 84th and 333rd Regiments on the club building occupied by the enemy submachine-gunners with their radio transmitter. This two-pronged attack was a success and the enemy soldiers were forced out of the building.

"On the 29th of June the enemy again delivered an ultimatum; the besieged troops would have to surrender or the fortress would be totally destroyed. One hour was given to reach a decision. Time ran out, but the citadel did not raise the white flag.

"A massive assault on the citadel was then begun. Dozens of bombers circled over the fortress and showered powerful bombs on it. These explosions caused cracks as deep as those caused by earthquakes to appear. Even buildings in the city were damaged. Inside the fortress itself, walls two-meters thick crumbled as bricks and metal melted. Enemy assault guns penetrated the citadel's courtyard and fired continuously at the gun-slits, windows and walls of the buildings that were still standing.

"The assault continued on the 30th of June. The major group defending the fortress was gradually being destroyed and broken up, and the defence headquarters were turned to ruin. It was here that the wounded and exhausted commanding officers of the joint force, Captain Zubachyov and Commissar Fomin, were last seen. As of this moment, contact has been lost. End of communication."

Gavrilov then stood up and hugged Korsak to him, both men knowing they would never see each other again.

"Make speed, comrade," said Gavrilov. "I shall take my men and draw fire. Your best chance is to head for the Mukhavets and wait in the reeds until nightfall. Good luck."

With that, the two men made their separate ways.

* * * * *

The familiar landmarks of the city of Berlin lay spread out beneath the wings of the Stuka. Approaching from the north-east, first Lichtenberg then Treptower Park slipped by under the gull-shaped wings. Soon Tempelhofer Park came into view, then Templehof Airport. It was busy as ever on that July evening. Civilian and military aircraft of all types were coming and going, so the sight of a lone Stuka dive-bomber coming into land drew little comment.

As the aircraft touched down and drew to a halt, a figure in a long leather coat got out of the waiting Mercedes and purposefully walked towards it. Despite the fact that he wore no uniform, there was something in the deportment of the man that marked him out as a policeman of some sort. RSHA Kriminalassistent Walter Lehmann advanced purposefully towards the plane. The pilot did not dismount. He tossed Lehmann a document pouch. Without exchanging a single word, Lehmann got back into the car. The driver immediately started the engine and the car sped off on the short journey towards central Berlin and the Gestapo headquarters on Prinz-Albert Strasse.

* * * * *

Dimitri Korsak lay in the ooze of the river bank as he waited for the long summer's day to end. When darkness came he would have a chance to slip out from his hiding place and begin the long journey eastwards. With the feeling of victory in the air, the German attackers had relaxed their vigilance and it had been relatively straightforward to slip out of the citadel and into the reeds by the river. All he had to do now was stay low and wait. In a few hours' time the sun would be gone and the short summer night would begin, bringing with it the concealment which would allow him to escape from the grip of events and start the next phase of his life.

All day long, as he lay hidden in the reeds, he had witnessed the dispiriting sight of groups of Soviet soldiers being led out from the fortress then formed into small groups and marched away northwards. Some of these men were terribly wounded. Some reeked of the noxious smell of gangrenous wounds. All were gaunt and emaciated. Their sunken eyes spoke of the torments they had undergone and time and again he heard their plaintive requests for *voda* ignored. This was the cruellest trick of all, as these dehydrated and broken men were tortured by their desperate need to refresh themselves from the river Mukhavets, which could be seen and smelled, sparkling tantalisingly in the summer sunlight. The river flowed softly by, only yards away from the parched and desperate men who were demented with thirst.

During the course of that long day in hiding he had looked on in horror as scenes of casual brutality were played out before his eyes. Four bodies scattered on the ground near his hiding place bore mute testament to the awful scenes he had witnessed.

Earlier in the day, an ageing cook had tottered by, unsteady on his feet, as he tried desperately to walk along with the group. Korsak remembered him as one of the brave defenders of the citadel who had manned a machine-gun post until the ammunition had been exhausted and a splinter from a German mortar bomb had ripped into his back, tearing his liver and intestines. The man urgently needed surgery, but instead he was being forced to jog along with a group of men. Eventually, he could do no more and had collapsed to the ground and refused to rise.

An order had obviously gone out instructing the men escorting the prisoners to show no mercy and to take immediate retribution if there was the slightest infraction. The German guards had no hesitation in battering his brains out with the butts of their rifles. The cook's body lay only a few metres from his hiding place and the scent of blood in the warm summer air had soon attracted a swarm of flies. Korsak then watched in horror, struck with morbid fascination, as a raven had descended and begun to feed on the bloody pulp of the luckless man's brains that had been dashed onto the river bank.

Another man had been shot in the back of the neck when he had fallen to his knees and failed to rise in time to please the guards.

A new group emerged from the gates and, if anything,

they were in an even worse condition. A young man was holding a useless arm that was strapped to his side and his face was horribly mutilated. His teeth and jaw were exposed to the elements by a horrible gash caused by a bomb splinter that had carved away the skin and flesh from his face. The youngster was clearly delirious and the pus-ridden wound suggested that, if he did not receive medical care soon, he was unlikely to survive.

The youngster was suffering beyond the limits of human tolerance and the waters of the Mukhavets were obviously too tantalising. Suddenly, the wounded man broke ranks and made a faltering dash for the river. He had not gone more than a few steps when he was felled by the swinging butt of a German rifle. The man fell heavily to the ground, about a metre from Korsak's hiding place. The young man's breath could be heard escaping from his tortured body as he thudded to the ground.

Then, to Korsak's horror, their eyes met and, seeing the shock of white hair, the desperate young man called out to him. "Grandfather! Help me, grandfather!"

Korsak had no time to react. A guard was soon on the young man and a bullet ended his misery. The young man's blood sprayed onto Korsak, who cowered down into the reeds, but it was hopeless. The guard immediately discovered Korsak and his hiding place.

"What's this? Come out of there, old man," barked the guard.

Korsak had no option but to give himself up.

"Fall in with the others."

Korsak, who was fortunately fluent in the language, was quick to obey.

Then began a living nightmare, as the exhausted prisoners were forced to move at the double along the dusty road. Tortured by thirst, exhausted and suffering from untreated and infected wounds, the men barely had the strength to walk. The dropout rate was high. The instant and brutal response was always the same. A swift bullet to the back of the neck or a rifle butt used as a club to dash out the poor unfortunate's brain.

As they proceeded along the road to hell, Korsak saw in the distance a long column of vehicles headed towards them. The guards swiftly pushed the prisoners off the road and they stood gasping for breath as the column slowly approached. At the head of the column was a battered half-track. Korsak instantly recognised the commander. It was Hans von Schroif. Korsak averted his face to avoid being recognised, but he needn't have troubled himself. His white hair and tortured countenance made him unrecognisable when compared to the man, then known as Wilhelm Stenner, who had served alongside von Schroif at KAMA.

Following the half-track was a line of battle scarred Sturmgeschütze. They were loaded down with every type of equipment and supply item. This far behind the lines, the crews were in relaxed mode. Only the drivers were in their positions. Despite the clouds of dust, the others rode along on top of the vehicles, enjoying the hot summer sun.

As the first of the StuGs approached the prisoners, the driver picked out Korsak from the chastened group at the road side.

"Hey, Knispel, it's your white devil!"

There was no time for Knispel to do more than make a dismissive gesture. "I hope you rot in hell!" was his passing shout as the StuG rumbled past.

The truth was that Korsak was already in hell. Defeated, exhausted, tortured by thirst and suffering pangs of hunger, he and his comrades were driven along dust-choked roads towards some distant prisoner of war camp.

Hans von Schroif and the remainder of the battalion were headed south, towards the railhead. Away to the distant south, the old division waited, and there were new battles to be joined. As the Steppe unfurled itself out in front of him, he could not help but remember the Führer's words. *The world will hold its breath.* Well, now Germany had exhaled, the might and power of this giant breath rolling across hundreds of miles of Soviet territory, sweeping all before it.

Hans von Schroif drew in a deep breath of sweet early-morning summer air, but at precisely the moment it began to fill his lungs, he was overcome by a sense of foreboding. Had they committed the cardinal sin of underestimating the enemy? What gargantuan tasks lay ahead of them in this huge land? What kind of foe were they preparing to meet?

The grim battle they had just encountered at Brest-

Litovsk had contradicted the essential message of every briefing he had ever attended. This was not some unbalanced, rotten civilization, which, once the door had been kicked down, would fall at their feet. These men, women and children were a brave, stubborn and resolute adversary. This was no last gasp of a rotten regime, but a people who would fight to their own last dying breath...

As the Sturmgeschütze drove into the distance, the occasional sound of small-arms fire continued to resound from tiny centres of resistance in individual sectors of the citadel and the Kobrin fortification. They continued from late June until the very end of July. Even then, rifle fire and short bursts of machine-gun fire continued to ring out from basements and half-destroyed casemates as small groups of soldiers continued their lonely struggle. When the groups were all gone, solitary fighters still battled bravely on. Even though they were starving and covered with wounds, they asked no mercy, nor sought to give themselves up. No one knows when the very last shot was fired in the fortress, who the last defenders were, or how they died.

Appendices

About Ritter von Krauss

R ITTER VON Krauss is the pen name of a former German army officer who was the author of a large number of manuscripts for novels based on his experiences as a tank man in the first and second world wars. Although von Krauss is not his real name, the literal translation, *Knight of the Cross,* has been widely interpreted as an indicator that the author is a Knight's Cross holder, gained as a result of his service in either the Wehrmacht Heer or the Waffen SS. There are at least forty surviving von Krauss novels in manuscript form, all of which are thought to have been written between 1954 and 1968, during the time when the author is believed to have lived and worked in Argentina. They range from fully-fledged novellas to story outlines a few thousand words long.

In 1990's, during the negotiations for the sale of the rights to the novels, the manuscripts and the supporting documentation, as part of an extensive legal due diligence exercise, were studied and verified by a number of experts. This allowed the sale to proceed, but with the strict stipulation that the author should not be identified and that no publication could take place during the lifetime of any of the author's children. In consequence of this condition, the manuscripts went unpublished in the 20th century.

The main barrier to publication during the author's life time was a legal challenge by the author's estranged children, based on the legitimate fear that the family might be identified and associated with von Krauss, who is reputed to have been active behind the scenes in the movement which became the *Hilfsgemeinschaft auf Gegenseitigkeit der Angehörigen der ehemaligen Waffen-SS*, the campaign to restore pension and other legal rights to Waffen SS veterans. His work in this sphere was strongly disapproved off by his family and, as a consequence, the publishing contracts contain strong non-disclosure clauses, preventing the publishers from identifying the author or commenting on his identity.

Following the death of the last of von Krauss' children, the way for publication was finally cleared and *Tiger Command!*, the first published Ritter von Krauss novel, appeared in e-book form in 2011. The film *Steel Tempest*, which was based on von Krauss' experiences in the Ardennes offensive, also appeared in 2011, with the author properly credited for the first time.

Ritter von Krauss was thought to have served in the Great War, where he was rumoured to have briefly been part of the unit which drove the A7V, the first of the German tanks, into battle. During the early years of the war, von Krauss is believed to have served as a motorcycle despatch rider and to have been an associate of Kurt Ludecke, who was later to emerge as a member of Hitler's inner circle. It has also been widely speculated that he was on good terms with Sepp Dietrich.

He is known to have been descended from an aristocratic family and suffered the humiliation of being reduced to poverty in the 1920's, when hyper-inflation wiped out the fortunes of both von Krauss personally, and the entire family. Following the Great War, von Krauss is thought to have served in the Freikorps and to have spent time in Russia, working on tank development at KAMA.

It is thought that his failure to find a place in the 100,000 man army of the Weimar Republic was the spur which led to his joining the Nazi party. It is also understood that von Krauss spent time in the SA, where he knew Ernst Röhm, as a result of an introduction by Ludecke. This is borne out by the fact that both Ludecke and Röhm appear in fictionalised form in the von Krauss manuscript *Freikorps*!

There are many references which are interpreted as being autobiographical and it is conjectured that, as a result of his experiences in the hungry twenties, von Krauss may have become a committed National Socialist and, in any event, undoubtedly harboured life-long Nationalist aspirations. He was obviously a strong supporter of the *Grossdeutschland* vision that led to the creation of The Third Reich. He may therefore have been an obvious and easy convert to National Socialism, however, von Krauss was clearly not an anti-Semite and his novels display no trace of this aspect of National Socialist policy. In common with Ludecke and many others, von Krauss appears to assume that the anti-

Semitic aspects of the party manifesto were a sideshow to the main event, which was the unification of the German speaking peoples into a Socialist state.

During the 1920's, von Krauss is thought to have come to a breach with Ludecke when a number of business ventures designed to revive the von Krauss family fortunes also came to grief, leaving von Krauss penniless. It is thought that this was the event which drove von Krauss to seek employment by joining the fledgling SS, although he was initially highly disparaging of this outfit, describing himself as nothing more than "a glorified advertising salesman."

It has been speculated that von Krauss joined Hitler's regiment of bodyguards, the SS *Leibstandarte*, in 1933. From the subject matter of many of his novels, it is also thought that von Krauss served throughout the war initially as an armoured car commander and later as a Tiger tank commander, either in the Waffen SS or the Heer, or possibly both. The Gross Deutschland division has also been suggested as a possibility.

In 1945 von Krauss is understood to have escaped capture by the Russians and also to have slipped out of a British POW camp. As a result, he was never officially de-Nazified and, lacking the appropriate papers, he was unable to work in Germany and so began a game of cat and mouse with the German authorities that saw him serve briefly in the ranks of The French Foreign Legion, from which he was invalided out, suffering from malaria, an illness from which he never fully recovered.

Notes on the Translation and Sources

It is never an easy task to render the thoughts of a writer from his native language into a secondary language, and one has to be careful to guard against creating a new work. Unfortunately, it is not possible to provide a complete translation of every word of the original manuscript. However, I feel it was important to preserve the essence of the German roots of the novel. I have preserved the original chapter headings and a larger than usual number of German words, which are hopefully sufficient to make it clear at all times that we are in a foreign army. This is especially true of the ranks of the political soldiers of the Waffen SS. I'd like to think the balance is about right, but please accept my apologies if you have to reach for the German dictionary more than you would like.

As with *Tiger Command!*, I've taken out a number of phrases such as "cleaned his clock", meaning to kill a tank, as there is no real English equivalent. Unfortunately, once again, a large number of the jokes told by Otto Wohl have been lost in the rewriting process as they did not survive the act of translation with any semblance of humour still intact. Other German references have also lost some of their charm. If you don't know, for example, that the German word *vogel* translates as bird, then you won't get the reference made by von Schroif concerning the pun on the liaison officer's name.

Other German phrases however have survived. "To bite into the grass" is recognisable as our own "pushing up daisies." As it is utilised in a German setting, I have used the German phrase in preference to the English version. For those of you unfamiliar with the ways of the German language, *Sturmgeschütz* is singular, while the additional letter 'e' on the end signifies the plural.

Panzertruppenschule Kama, or *KAMA* for short, was a top-secret research and training facility, located near Kazan in the USSR. It was jointly operated by the Soviets and Germans between 1926 and 1933. Oberstleutnant Malbrandt was the Reichswehr officer who selected the location for the training and testing of military technology. The site was chosen to be as far away as possible from the prying eyes of League of Nations inspectors. It was a school for the study and development of armoured warfare. KAMA was the short form codename created by the fusion of the words Kazan and Malbrandt. KAMA came out of the brief period of Russo-German cooperation that was agreed upon as a part of the Treaty of Rapallo of 1922, and the Berlin Friendship Treaty of 1924.

Between 1926 and 1929, at least 146 German officers are known to have completed training at the Panzertruppenschule Kama. A great many more NCOs and perspective officers received clandestine assistance. The most famous 'graduate' of KAMA was Ewald von Kleist, future Generalfeldmarschall of the Reichswehr.

Generaloberst Lutz and NKVD Kommissar Josef Unshlicht were jointly responsible for conducting the training. Security for the facility was provided by troops of the NKVD.

Several armoured fighting vehicles were developed at Kama, under the alias of agricultural tractors. The German companies Rheinmetall-Borsig, Krupp and Daimler Benz were responsible for most of the development. The preliminary work at Kama resulted in the designs for the Panzer I, II, III and IV. The training and development which took place at Kama made the *Panzerwaffe* a reality.

Also in the series...

When Germany's leading tank ace meets the Steppe Fox it's a fight to the death. Faced with overwhelming odds Kampfgruppe von Schroif needs a better tank and fast; but the new Tiger tank is still on the drawing board and von Schroif must overcome bureaucracy, espionage and relentless Allied bombing to get the Tiger into battle in time to meet the ultimate challenge.

Based on a true story of combat on the Russian front, this powerful novel is written by Emmy™ Award winning author Bob Carruthers and newcomer Sinclair McLay. It tells the gripping saga of how the Tiger tank was born ad a legend was forged in the heat of combat.

Gritty, intense and breath-taking in its detail, this sprawling epic captures the reality of the lives and deaths of the tank crews fighting for survival on the Eastern Front, a remarkable novel worthy of comparison with 'Das Boot'.